With Extreme Pleasure

With Extreme Pleasure

ALISON KENT

KENSINGTON PUBLISHING CORP.
www.kensingtonbooks.com

BRAVA BOOKS are published by

Kensington Publishing Corp.
119 West 40th Street
New York, NY 10018

All Kensington titles, imprints and distributed lines are available at special quantity discounts for bulk purchases for sales promotion, premiums, fund-raising, educational or institutional use.

Special book excerpts or customized printings can also be created to fit specific needs. For details, write or phone the office of the Kensington Special Sales Manager: Kensington Publishing Corp., 119 West 40th Street, New York, NY 10018, attn. Special Sales Department; phone: 1-800-221-2647.

ISBN-13: 978-0-7582-1758-5
ISBN-10: 0-7582-1758-7

First Kensington Trade Paperback Printing: December 2009

10 9 8 7 6 5 4 3 2 1

Printed in the United States of America

For the readers who've loved the SG-5 and connected stories.

For Kate Duffy who gave me the opportunity to tell them.

For Walt who made writing them possible in ways only he knows.

Prologue

The office was like thousands of others looking out over Manhattan, dressed in sleek black marble, brushed chrome, and glass tinted the green of the sea.

There was carpeting done by the Persians, and furnishings done by designers whose names continued to be worth a fortune though their creativity had gone flat.

Or maybe it just seemed that way, aesthetic appreciation one more thing lost to the man staring out the room's window at the skyline he'd once loved.

He didn't love anything anymore.

Oliver's greed and stupidity had decided his own death. Elise first had died of grieving, and later by her own hand found clutching an empty prescription bottle.

The concept of love had been lost to the man next, killed by those two brutal blows.

He no longer loved his money, of which he had more than any man could spend. He no longer loved the car he drove that turned heads left and right.

He turned heads, too, and he no longer cared that he did so, or how much he was loved. The only thing he had left was his power.

What he felt for that was too consuming for a simple four-letter word. And so he left it undefined.

A buzz in his ear brought him out of his trance. He tapped his earpiece to receive the call he'd been waiting for since yesterday's break sent his team scrambling.

"Yes?" His voice pierced the room's stillness, a gunshot to his own ears.

"A dead end, man. We got zero," said the gruff voice on the other end; then it fell silent, the air empty with a hum of nothing.

The man wasn't surprised by the news. He'd never expected that reaching his goal would be easy, or that he'd accomplish it through obvious channels.

Which was why at the outset he'd explained to the people he employed through a privately funded payroll exactly what needed to happen. They had agreed to see to it.

He supposed if there was anything left that moved him it was their loyalty as much as their consummate skill. His global influence had ensured him the first; his fortune had bought him the second.

Were he to lose it all tomorrow, his team would remain at his side, pledging to him the fruit of their endeavors and going above and beyond.

They did so because he believed in them, because he allowed them free reign. And he would continue to do both—as long as he was never linked to their actions. They made sure no one could.

His motions as automatic as his thoughts, he returned to his desk, tapped the screen of his notebook pc, and brought up his encrypted contact program.

On the keyboard, he pecked out the password, then initiated the call that would set in motion the next step decided on at the beginning of this road.

When the phone connected and was answered, he waited for the two clicks that told him the line was secure.

And then he said, "I want to know everything there is to know about the murder of Kevin Kowalski."

One

New York City, the greatest city in the world, was a long way from Louisiana's Cajun country. So far, in fact, that Kingdom Trahan found himself measuring the distance in things other than the miles that separated the Big Apple from his Vermilion Parish home of Bayou Allain. For one thing, there wasn't a decent boiled crawfish to be found.

It was coming up on April, and he was more than ready to get back to the Gulf Coast for his favorite time of the year. Crawfish, red potatoes, corn on the cob, and Tabasco sauce, with ice cold beer, ESPN, and friends gathered to feast. *Mmm-mmm-mmm*. Life didn't get any better than that.

But it *did* get a whole lot better than now. While hating most every minute of the last three weeks spent in the northeast corner of the continent, he'd been reminded daily—and uncomfortably—that he was not cut out for the cold. He was all about the heat of the sun. Baking. Sweating. Burning up like bare feet on asphalt. It made him feel alive.

His cousin Simon, and Michelina, Simon's wife, had been getting a kick out of his shivering and cussing and working to keep his blood from turning to ice. Since he'd been getting one out of watching the newlyweds try to keep their hands to themselves in public, he called it a draw.

King had come to Manhattan for the couple's elopement party at the Mandarin Oriental. They'd sent out invitations the day they'd flown to Vegas to tie the knot, inviting a couple hundred of their closest friends to celebrate their union the weekend of their return.

Their stealing away to get married had provided a source of society gossip for days. King couldn't imagine dealing with the paparazzi and the press the way S & M had to do on a regular basis, what with Micky being the international face of Ferrer Fragrances.

And that was the other reason King was here. He'd come to pose for some men's fragrance ad test shots at Micky's request. Only days after meeting him, she'd told him he had the perfect look for Ferrer's new *Trieste* campaign, and made him promise he'd let her see how he looked in print.

He was a white T-shirt, blue denim, and brown leather boots kinda guy. Dealing with photographers and makeup, hair stylists and wardrobe . . . way too much drama when he could be home on Le Hasard working his drilling rig with the roustabouts he'd hired, or pounding nails with the crew building his house, or even out in the Gulf, shrimping with the fishermen manning the trawler he'd christened *My Precious*.

Finding a treasure of gold coins buried for over a century on his property had gone a helluva long way to helping turn his sorry life around. But it hadn't done half as much toward setting him on the straight and narrow as hooking up with his cousin again after twenty years spent apart and at odds, the *dumbest* thing he'd ever let happen.

In fact, hanging with Simon and Micky had been the only thing making the trip to New York bearable. It had helped, too, that Simon had been put through the very same photographer, makeup, wardrobe, hairstylist hell. Misery loving company—and that company being his cos—had pretty much been the glue keeping King from walking off the set.

Two weeks ago . . .

"No, goddamnit. Enough with the hairspray. My eyes feel like I walked into a stack of burning tires."

King snorted, looked over from the chair where he sat wearing a bib that matched Simon's, and watched his cousin bat at the persistent stylist flitting around and wielding her can and comb like the stinger end of a wasp.

"Better let her spray, Cos. Else she'll come after that tail of yours with a blade. Chop you right down to size like Delilah did to poor ol' Samson."

"I'm not so sure it wouldn't make Micky damn happy if she did." Simon yanked the cape from his neck and shoulders, and surged out of the chair, his shoulder-length hair flying behind him like a black stallion's mane.

He headed around the makeup stations toward the green screen in front of which the two of them, along with the female models posing with them as sex objects, would be twisted and tortured and turned this way and that until the photographer got what he wanted.

Or what Micky wanted, since Mrs. Ferrer-Baptiste was the one in charge.

Facing forward again as he snickered, King found himself eye to eye with the only stylist who'd had the patience—and the moxie—to work with him. Cady something. Cady Kowalski. Cute girl. Pale. Big brown eyes.

Black hair spiked all over her head like a porcupine plugged ass-first into a live socket. Waifish looking, if waifs could stare a man down until he cried uncle. King didn't know much about waifs except that this one was a wolf in sheep's clothing, and scared him.

In fact, as he looked on, she bared her canines in what he supposed most folks would call a smile. He did what he could to wave her off, and make himself look good. "Hey, don't go blaming me for Simon being a dick. I'm sitting here like the royalty I am, haven't moved a muscle."

"You turned your head," Cady growled, pushing out the words from behind her teeth. "I told you to sit still, and you turned your head. Royalty my ass."

"Well, then. You should've fixed up the backside while I was looking away," he told her, shaking his head wildly and undoing all the styling she'd done before giving her a wink that usually brought women to their knees.

Not this time.

"I should've been a nun. Seriously." She turned away, cleaning the comb she'd been using and straightening all the cans and tubes and bottles of product scattered around her station. "I should've joined a convent like my grandmother Josephine promised God she'd make me do. If I never have to deal with another man in my life, it won't be too soon."

She closed up her laptop, packed up her bag, continued her one-woman conversation. "Maybe it's not too late to give the nun thing a try. I can still make my grandmother happy. I can have that surgery, get my virginity stitched back together. I'm pretty short on worldly possessions anyway, and since I really should find a new crash pad before I get kicked to the curb, Tibet's probably as good a place as any."

King listened to her mumble and mutter, knowing she was talking to herself and not to him, but he had to interrupt before someone carted her off to the loony bin. "I think you're confusing a convent with a monastery."

"Same thing."

"Nope. Don't think so. Catholic nuns, Buddhist monks. Worlds apart."

"Whatever." She whirled around, jerked the cape he wore from his neck. "Just go. Be beautiful. Paw the models and make them squirm. See if I care."

He levered himself out of the chair, towered over her, stared down. She had her arms crossed holding herself tight, her gaze focused on her feet. He shouldn't care, and really he didn't, but that didn't stop him from making a loose fist, lifting her chin, and giving her a true blue smile.

"Simon's a dick. I'm a jerk. Don't let us get to you, boo. We'll be outta here in a few days. We're not worth you shaving that porcupine off your head and wearing nightgowns and sandals for the rest of your life."

"Thanks, but really. It's not about you," she said, stepping away from his touch and walking off, leaving him there with her mirror and his reflection.

And no matter how much King's life had changed this last year, the man looking back at him had nothing to say.

Two

As much as he'd been tempted, King hadn't walked off the set until yesterday, the last day of shooting, but now that he was done with all of Micky's ad campaign nonsense, it was time to get his personal show on the road.

The elopement party was long over. The photo shoot was finished. The catching up he'd needed to do with his cousin was done. King may not have worn out his welcome, but he had worn to the nub his patience with this life and this place that wasn't his.

He'd said his good-byes to Simon and Micky over a private dinner last night. Today, he'd smiled and shaken hands with everyone at Ferrer Fragrances who'd stopped by the conference room for a sandwich, a bag of chips, and a soda—a going away lunch to wish him well.

He'd flown up for the party and the shoot and the catching up, but had decided he was due a real vacation. And since he wasn't of a mind these days to worry about the price of gas or global warming, he'd had Simon take him shopping last week for a vehicle worthy of the cross-country trip.

The shiny black Hummer H3 Alpha had been parked in the garage down the block from the Ferrer office now for five days, and ever since it had been delivered and valeted, King had been itching to get behind the wheel.

Simon, knowing the terror his cousin was on the two-lane blacktops that he traveled through Vermilion Parish, said King would do better to keep it parked and use their car service—unless, of course, he didn't mind being hit with insurance claims, traffic tickets, and lawsuits that would tie him up in court for years.

Yeah, and no thanks.

But finally, *finally*, it was time to go.

He heaved the military duffel filled with his clothes and other crap behind the front seat, and checked the supplies in the cargo space he'd ordered laid in—a cooler he would fill with ice, food and drinks once on his way, along with a sleeping bag, one-man tent, and enough camping supplies to outfit his own scout troop for a month off the grid. This was going to be a hell of a road trip.

Damn if it wasn't good to be King.

He slammed the rear door and headed for the driver's, pulled it open, and climbed behind the wheel. He started her up, loving the sound of all those hungry horses, and checked the gauges, then programmed the GPS to get him from here to Pennsylvania. He'd figure out where to go next once he got there.

He was just shifting into D, which he'd decided stood for "drive like a madman until getting caught," when the passenger door opened and Cady Kowalski climbed in beside him.

Without a word, she tossed a backpack half the size of his duffel behind her seat. And then she buckled her seat belt and faced straight ahead, still silent.

King waited, and waited, the engine running, finally shifting to the side and giving the spiky-haired waif an eye, "I think you've got the wrong bus, boo. I'm not making any side trips to Tibet."

"Wherever you're going is fine."

"I'm going to Louisiana."

"Like I said. Fine."

"Let's try this again." He'd told her he was a jerk. It was time to live up to it. "Get out."

She shook her head, sat on her hands, and hunched forward. "I can't."

"It's easy." He reached behind him for her heavy-ass backpack, shoved it into her lap. "You do the reverse of what you did to get in."

Still nothing. No eye contact. No movement except her knees bouncing. And now no more talking.

She had on skinny frayed jeans, what looked like red plaid Converse sneakers, and a faded black logo T-shirt beneath a maroon hoodie left hanging unzipped.

The clothes made her look a lot younger than she'd appeared when wearing the black on black uniform of the stylists hired by Ferrer. And her looking younger made King feel every one of his close to forty years.

Screw it. He wanted to know. "How old are you?"

"Twenty-nine, why?"

Well, shit. Now he wasn't feeling so old at all.

What he was feeling—besides irritated—was something that still felt big-time wrong, so he went back to being irritated instead. "Good, then you're old enough to understand a threat when you hear one. Get out."

"I can't," she said, and though he knew she hadn't moved, he also swore her voice had flinched.

Christ Almighty.

He shoved open his door, jumped down, and stalked around the front of the SUV to her side, yanking it open and grabbing her wrist where she'd buried her face in her hands. He didn't pull, he just held her, and he didn't even hold her tight.

"Cady. I'm going home. To Louisiana. Understand?" When she still didn't move, or even look at him, he weakened. "I can give you a ride to wherever you want to go, but that's it. I don't have time for games."

"This isn't a game," she said, her voice muffled by her fingers and palms.

He let her go, grabbed her backpack from her lap, and before she could stop him, spun it like a Frisbee and sent it skidding across the floor of the garage. It hit a concrete pillar and stopped.

"What are you doing?" she screamed, launching out of her seat. "My laptop, everything I own is in that bag!"

He stood in the V of the open door, blocking her way and forcing her to meet his gaze. He was done with this. He didn't know what she wanted or what she thought she was doing, and he didn't give a goddamn care.

Head down, she struggled to get past him. He wouldn't let her. He wouldn't budge. He was serious about not putting up with her shit, and he wanted to see that she got it.

Only that wasn't what he saw when she finally gave in and looked up. What he saw was a viciously brutal black eye. And that wasn't the only damage. Her cheek, her lip. She was mighty busted up.

She met his gaze for a second, then glanced quickly away, lifting tentative fingertips and touching the butterfly bandages on her forehead and cheek. "Believe me. I understand a threat when I hear one. But you've got to understand that I need to get out of here now."

"Yeah," he heard himself saying, while his mind got ready with the twenty questions he wanted to ask. "Get in. I'll get your bag. I've got an ice pack in my gear. I'll get that, too."

"Thank you," she said, boosting back up into the seat. "And I'm sorry. I didn't know what else to do."

If this girl who he'd met last week, this girl who he'd spent a few afternoons harassing had no one to turn to but him, there was something very large and very wrong going on here.

Something somebody needed to fix.

A hell of a road trip. Wasn't that what he'd been thinking just moments ago? Hmph. Looked like this one was going to start out with a detour before he'd even driven a mile.

Three

As he pulled out of the parking garage and checked traffic, King caught a glimpse of the backpack Cady clutched to her chest as if it contained a million bucks.

The backpack she'd said held everything she owned.

The backpack he'd flung across the floor like he would a bag filled with garbage.

Nice.

She'd had it with her every day at the shoot, and she'd pulled out her laptop more than once, grumbling when she couldn't find an unsecured wireless network to get her onto the Web.

He couldn't have known she had it with her now. He should've suspected, but he couldn't have known.

That didn't make his lack of respect for her property go down any better. In fact, it hung in his chest like a wad of day-old dry cornbread soaked in bad buttermilk, and he had to clear his throat twice to speak.

"Your backpack. Is that really all the stuff you own?" He glanced over, saw her turn her head and stare out the passenger side window.

Her voice bounced back at him off the glass. "It's all I could get out."

Get out? "Get out of where?"

"My apartment."

"Before it burned down? Before the rats and roaches took over?" He wanted a real answer, one that said something, not one leading to a string of questions that would take too long to reel in.

He wanted to know what he'd find dangling at the end of the line, and he wanted to know it now.

"Before either of my roommates came home."

King braked abruptly as a cabby cut in front of him at the next light. He was too busy frowning over what Cady had told him to even think about honking or being pissed off. "Who do you live with? Jealous boyfriends? Jealous welter-weights? Jealous black belts?"

She blew out a loud puff of breath. "Who *did* I live with is the question."

He remembered. She'd mentioned something about needing to find a new place to crash. Now he was really curious about what her face had run into.

When she didn't say anything else, he prodded. "And the answer would be?"

"Two girls I met on Craigslist," she said, shrugging it off as she added, "They needed a third to split the rent. My building was going co-op, so I had to get out. I moved in six months ago."

The light changed. The driver behind him sat on his horn. King checked his rearview and saw the delivery service's logo and a middle finger flipped his way.

He kept his attention on Cady, ignoring the asshole driver behind him. "You moved in with them but didn't know them? Before hooking up online?"

She was facing forward again, and she shrugged as the H3 crushed its way through the intersection to a loud blast of horns from all sides. "It was a three-way of convenience. It happens. You don't live alone in the city unless you're in a rent-controlled building, get paid way more than I do, or are sleeping with Donald Trump."

He'd looked at real estate while he was here. He didn't know why. Maybe the temptation of having Simon and Micky living just down the road instead of thousands of miles away had been too much to resist.

He'd resisted once he'd realized he could run a small fleet of shrimp boats for the price of two thousand square feet ten flights up.

He checked his mirrors again, changed lanes, watched a car behind him crunch bumpers with the delivery van, and found himself grinning ear to ear. A grin that faded when he remembered Cady. "You said you got out what you could before your roommates came home. Does that mean you left a lot of stuff behind?"

"Not a lot, no. My bed and dresser, which I'm sure they'll give away when they realize I'm gone. Same with the clothes I didn't have room for."

"You've got room now," he said, gesturing with a tilt of his head toward the Hummer's backseat and wondering when he'd become a good Samaritan.

She looked over her shoulder in the same direction, then turned to stare straight ahead once again. "The furniture's secondhand and not worth worrying about. There are some outfits I'd like to get, but I can live without them. Vintage stuff I found in resale shops.

"Oh, and my shoes," she hurried to add as if suddenly realizing her good fortune. "I've got a lot of shoes. Mostly, though, I could use more clothes than I had time to grab. I was in a hurry this morning, and not thinking too clearly after the emergency room."

King's stomach tightened around the drill bit churning there. "Who sent you to the emergency room? One of the girls? These wonderful roommates?"

"I never said they were wonderful," she reminded him, then stopped talking, making King wonder if that was all or if she was going to say more.

Finally, she moved her backpack to the floor and pulled a

knee up into her seat, turning to face him. "Does the offer of your backseat come with a list of conditions?"

He supposed it should, but . . . "No."

"So I don't have to tell you what happened?"

To her face? Or to her spirit? Because this girl . . . ? She was not the same Cady Kowalski who'd had her hands all over his hair, whose breasts he'd mentally felt up when she'd leaned over him to spritz and spray.

Yeah, he wanted to know what happened. And the Kingdom Trahan who'd spent his first four adult years at the farm in Angola, Louisiana's State Penitentiary, would've said, "Damn straight."

But those days were long gone, and he was no longer that man. Hell, he was a different man today than he'd been just last year when his cousin had walked back onto Le Hasard after half of their lifetimes apart.

And so what he said was, "You only have to tell me what you want me to know. And how to get to your place. I don't know which way is up around here."

She gave him directions as he drove, taking him into a part of the city he hadn't yet seen during his trip. He wasn't sure where he was, upper or lower or east or west, but he did know that whatever Cady's split of the rent—

It was too much. The place was a dump.

"I'm on the fourth floor," she told him as he pulled up in front of the building sandwiched in the middle of a block of similar ones. "I know it looks like crap, but the apartment itself is nice."

"I won't be taking your word for that," he said, shoving open his door and circling the front of the vehicle to her side. When it became clear she was making no move to follow, he opened her door and offered her a hand. "I don't know vintage from Velcro. You have to come in."

Four

Cady didn't seem the least bit interested in coming in, a situation that would've been more hassle than King was willing to deal with had she not decided instead to talk.

"It wasn't one of the girls," she told him. "Not all of it anyway."

His gut tightened up again, her voice was so small, so fragile. "Who was it?"

"Alice's boyfriend, Tyler."

Heat flared behind his eyes. "Are you going to tell me what happened? In case I run into him on the stairs? I'll need to know whether I should let him pass or dump him over the banister."

It was the first time since she'd climbed into the SUV's front seat that he'd seen her smile. At least it looked like a smile. It was hard to distinguish the movement of her mouth from the grimace that followed when she brought her fingers to her split lip.

"We were drinking last night. Me and Alice and Tyler and Renee."

"Renee's the third roommate," he guessed, and Cady nodded to confirm.

"I woke up around four to pee, and realized Tyler was in my bed. He was passed out, but neither one of us were dressed. I grabbed my panties and T-shirt from the floor and ran to the bathroom. Alice gave me this"—she said, pointing to her lip—"while I was sitting on the toilet."

Christ Almighty. "Did he rape you?"

"I don't think so. Things didn't smell like sex, if you know what I mean, and I wasn't sore or raw, not that I necessarily would be."

Yeah, definitely TMI. All of it.

"But I really don't think we had sex. Tyler was wasted long before I even started drinking. And he was still going at it when I went to bed. If he was able to get it up after that, then Alice's one lucky girl."

King had thought before that something was wrong, but this was even too weird for him. "The sex thing. It's not a big deal? Not knowing if you were raped?"

"Like I said. I doubt Tyler did more than crawl into the wrong bed. The clothes thing, I don't know about. Last night's not a blur, it doesn't even register."

"At least until four A.M."

As if she had no intention of leaving her seat, Cady pulled both of her knees to her chest and wrapped her arms around them. "The bashing hour."

King wasn't much for coaxing, but if that's what it was going to take . . . "What happened after Alice hit you?"

"She hit me again. And again. Renee finally dragged her out of the bathroom long enough for me to wipe and pull up my underwear. By then, Tyler was up stumbling around, deflecting Alice's accusations that he'd been after me for months and telling her I'd seduced him. He slapped me once, called me a liar when I told him he was full of shit."

"Had he? Been after you for months?"

Cady shrugged, the motion small. "It's news to me if it's true. I'm hardly ever home to see any of them. I work long hours. I go out with friends."

"Your roommates aren't friends?"

"We're friendly, but we don't hang out."

"Who do you hang out with?"

"Depends on the occasion. Girls I work with, usually. One who works at the coffee shop on the corner."

"Then why climb into my truck instead of going to one of them?"

She cut her gaze up to his. "None of them were leaving town."

"A girl beat you up because she thought you slept with her boy toy. And you're leaving town?" Yeah, she'd given him a story, but it wasn't making sense in the scheme of the other things going on here.

No one left town because of a split lip, a busted cheek, and a hellacious black eye. Move out, sure. Lay low, keep her distance, disappear, okay. That he could see.

But hitching a ride to Louisiana—or a yet-to-be-determined point along the way—was taking things way too far considering she wasn't even friends with the jerkwads who'd done the job on her face.

Before he could press further, Cady jumped from the Hummer and hurried down the sidewalk to the stoop. Hands in the pockets of her sweatshirt, she jogged up the short flight of stairs, stopping when she got to the door.

She looked back, her eyes big and wide and scared as she met his gaze. "You coming with me or not?"

He slammed the door she'd left open, set the locks and the alarm because he was no man's fool, and followed, hunching his shoulders against the wind that decided to blast down the canyon of the street and ruin his day even more. Goddamn cold-ass spring.

She took the four flights of stairs at a quick climbing jog. He took them two at a time to keep up. The lighting was dingy at best, the paint on the walls peeling at the bottom and water stained at the top. The smells of garlic and curry and bad tennis shoes hung strong in the air.

When they reached the fourth floor, she dug a loose key from her jeans pocket. He took it from her hand and went in first. He wouldn't know if anything was out of order, but he'd much rather have someone come at him for trespassing than go after Cady when she walked through the door.

He knew that Alice had turned her lip into a Bing cherry and her eye into a puddle of mud, while big bad brave Tyler had slapped her. Who knew what the other roommate was capable of, or who might be lying in wait? And one more blow? Her face was liable to cave in.

No one met them at the door, and Cady locked it behind them, then headed down a short hall to her room. King, on the other hand, took his sweet time. She'd been right when she'd said the apartment was nice.

It wasn't nice in the uptown and upscale way Simon and Micky's place was, but it wasn't the shithole he'd expected, having judged this particular book by its run-down cover that faced the street.

The living area had a big cushy sectional in a red and blue plaid, end tables holding ceramic jug lamps with navy shades, and a matching throw rug over the hardwood floor and under the coffee table with its thick glass top.

Another part of the same big room, the kitchen and eating area continued the color scheme, and the whole place was neat and clean with no sign of violence or bloodshed marring the furniture or floors.

He left the front of the apartment and walked down the hall. Framed photos taken in nightclubs and bars hung on the walls. He stopped in the doorway of Cady's stamp–sized room, watching as she crawled into the closet with a roll of black trash bags.

"Who's the photographer?" he asked, gesturing with a lift of his chin toward the pictures.

"Alice. I've actually worked on some of her shoots." Cady jerked clothes from the rod and rolled up the garments, hangars and all. She filled one bag, grabbed another, needed a third when she started in on her shoes. "Who knew she'd turn out to be a lunatic bitch?"

King glanced around the small room. The twin bed with the purple velvet spread would've been a tight fit for two adults—or even for one, bumped up the way it was against the walls between which it was wedged.

The rest of the tiny space was taken up by a scarred dresser with a bench and vanity mirror. That held rows of more lotions and sprays and other girl goop than he'd seen anywhere but on store shelves.

Women. "You taking all that stuff, too?"

Cady looked up from sorting her shoes, then leaned back against the wall of the closet, finally tossing him a small carry-all. "If you want to just scrape it all into this, that would be great."

Scrape. That he could do. And then he cringed at the sound of glass on glass as the bottles tumbled to the bottom of the bag.

"Glass? Hello? Breakable?"

"Hey, you get what you pay for, and my name's not United Van Lines. Besides, I figure we're in a hurry here. You can grab some tape and bubble wrap later."

"Assuming there's anything left to salvage," she said, tossing a bag of shoes to the bed and crawling out of the closet. "That should do it. They can do what they want with the rest."

"Let's go then," King said, hefting the two heaviest bags, one over each shoulder, before stepping from the room into the hallway and into the barrel of a gun.

Five

"Who the hell are you, and what the fuck are you doing in my house?"

At the sound of her roommate's voice, Cady pushed by King and swatted at the handgun the other woman gripped in both hands like she was some kind of cop trained to use it. "He's with me, Alice. Back off."

She headed for the kitchen and the case of peanut butter cracker packets she'd bought the other day, figuring she could live on those and not have to worry about starving as well as being homeless until she came up with a better plan than forcing King Trahan to let her stow away.

But Alice was in no mood to back off. When Cady turned, she found her roommate and the other woman's wrath blocking her exit from the kitchen, the gun in her hand way too cop-trained steady as she pointed it at Cady's forehead. "What's in the trash bags?"

Cady wrapped her arms around the big box of crackers, braced her feet on either side of the bag she'd set on the floor. "My stuff. Shoes, clothes. You can do what you want with everything else. Sell it, trash it. I don't care. Just move so I can get out of here."

"You're not going anywhere until I see what's in the bags." Alice blew her overlong black bangs out of her eyes, pursing her bright red lips when she did. "You obviously think anything you can get your hands or cunt on is yours to take, but it's not the middle of the night, and I'm not drunk."

"Yeah, but you're still a lunatic bitch. I'm done playing punching bag, Alice, and I'm done taking the blame for your boyfriend not being able to tell which bed the real cunt sleeps in," Cady said, and hefted the box to one side, reaching down for the bag—stopping short when she heard the click as her roommate released the safety.

Well, shit.

She straightened slowly, her stomach rising into her throat. Forget the "C" word. She'd called the woman a lunatic intending it as an insult, unaware it was the whole truth and nothing but. "Fine. Look inside. You won't find anything but my shoes. And not even all of them at that. I left a dozen pairs in the closet, including those red velvet Jimmy Choos you love from the Chelsea resale shop—"

Alice's yelp cut off the rest of whatever Cady had been blabbering about. As she looked on, King, who'd taken his sweet time getting here, grabbed Alice's arm and slammed it to the side and back, twisting the gun from her grip while she fought like a heathen she-devil, snarling and scratching and screaming nasty words Cady didn't think she'd ever heard come out of anyone's mouth.

But he didn't stop there. He shoved Alice into the closest dining chair and kept her there with nothing but a look while he removed the ammunition from the gun. "Do I need to call the cops here? Or can we play nice?"

"Call them," Alice spat, sitting on her hands, her blunt cut hair wild and sharp around her pinched face. "Let them see how much of that shit she's hauling out belongs to me or Tyler or Renee."

"Done," King said, his gaze moving from Alice to Cady as he walked toward the kitchen and picked up the phone, tucking the gun into his waistband before dialing. "Then your roommate can file assault charges. And while the boys in blue are here, she can explain you threatening her with a deadly weapon. Should make for an interesting visit."

"Wait," Alice said, her capitulation even faster than Cady had anticipated, stopping King from punching the third number to complete the 911 call. "Just get out of here. Both of you. Leave and don't ever come back."

"There's not enough money in the world," Cady muttered, more than happy to get going.

"Are you kidding? The right price, and you'd do anything, you whore," Alice snarled. "Take your crap and your mangy skanky ass to Jersey where you belong."

Cady ignored the slur, letting it slide off her back as she reached for her things, slapped her key on the table, and headed for the door, hoping King would do the same. She should never have let him talk her into coming here.

"Hold up," King said, and since he was the only reason she was still in one piece—forget that he was also the only reason she'd returned at all—she held up, asking, "What?"

He cocked his head toward Alice. "Does your roommate here owe you a refund on the rent? There are twenty-five days left in the month."

"If you think after what she did that I'm going to give her a dime—" Alice began, closing her mouth when King reached again for the phone.

"It's not worth it," Cady said after looking from King to Alice and back, and seeing as much pity as she did loathing. Neither one did much for her self-esteem.

She wanted out of here. That was all. She didn't care about the money, which was stupid considering she didn't have much expendable to her name.

She just wanted to finish the moving out she'd started this morning and get on with her life. If that was even possible. Which after eight years of trying, she wasn't betting on.

Her face was hurting, and she was glad it did. That centered, focused pain kept her from dwelling on the others pounding both her body and her soul. She wasn't used to feeling sorry for herself, but she needed someone to, and right now, she was her only choice.

She jerked open the door, shouldered through to the landing with her bags, and dragged them behind her down the stairs. She didn't wait for King, but heard him a flight above following.

At this point, she didn't even care if he was bringing the rest of her things. All she cared about, all she was hoping for, was that he'd kept Alice's gun and the ammunition.

She had a feeling that sooner or later she was going to need it.

Six

King drove them away from the apartment and wound his way through the city to the sounds of squealing tires, shouted curses, and blaring horns. They were halfway across the George Washington Bridge before Cady snapped and realized where they were.

Crap.

And she'd thought the day so far had been a titanic disaster.

"Where are we going?" she asked, hoping the bridge as his choice of exit route from the city had been purely random, and that he hadn't picked up on Alice's Jersey remark.

He had. "You bein' a Jersey girl and all, I figured Jersey was the best bet for finding you someplace to stay."

"Then you need to figure again. There's nothing for me there anymore."

"Meaning there once was."

God, this day! What next? A stake through her heart? A telephone pole through her eye?

"Not to pick at the scab," King said. "But what did Alice mean, the right price and you'd do anything?"

No stake, no telephone pole. Just a plunger, sucking at all the crap she'd flushed away a long time ago. "She didn't *mean* anything. Except to *be* mean. She's just talking out of her ass, which is nothing new for Alice."

King made a noise that sounded like, "Hmm," but Cady feared if she asked what it meant, he'd tell her. Then they'd get into a big fat discussion about all the things in her life she had done for money.

That was a discussion she didn't want to have, because if they did? Like everyone else she got into it with, he'd want to know why a nice girl with a business degree couldn't stick with a job.

She didn't want to tell him about the gossip and rumors, about giving up her car, about constantly moving—the things that made sticking with a job hard to do. Right now, the only thing she wanted was to get out of the city.

He was taking her, sure. But Jersey? She found herself gritting her teeth. "Drop me at the bus station. Greyhound and I go way back. I'll find my own way outta here."

He sputtered out a snort. "What about the ton of crap you're hauling in those garbage bags? You need a semi, not a bus."

"My problem, okay?"

King didn't respond. He kept driving, pulling his cell from the clip at his waist and using one thumb to type more numbers than required for a phone call. Then he waited. Ten seconds later, the phone buzzed.

He flipped it open and glanced at the display. "Got a Cady Kowalski listed right here. Freehold Township."

Her past. It was destined to haunt her forever. "And if you call that line, you'll find it's no longer working."

"Yeah, but there's an Edgar Kowalski at the same street address." King secured his phone, flipped his blinker, and changed lanes. "I'm guessing he's either an ex, a brother, or your dad. If it's the first, then never mind. If it's one of the others, I can't see that it would kill you to go there until you can figure things out."

That's because he was blind to the ways of the Kowalski

world. Spelling it out would only be inviting trouble, and so she didn't say a word, trying not to imagine what would happen—and failing because her imagination wasn't really required—if she showed up at her parents' front door.

If her mother was there, the reception wouldn't be much better than what Cady had received in the bathroom from Alice this morning. But if Edgar Kowalski was indeed at home instead of living the high life at McLanahan's Pub . . .

And then a light went on, a cartoon bulb dangling above her head. The best way to prove to King that she couldn't go home again might be to do just that. Show him how long it would take to have things figured out for her.

She wasn't so stupid, however, as to do so without first checking to see if the coast was clear. What Alice had inflicted on Cady's face was nothing compared to the damage Edgar Kowalski could do.

She took a courageous breath, knowing no amount of courage would change things. "If I tell you how to get to my parents' house, you have to promise me that you won't drive off and leave me the second I climb down from this seat."

"I'll wait as long as you need me to. Hell, I'll carry your things inside."

Cady held back a grunt. He didn't have to sound so relieved to be getting rid of her, did he? Then again, she could see how he'd think her a nuisance, the way she'd dragged him into her drama. As if her cuts and bruises weren't enough, there was the business end of Alice's gun.

They had an hour or so ahead of them. She could share her life's story between here and there, or she could sit back and stew and hope her hands didn't shake so much that he noticed and started in with the platitudes, or worse, with wanting to know what was wrong.

She didn't want to tell him. What she wanted was to show him the greeting she'd receive, the one for which she was already bracing. Then maybe he'd get it. Then maybe he'd see that there was no way she was staying in Jersey when so many people here wanted her gone.

After that, he'd have to take her with him, right? Or at least put her on a bus. She could always get in touch with him once she was settled and have him ship her her things, assuming he would agree to keep them and not toss them in the first Dumpster he saw.

Hey, a girl could dream, couldn't she? Maybe this one wouldn't turn into the usual nightmare. No, this plan might not be the best one she'd ever come up with, but with the way this day was going and time not being her friend, it was all she had in her.

And so she said, "Fine. But I'll need you to make a quick detour."

"What kind of detour?" he asked, all suspicion and hooded eyes again.

She didn't even know why she'd said that. He wouldn't know if he was detouring or not. "If I tell you now, that'll ruin the surprise, won't it?"

Of course, there was no surprise.

She just wasn't up to explaining that going by the house where she'd grown up depended on her father having stopped off for a round—or ten—of drinks before going home from work to the dinner he wasn't going to eat that her mother hadn't wanted to cook in the first place.

Cady wasn't sure if staying in Manhattan wouldn't have been the better choice between the two hells.

"I'm not much of a surprise kinda guy," King said, cutting into her musings.

"Good. Then you won't be disappointed. Since this isn't much of one."

"Cady?"

"Fine," she said, her easy surrender saying a lot about her state of mind. Alice's beating must've been some sort of last straw because she hadn't backed down after any she'd suffered in the past. "I want to know who's home before I knock on the door. Last I knew, my father, that would be Edgar, topped off the workday with several pints. If he's at the pub, that means I'll only have my mother to face."

"You make it sound like a death sentence."

"You don't know my mother."

"Tell me about her."

"I'd rather not. Besides, there's nothing to tell. She cooks breakfast and lunch in a school cafeteria, then cooks dinner at home."

"Is she a good cook?"

"Let's just say she's never met a canned food product she couldn't find a use for." Not that Cady would say no to a big plate of corned beef hash right about now.

She popped free her seat belt and squirreled around, digging a couple of cracker packets from the box in the back. She hadn't eaten all day.

Behind her, King huffed. "I see cellophane's not quite the same evil as aluminum."

"Sure it is. But I'm starving." She offered him the second pack anyway.

He shook his head. "Ferrer had a bon voyage lunch thing today. I think I ate at least three boxes of sandwiches and chips."

"How long have you been in the city?" she asked, grateful for the opening. A change of subject was way overdue.

He glanced in his rearview mirror, signaled, and changed lanes to pass a slow-moving car. "I came up originally for the elopement party then stayed for the fragrance ad test shots. Three weeks, I guess."

"Awful long time for a party and some pictures," she said, then popped a whole cracker into her mouth.

"Yeah, but the biggest part of the visit was about seeing my cousin. You remember Simon?" he said, and she nodded, her mouth full. "We spent a long time out of touch, and just reconnected last year. Hanging out for a while seemed the thing to do."

"Why the estrangement?" She was curious to see if he'd contradict her, correct her, tell her that he and Simon hadn't been estranged, just living their own lives, doing their own things. It was hard to imagine them being out of touch. They'd seemed close the times she'd seen them together.

When he didn't object to her question, she was thrilled. Not because she was right, but because her being right gave them a common ground.

He shook his head, returned to his lane. "An old sad story from a long time ago that's not worth me taking the time to tell you."

Meaning, it would be worth every gory word. "Juicy details?"

"None."

"A woman?"

He hesitated a fraction too long.

"A-ha! There was."

King gave a loud, "Hmph," as he checked traffic again, the setting sun glinting off the pricey sunglasses he pulled from the visor and put on. "Not in the way you're thinking, but yeah. Lorna Savoy. She was there for what went down."

"What did go down?"

He cocked his mouth into a half wicked smile. "You don't need to know, boo. Hell, you don't want to know."

More like he didn't want to talk about it. She knew what that was like, steering clear of those things too personal to be kept as anything but secrets. Which, of course, had her curiosity climbing the proverbial walls.

"Sure I do." And she did, though the story could wait. Hearing it wasn't the goal. "But what I really want to know is that you understand being family doesn't guarantee sunshine and rainbows, or even open arms."

"Yeah, I understand," he said, and then he shut up.

Since there was nothing more to be said, Cady shut up, too. She dug for and found a bottle of water in her backpack, then rinsed the cracker crumbs and peanut butter from her mouth.

After that, she would've closed her eyes and slept through the rest of the ride, but King didn't know where to go, so she stayed awake and watched the familiar landmarks fly by.

She'd grown up in Freehold Township. Springsteen's home. She, her mom and dad, her older brother Kevin.

Both of her parents were only children, meaning she and Kevin hadn't spent their young lives tussling with cousins the way many of their classmates from large families had. They'd only had each other, which made everything that eventually happened so much worse.

Twisting her hands nervously in her lap, she told herself not to think about that now. She didn't want to think about it ever again though the way the events of eight years ago continued to drive her life, it was hard not to.

But right now, with this morning fresh on her face and reminding her that she had no life, that she was a nobody, that she'd had to go to a complete stranger for help, she couldn't wallow in the past, especially when she was on her way to confront it.

And so she made herself a deal. She wouldn't think about Kevin's murder while she was with King—a deal that got harder and harder to stick to the closer they drew to their destination.

She gave him directions to her family's neighborhood, and tried not to grow melancholy as so many good memories assailed her and reminded her of all she'd lost.

Yeah, things had gone to shit in a very big way, but she'd grown up here, celebrated birthdays with Barbie and My Little Pony parties, learned way too young that there wasn't really a Santa Claus, cheered on her junior high sports teams from the middle of the cheerleader pyramid, lost her virginity to Wayne Hoppes in the back of his yellow Ford Pinto.

Okay, so that last one wasn't exactly a memory she wanted to revisit, but this had been her home, her *home*, goddamnit, for twenty-one years. Now it was a place where she was no longer welcome, where she no longer fit.

Coming back here just to prove that truth to King Trahan was not something she was looking forward to, but right now he was her best hope for getting far far away from here and doing so in one piece.

"Turn here," she told him, pointing to the right as they approached the next intersection. He did, and once the red and green neon lights of McLanahan's sign came into view, she added, "Slow down."

"What is it that we're looking for?"

"Edgar's always been a fan of the big American auto. Last I knew, he was driving a late nineties' Buick."

And there it was, the maroon LeSabre parked at the curb in front of the pub's front window. The car she remembered him bringing home new her junior year of high school.

The car he'd let her use after a lecture on buying American he'd made when her ancient Toyota wouldn't run. The car Kevin had pummeled with a baseball bat the night Sunny, his girlfriend of six years, dumped him.

Cady smiled remembering how many jobs Kevin had worked to pay for the repairs, Edgar never saying a word when he'd been handed the check. Then she stopped smiling because she remembered why they were here.

"Two streets up, make a right, then a left at the third intersection. We're the second house on the left." *The one where my whole life imploded.*

King nodded and followed her directions without asking her to repeat a single step. Since her throat had swelled, making it highly unlikely that she would've been able to answer, she didn't mind the silence. In fact, it made it easier for her to come up with something to say to her mother.

She was still working on that when the SUV rolled to a stop in front of the two-story Georgian that had once been white but had long ago gone to gray. The shutters on the upstairs windows were closed tight, keeping the memories inside. Two big oaks hugged the house in gentle shadows with the wide spread of their sheltering limbs.

If she'd had the time, Cady would've sat down on the sidewalk and cried. But she didn't, so she took a deep breath and steeled herself for the confrontation to come, wishing things eight years ago hadn't gone so wrong—wishing even more for a magic forgiveness fairy to sprinkle dust over her parents' house.

She opened her door. King opened his. She looked over. "Where are you going?"

"To unload your stuff."

She shook her head. "Just wait, okay? Stay here and wait."

He frowned as if inconvenienced by the delay, but remained where he was, nodding when she told him, "Thank you."

The trip from the Hummer up the sidewalk to the porch took a small eternity.

Cady kept her gaze on the front door, knowing curtains would be fluttering away from the windows of the neighbors' houses and phones would be jangling in their cradles up and down the block.

More than likely, her mother would know she was there before Cady even knocked—an upper hand certain to go the other woman's way.

Cady was right. She was only halfway up the steps when the locks snapped back.

By the time she reached the top, the door was swinging open, the hinges squeaking, spilling a rectangle of yellow light onto the worn boards of the porch. And then the light disappeared, her mother's body blocking it.

Except for her fleshier jowls, Lorraine Kowalski looked the same as she had the last time Cady had seen her. She wore the white knit shirt and black knit pants of her cafeteria worker uniform, the thick-soled shoes that made it possible for her to stand on her feet all day.

She held a dish towel in her damp, reddened hands. Her gray hair was pulled tightly to her head and covered with a fine net. Her face was devoid of makeup.

It wasn't, however, devoid of emotion. Her eyes sparked. Bright red circles glowed on her cheeks. The wrinkles above her cracked lips deepened as her mouth moved, though no words ever came out.

"Hello, Mum," Cady finally said, looking beyond her mother's shoulder and blinking away tears.

And because she'd focused her gaze on the Thomas Kinkade painting hanging between two sconces on the living room wall, she never saw the punch coming.

Seven

King had been seconds from unloading Cady's trash bags from the backseat of the Hummer when the woman who'd met Cady on the front porch slammed her hand into her daughter's face, then slammed the door so hard the sound echoed all the way to the street.

He bolted away from the vehicle where he'd been waiting, skidded around the front end, and ran up the front walk, taking the six steps in two leaps.

Cady was just getting to her feet when he reached her. He made sure she had her balance and wasn't going to fall, then he pounded his fist on the door.

She grabbed at the sleeve of his denim shirt with one hand, probed her face with the other. "Don't bother. She won't answer."

"She just assaulted you." He didn't know what was going on here, but Cady had been through enough. He wasn't going to let this one go. He didn't give a shit that it was her mother behind the battering. "I'm calling the cops."

This time she grabbed at his cell phone before he could flip it open and punch 911. "Let's just get out of here. The neighbors have enough gossip to hold them for a while. And I need an ice pack. Again."

As much as he wanted to bring down the broad behind

the door, he knew Cady was right. The bitch could wait. Cady's face could not. "Is your nose bleeding? Broken? Where's the nearest ER?"

She shook her head, held onto him as they descended from the porch to the sidewalk. "She's not that strong. I'll have a new bruise on top of the others, but I might as well get the abuse out of the way so I can get on with my life."

He waited until they were both buckled in and he'd started the engine, the truck rumbling softly beneath them, before glancing toward her and asking, "You knew that was coming, didn't you?"

She shrugged, sucked in a breath as she gently touched the newest damage to her face with the second cold pack he'd supplied her from his camping gear. It took her a minute or two to get settled, and even in the waning light he could see her wince when she moved.

"I wasn't sure if it would be a fist or a palm, but yeah. I knew." She groaned, finally pulled her knee to her chest and propped her elbow there, bracing the hand holding the pack. "At least it was Lorraine and not Edgar. Her punishment I was willing to take to prove you wrong."

He didn't like the sound of that. Or the blame her words lobbed his direction when he didn't want to be involved. He wasn't involved. She wasn't his problem. She was a stowaway he was going to help find another ride.

He could not be her ride. "What do you mean, prove me wrong?"

She turned her head, her hand moving as if part of her face. All he could see was the cold pack where she held it, and the puffy purple skin around her original black eye. "You said it wouldn't kill me to go home until I figured out what I was doing with my life."

He looked back at the road, accepting that he had, indeed, said just that. But he'd said it back when he'd thought her objection to bunking with her folks was her being too proud to ask them for help.

He didn't know Cady Kowalski wouldn't be welcome—or safe—in her own family's home.

Now he wanted to know why.

But first he wanted to know something else. "Why put yourself through that? You couldn't think of a less damaging way to make your point?"

She settled more comfortably in the far corner of the seat. "You threw my backpack across the garage to get rid of me. You made it clear you didn't want me around. A dramatic gesture seemed the best way to convince you that I wasn't throwing a tantrum about not going home."

"I threw your backpack before I saw your face," he said, completely convinced. She wasn't the tantrum type. Dramatic, yes. Hissy-fit, no.

"Yeah, well. Oomph." She sucked back a sharp breath when he hit a pot hole and jolted her. "Most white knights don't need a literal blow-by-blow. They take the damsel in distress at her word."

"Most white knights know the dragon they're being asked to go up against," he said, thinking of several he'd walked away from, choosing to save his own ass instead, having been that kinda guy long enough to have put it to the test.

He twisted his mouth, added, "Then again—"

"You're no white knight," Cady finished for him.

"Exactly."

Yet even as he made the admission, he felt the label constrict him in ways that no longer fit. He should have listened to her. He should have done more than hear the words coming out of her mouth.

He should have paid attention to what she was saying, especially after seeing for himself the nut job who was her roommate. She'd told him the truth about that, hadn't she? He'd just found this more convenient to ignore.

He might not be much for rescues, but that didn't mean he had to be a jerk. She needed help, and giving it wasn't going to put him out. It was the least he could do since he was a whole lot of responsible for her newest shiner.

He pulled into the next fast food joint he saw. They were fifteen minutes from her parents' house. What were the odds she'd run into someone she knew? "Hungry?"

"Starving. I would never make it on *Survivor.* I can't even get by on peanut butter crackers." She grabbed her backpack and followed him to the door, once they were inside telling him, "I'm going to see if I can do something about my face. Just get me something with cheese and bacon and fries, and size it as big as you can."

"Yes ma'am," he said, thinking she didn't look big enough to hold that many calories. She was either a bottomless pit, an emotional eater, or starving like she'd said.

He also got to thinking, while he was waiting for their food and for her to reappear, that she really didn't need to do anything to her face. Aside from covering up the cuts and bruises. And even that was more about her own comfort level with having people see her beat all to hell.

She was cute, in a perky elf with hair like a field of charred alfalfa kind of way. She was tall, and he liked tall. She was curvy enough, with a lithe, limber, athletic build, nothing out of proportion, overdone, or fake.

Not that he minded fake or overdone. Both made for good eye candy, one night stands, and centerfolds.

But he'd discovered a lot about himself this last year, and one of those discoveries was that he wanted what his cousin Simon had found with Michelina . . . except that wasn't quite right.

He wasn't Simon. He lived just as dangerously, though in his own way, fighting personal demons instead of bad guys, losing as often as beating them down.

He'd thought for a while that it would be nice to have a cheering section if not an equal partner at his side—except he was too old for the first, and too old-fashioned for the second because he liked things done his way. So he wasn't much for compromise. Sue him.

No, what he found himself wanting was a friend who was also a lover, someone to go home to, to talk to about his day and hers, a reason to look forward to the end of the day besides a bath, a plate of food, and a bed.

And why Cady Kowalski was making him revisit all of this while waiting for his onion rings and double cheeseburger, he couldn't have said.

It wasn't like he'd been the one on the wrong end of her roommate's gun this morning, his life flashing before his eyes in too many unresolved shades of gray.

The gun was now stored in his camping gear along with his own. He probably should have left it with Alice, or ditched it before leaving the state.

Now he'd have to deal with the stolen weapon he was hauling around, as well as figure out what to do with Cady before he hit the road for the long drive home that was supposed to be his vacation.

He supposed he could put her on a plane to wherever she wanted to go. He had the money. Enough that he could give her a nice start on a new life on top of the plane ticket. Hell, she could buy all new stuff instead of secondhand.

That sounded like a win-win plan, the best thing for the both of them—even though he knew he was going to have a hell of a time persuading Cady of that.

"Order two-sixty-four. Two-sixty-four. Hello, mister? Two-sixty-four!"

"I'll get it," Cady said, nudging him as she walked to the counter to take the tray from the woman in the red chef's hat holding it out as if doing them a big fat favor in her free time.

He followed Cady to the table she chose, trying not to notice the fit of her jeans or her sweet curvy ass or her long, long legs.

He'd enjoyed flirting with her during the Ferrer Fragrance ad photo shoot. He'd liked a lot feeling her hands on his face and in his hair. He'd gotten a charge out of having her rub against him as she tried to turn him into someone he'd never wanted to be.

But he'd never expected to see her again once Micky had her pictures in hand. And he was finding it really strange to be remembering the flirting and the touching when more than likely he and Cady would be sharing a room—though he doubted a bed—tonight.

"You looked like you were lost in thought," she said to him, sliding into the booth after returning the tray to the counter.

"You could say that," he said, popping his straw from its wrapper and shoving it through the plastic lid into his caffeinated drink. He probably should've gone for no sugar and decaf. He sure didn't need the jolt.

Cady watched him intently. "Worth a penny, or worth a pound?"

"You're mixing your currency."

"And you're avoiding the question," said she who looked like the lucky survivor of a killer auto accident. He wondered how long she'd have to wait to see a doctor about pulling the stitches.

"After everything that's happened today? I'll be the interrogator. You're the interrogatee," he said, then bit away a good third of his burger.

"I suppose that's only fair," she responded, then bit away almost as much of her own.

In silence, King watched her flinch and grimace as she chewed and swallowed, watched her wash down the food with a long gulp of her soda, chase the drink with enough French fries to choke a horse.

He chuckled under his breath, went back to feasting on his own greasy heart-attack-in-a-box.

"I'm hungry, okay?" she asked, around a mouthful of food. "And I'm rarely Miss Manners even when I'm not starving to death."

"Then who are you, Cady Kowalski? Why don't we start there?"

"You know just about everything there is," she said, reaching for her napkin and gently dabbing her mouth. "I'm an unemployed, homeless, twenty-nine-year-old woman with no real friends and no family ties."

That sounded a lot like where he'd been a year ago. Except for the woman part. And the twenty-nine-year-old part. And the part about having a home; the trailer he'd been living in could've been a cardboard box for all the comforts it gave him.

"No family ties." A good place to start. "Tell me what went wrong there. What happened to make your mother think a fist is any way to greet her daughter?"

Cady shrugged, tore off a big hunk of her sandwich, and popped it into her mouth. King waited.

A lifetime ago, he'd spent four years in Angola. He still had the patience of a saint, and the tenacity of an inmate determined to come out of that hellhole in one piece.

No black-eyed waif, fine ass or not, was going to get rid of him by blowing him off.

Once she was through her food and staring wistfully at what he hadn't eaten, she seemed to realize it, too. "Are you going to eat that?"

He nodded. "But I'm happy to order you seconds."

She deflated like a bike tire hitting a nail. "As long as I tell you what you want to know, you mean."

"Sounds like a fair trade."

"To you, sure," she said, snitching one of his onions. And then she sighed. Capitulated. "Okay. A junior burger and an order of onion rings for this. I got my older brother killed. There. Is that enough?"

It was enough to hold him while he headed to the counter to place her order, leaning back while he waited and watching her wolf down the onion rings he'd left on the table.

Bottomless pit. Nervous eater. Starving woman. He wasn't sure that she wasn't all three.

But a killer? That he would never believe.

He'd lived with killers behind bars. He knew what they thought, how they thought. Cady might be capable of massacring a cheeseburger, but that was the extent of her murderous tendencies.

Hell, she was sporting railroad track stitches across her cheekbone and two of the blackest eyes he'd ever seen—all that without filing assault and battery charges against any of her assailants.

She hadn't even wanted to bring the heat down on Alice for the incident with the gun.

Added up? The girl was on the run. She might not have defined her lifestyle in those terms, but she didn't have to. He'd just done it for her.

"Order two-seventy-two—"

"I've got it," he told the woman at the counter before she started in with the attitude, adding a "Thanks" that earned him an unexpected smile.

Back at the table, he gave Cady the burger, but kept half of the onion rings for himself. "What happened to your brother?"

"He was shot during a home invasion. Killed. Bled out all over the floor of the front room."

Whoa. He'd expected to hear that she'd rolled the car she'd been driving. Or that she'd given him pneumonia. Maybe that she'd sent him on a late night burger run and he'd interrupted a robbery. But not that. Not that.

He held her gaze, genuinely sympathetic. "I'm sorry. Truly."

"So am I," she said, staring down at her food. "Kevin was a real sweetheart. He didn't deserve to die that way."

"Does anyone?"

A corner of her mouth twitched. "I can think of a few people."

"Like those who shot him?"

She'd unwrapped the paper from around her small burger while talking, but as his question settled around them, she wrapped it back up. Then she pushed it across the table. "Here. I changed my mind. It's not a fair trade."

"You already gave me more than you said you would," he said to set her at ease—though he was still wildly curious about how a home invasion was her fault—as he pushed the burger right back.

She took it, but didn't eat it, and her gaze remained on her fingers, the polish on her nails chipped and black, while she toyed with the yellow wax paper. "Maybe I'll save this for later. I'm pretty stuffed."

"After all of that?" He nodded to indicate the pile of trash next to her arm "You should be."

He'd been hoping to see a spark of the smart-mouthed stylist who'd moussed and gelled his hair into the same natural bed head he woke up with each day. For the moment, that girl was gone.

This one had drifted back to her brother's death, and was going to need more than a junior cheeseburger or King's digs to bring her around.

What he had to say next probably wasn't going to be much help in making that happen. "We should get going. We need to find a place to bunk down for the night before you fall out from exhaustion."

That had her lifting her head. "What do you mean, bunk down?"

"A bed. A place to sleep," he said, keeping his eyes on her as he swirled what was left of his drink in its ice and brought the cup to his mouth.

"Together?"

"If we can't find a place with two beds, I'll take the floor.

I've got a sleeping bag." And if he was going to take her with him, he'd have to get her one, too. Something to think about tomorrow. Once he was thinking straight again.

He obviously needed sleep as badly as she did. Why else would he be considering taking her with him?

When she still hadn't responded, and the silence between them had taken on an uncomfortable life of its own, he said, "You jumped into my ride like a stowaway. You didn't think about sleeping arrangements?"

"I wasn't thinking about anything but finding the cheapest way possible out of town."

He gave her an eyeful. "You tried to get me to drop you at Greyhound. That dog don't run for free, boo."

"Which is why you were my first choice," she said, sitting back, crossing her arms, her chin up, trembling though defiant. "You can take me farther away than I can afford to get on the bus. But now I'm wondering what traveling with you is going to cost me. And if you're worth it."

Again. She was running. He was certain. He was also certain he hadn't told her she could come along because he was still fighting himself over letting her. "I said we need to find a place to get some shut eye. That's it. Nothing about you traveling with me or any sort of cost."

"Does that mean you're not taking me with you?"

"It means I don't know what I'm doing." And if that wasn't the biggest understatement he'd ever made.

"When will you know? Because if you're not—"

"Cady." He reached over, covered her hand that was back to nervously playing with the burger wrapper. "I'm not going to leave you on the street."

"That doesn't make me feel a whole lot better," she said, turning her fingers into his and squeezing tight.

Tears welled in her lower lids that were already rainbow-colored and swollen. Talk about ripping a guy's heart out. "Trust me, okay? Things will look better tomorrow."

She snorted. "Assuming once I close my eyes, I'll be able to open them again."

Ripped out and stomped into the ground. Damn if he wasn't going soft in his old age.

Even so, he continued to hold her hand while sliding out of his seat, using his free one to snag their trash and drop it in the receptacle on their way out the door.

Once they were back in the Hummer, he made yet another command decision that would put off his man versus nature vacation road trip. "I figure I've got another hour in me, so we'll put this place a few miles behind us before stopping."

"Thank you," she said, and then he swore she fell asleep.

Eight

She was going to spend the night with Kingdom Trahan. The same Kingdom Trahan whose hair she'd tousled then smoothed then rumpled with her hands at the photo shoot director's request, whose face she'd dusted with matte powder to dull the camera's flash and the glare of the lights on the set.

He'd said no to anything else. No kohl or color on his eyes, no lowlights or highlights in his hair. The ad people could take him as he was, or not take him at all. He was a Cajun, not a queen. Yeah, that Kingdom Trahan. The politically incorrect jerk who'd stirred something female in her that hadn't been stirred in forever.

And because she had yet to process what it would mean for them to share a room without a full production crew flitting around, Cady feigned sleep so he wouldn't catch her trying to come to grips with a situation that she feared would test her in ways she was too tired to pass.

She had no plans to become intimate with him, and doubted he had any where she was concerned, though she couldn't deny she found him distractingly attractive, and in a more sane time and place, she might think about giving it a go.

Right now, however, insanity was her reality—even

more, she was certain, than at any time since Kevin had died. It was a scary place to be, and thinking about spending the night with Kingdom Trahan didn't help.

He'd rescued her in the garage at Ferrer Fragrances. He'd rescued her from her psycho roommate. He'd rescued her on the front porch of her parents' home, and rescued her when hunger had stolen her strength.

She didn't like being a damsel in distress, but she liked even less the idea of being in close quarters with a knight in glossy black armor. She didn't know if he would turn out to be like so many of his gender, expecting her to show her gratitude by taking off her pants. And she really didn't like knowing if she had it in her not to.

What made things so bad was that he'd witnessed the Kowalski family dynamic in action. That left her feeling vulnerable. She didn't like feeling vulnerable. She'd worked so hard to fit comfortably into the protective façade she'd donned to attend Kevin's funeral. Not once in the past eight years had she taken it off.

And even though she hadn't said much, she still couldn't believe she'd told King what she had about Kevin. She didn't talk about Kevin with anyone. Ever. She hadn't since the trial. Not even after being kicked out of the Kowalski family and the bombardment of questions that followed.

Instead of being stalked, hijacked, and ambushed into answering, she'd moved from her campus apartment into the city and vanished, juggling part-time jobs while taking an extra year and finishing her business degree online.

She'd moved as often as she'd changed jobs. She'd kept her number unlisted until she could no longer afford a phone. She'd done anything she could think of to keep from being found by reporters who refused to let go of Kevin's story, by old friends who really weren't, by new enemies who really were.

Anything except changing her name. That had stayed.

Yes, her parents had made it clear that she was no Kowalski to them, but changing her identity would've been the ultimate admission of defeat, and because she was a Kowalski, she would never let things go that far.

How far she was going to let things go with King in exchange for his help, however . . .

She shifted in her seat, letting her head loll sleepily on her left shoulder. The interior of the Hummer was dark, the tinted windows making it seem even darker, so she opened her eyes just a slit and peered at him while he drove.

It wasn't hard at all to see why Ferrer Fragrances wanted to use him in their ad campaign. Even if he hadn't been distantly related to Michelina Ferrer, he would've been the perfect choice to sell her products.

He had the sort of smoldering look that drew women and their disposable income like flies. Cady wasn't immune, but she wasn't in any sort of situation to take advantage of his honey. And, yeah. That's what he made her think of. Honey.

He was smooth. He could be sweet. Being in his company was definitely going to get sticky. And if she got too close, she was certain she'd feel his sting.

"What's so funny?"

Funny? Had she laughed aloud and given herself away? "What do you mean?"

"So you're *not* asleep."

"Not now," she grumbled, stupid for thinking she could get away with playing that she was.

"Good. Then you can tell me what's so funny, because it's dark and quiet, and I'm boring myself to death over here."

The lights from the dashboard lit up bits and pieces of his profile. His cheekbones, his lips, the rough stinging stubble on his chin . . . "Nothing is funny."

"You laughed."

Laughing was good. It meant she hadn't called him honey out loud. "I must've been dreaming."

"What about?"

Even though he wasn't looking at her, she frowned. "Are you always so nosy?"

He shrugged then rolled his shoulders as if to ease the stress of driving. "If I'm curious enough, interested enough. Sure."

"What are you?" she asked, changing the subject to keep the conversation off her dreams about sticky sweet substances and licking them out of the hollow of his throat. "Curious or interested?"

"Bored."

"Yeah. So you said."

"Hey, you pretended to go to sleep and left me alone in the dark, boo."

"You have a radio."

"I didn't want to disturb you."

"Why would it matter? According to you, I was only pretending."

"To sleep, yeah. Doesn't mean you weren't lost in thought."

Her thoughts could've used an interruption, she mused, straightening in her seat and realizing how nice it was to have someone be considerate of her. "That was very thoughtful of you. Thanks."

"You're welcome."

She let several miles go by before speaking again. Then she broached the subject that had been simmering in her mind since he'd first mentioned their stopping for the night. "I think I'd prefer it if we shared a room. But with two beds. I'd feel safer."

He didn't answer right away, and that bothered her. She wanted to know what he was thinking. About her. About what he'd learned, what he'd seen. She wasn't happy that she'd become a burden. It was so much easier being his stylist than his stowaway.

Leaning over him, being close enough to count the scattered gray hairs at his temples, near enough to see the details of the scars criss-crossing his jaw . . . Honey or not, that was as personal a relationship as she was comfortable with.

His knowing about Kevin and her parents, even about Alice and what Tyler had done, cut too close to the bone. Gah, what was it going to take to have a life worth living? Would she be paying for a mistake that was as stupid as it was innocent for the rest of her days?

"Why would you feel safer?" King finally said, his words slicing like rays of harsh sunshine through the cloud of depression cloaking her.

She was some kind of melodramatic, wasn't she? "Uh, because I wouldn't be alone?"

"That's not what I meant," he said, shaking his head as if his question hadn't been worded right either.

"Well, then? I'm not a mind reader here."

"Safe implies danger," he said, his tone that of a guardian to a charge. "Since I don't see your mother or father or your roommate following us, I would think being in a room of your own would be the safest bet."

"Why?" she asked before she could think better of it. "Are you out to get me now, too?"

"Who's out to get you, Cady?"

"Just because I'm paranoid . . ." Head back, she crossed her arms to hold onto the painful tightness in her chest that seemed the only thing keeping her in one piece.

She should never have told him about Kevin. Or let him see that she was no longer a daughter a mother could love. If she slipped again, let down her guard and told him her whole life story . . .

She wondered what he would say if she asked him for plane fare to Alaska. Fairbanks sounded good. Juno. The North Pole. Then she wondered what he'd say if he knew the truth about why she would never feel safe again.

She didn't say anything, and he didn't push though she

knew the subject would rear its ugly head again once they'd checked into their room.

Instead, as he took the next exit, pulling the Hummer under the awning of the chain motel's entrance, she pressed her lips together to keep her teeth from chattering and broadcasting the state of her nerves.

She watched him skirt the front of the big vehicle and head inside. Watched him hand over several bills and his ID to procure the room. Watched him laugh as the female registration clerk flirted and smiled and probably gave him her number along with the key.

Then she watched him come back, climb into the driver's seat, and show her what he had in his hand. One key. Meaning . . . one room. Just like she'd requested.

Now if anything went wrong and morning arrived filled with regrets, she'd have no one to blame but herself. She snorted, because really, was that any different from any other time she woke up to start a new day?

She nodded her thanks, hoping one of them had some aspirin, hoping he didn't try to talk her out of her pants, hoping that when she woke up in the morning, tomorrow would indeed be a another day and not just this one continued.

If it was, she swore she was going to go back to sleep until she withered away like a plant tossed around and left rootless by a big bad storm.

Nine

One room. Two beds.

Two bodies. One big fat secret.

King wondered what all of that added up to, and whether going to the trouble to do the math would yield him anything he needed to know or whether he'd be better off dropping the problem of Cady's secrets and getting some sleep.

While the waif with the mysterious past dug through one of the garbage bags in the SUV's backseat, King rifled through his supplies for the things he'd want before morning, wishing he had a better handle on her need to feel safe so he'd know whether to bring his gun.

He didn't think the threat she felt was one that would come knocking on their door. He didn't see her parents loading up in the LeSabre and following.

He didn't imagine her jealous roommate had that big of a beef with her, or that the boyfriend was desperate to apologize or try to finish what he'd started.

But King ended up grabbing his gun—and Alice's—just in case.

Once he and Cady had their gear together and their hands more than full, he pointed the way and walked her down the hotel's first floor hallway to their door. Neither one of them said a word on the way. Cady clutched her overstuffed backpack like a satchel of stolen cash.

He'd brought his fair share of women to similar places, nicer places, ones not half so, and there never had been a lot of talking involved on the way in, or the way out. But this situation wasn't like those where talking didn't have anything to do with renting a room.

The fact that he wanted Cady to talk, that he wanted to hear what she had to say proved it. He needed to find out what was going on with her so he could figure out what the hell to do with her after tonight.

He slid the card key into the slot. The green light lit up and the lock clicked. He pushed the door open and gestured her inside. She passed the closet on the left, the bathroom on the right, and stopped.

"Take whichever bed you want," he told her, slinging his duffel onto the closet floor and checking the room's thermostat. The place could've served double duty as a freezer.

As long as he wasn't cold, he didn't care where he slept. If Cady hadn't decided to stowaway in his SUV, he'd be stretching out tonight in an insulated sleeping bag under the stars. This room was for her.

Still holding onto her things, she crawled up into the center of the bed closest to the exit, and sat cross-legged. "I'll sleep here."

"Fine," he said, walking to the other side of the room to pull back the curtain and look out the window. He wanted to see how far away his H3 was parked and make sure the lights from the parking lot reached it. "I'll sleep all the way over here."

Cady groaned her frustration. "I trust you, King. I'm the one who wanted us to share a room, remember?"

He let the drapes fall into place and faced her. She still sat in the center of the bed, legs crossed, closed in on herself, her backpack a shield. Only her head had moved, allowing her to keep him in sight.

He felt like some sort of predator being eyeballed by his suspicious prey. "I remember."

"And yet, here you are, being petulant."

He snorted, arched a brow, took a step toward her. "Petulant?"

"What else would you call it?" she asked, gesturing with one hand. "'I'll sleep all the way over here.' You act like I'm putting you out."

Challenge accepted. Another step taken. Hands at his hips as he stared down. "Aren't you? This isn't exactly the route I'd planned to take home."

"And you wouldn't be here now if you hadn't insisted on taking me to my parents' house. I would be on a bus and you would be miles away." She wasn't going to give him an inch, flouncing there, crossing her arms.

"I have no one to blame but myself, then. Is that what you're saying?" Because if that was what she was saying, he had a few things to say of his own.

She shook her head. "No. I'm the one who climbed into your truck in the first place."

"Good. At least that part you remember."

"With you to remind me, it's not very likely I'll forget," she grumbled, adding, "ever," before she unzipped her backpack and began rooting around.

King waited for her to finish, but it quickly became clear that she wasn't really looking for anything or planned to get back to him on the topic of blame. She was distracting herself, or him, or the both of them. The distraction had worked. He'd lost his train of thought.

Crap.

"I'm going to shower," he finally said, heading for the bathroom before she gave him a reason to change his mind.

He was itching for a fight, and it didn't matter that she wasn't the one who'd pissed him off, that he was frustrated by the situation he was stuck in. She was the one here, the one within shouting distance.

He wasn't that much of a beast not to recognize the danger in such a situation. Convenience played too big a part in abusive situations. Anger taken out, aggression spent on innocents was too commonplace.

King had seen it. He knew it. He wasn't going to fall victim to that behavior, or use Cady as an emotional punching bag. He'd freeze his ass off under the needlelike spray of cold water first, though steaming himself pruny instead sounded really, really good.

He was tired. Who knew time spent playing white knight could wear a guy plumb out, he mused, shucking off his clothes? Here he'd thought he'd end his day with a cup of campfire coffee beneath a blanket of stars. He wouldn't bathe, he wouldn't shave. He'd just be.

Spending it in a tiled tub enclosure with fruity smelling soap did not have the same sense of adventure. And knowing he was going to have to do something about the woman in the other room lessened his enjoyment of the pounding wet heat.

Storing her things and dropping her at the bus station was sounding better and better. She'd be out of his hair, and they both could get on with their lives. He had beer and crawfish waiting for him in Bayou Allain, and she had . . . nothing, nowhere.

Nobody.

Back when he was a heartless bastard, that wouldn't have caused a twinge. But he seemed to have found a heart. And after seeing the job Cady had been doing fending for herself, the idea of sending her on her way had his ticker clanking around in his chest.

Sometimes he wasn't sure being hollow wasn't an easier way to get by. It sure as hell helped when he'd been told a few years ago by the boy's mother that he had a son—a kid who was now fourteen. If any part of him had been able to care about anything back then . . .

He reached for the shower's controls and turned up the

heat. The thought of having a child whose life he wasn't part of would've sent him tumbling into an even blacker mood had it not been interrupted by the bathroom door opening.

He stilled in the act of scrubbing the day's sweat from his face and waited to see if Cady had something to say, or if she'd only come for the facilities because she couldn't wait. He didn't want to make her uncomfortable if she had.

But she didn't say or do anything. Best he could tell, she was standing unmoving just inside the door. And since his clothes were in a pile somewhere near her feet and his towel on the edge of the sink, he needed her to do whatever it was she'd come to do and get out.

So he nudged her. "First my truck, and now my shower. Is nothing sacred?"

"Sorry," he heard her mutter. "The TV wasn't working."

What the hell? "You came to get me to fix the TV? Did you try calling the front desk first?"

"No. I mean, the TV works fine. It just wasn't . . . working. As a distraction." She groaned beneath her breath, the sound giving off an emotion he hadn't heard before. "I needed a distraction."

She had dozens of channels broadcasting more distracting crap than a person could need in a lifetime. She wasn't making any sense. And he wasn't exactly comfortable here with the situation.

"You're looking for a distraction? In here? Where I'm bare-as-the-day-I-was-born naked? Cady, Cady, Cady." He clicked his tongue. "You devil."

"It's not like that."

"Then what's it like, boo, because you coming in here saying you need a distraction kinda leads me down that road." He stared at the shower curtain where he could see her shadow on the other side. It was the strangest way to be having a conversation, not one he was exactly good with.

The water was beating down on his shoulders as he stood with his hands at his hips, keeping his secrets out of sight the same way Cady was on the other side of the cheap white vinyl keeping hers.

His were of a physically personal nature; he didn't hang it out for everyone to see. But her own package of mysteries was obviously pretty damn heavy. After all, it had sent her seeking refuge in a steamy wet bathroom when she had a perfectly comfortable bed to hide out in.

King leaned into the spray, rinsed the shampoo from his hair, the soapy water from his face, neck, and chest. He was clean and ready to get out, but he was also butt naked, and she was standing between him and his towel.

Except standing wasn't exactly the right word. Even through the curtain he could see her nervous movements, pacing, rocking, leaning over the sink and talking into her hands instead of to him.

He'd had enough. "Cady, either talk to me or get out so I can get out."

"I can't go back out there."

Then talk it was. "Because?"

"I just can't. In the city, I felt safe. The incident with Alice aside," she added. "In the city, I was just another nameless person in the crowd. It was easy to stay out of sight, lost, bland, blending in."

She was not bland. She was anything but. "And somehow that all changed with me taking you home?"

"That place is not my home."

No, but it used to be. She had a lot of history there. Was standing out now what was bothering her? "You think the gossip mill is all churned up with tales of your face meeting your mother's fist?"

"It's not the tales and the gossip that scare me."

Scared? That's what she was feeling? He would've thought something like rejected, dejected. Embarrassed. Any one seemed more in order. "Then what scares you?"

"That after all these years, they're finally going to catch me. And kill me when they do."

Okay, now this was getting spooky weird, but the thing about feeling safer sharing a room? If she thought someone was after her, it made sense. Made him glad, too, he'd kept his gun close. At least until he knew more.

Like whether she had a real reason to be frightened. Or whether she was some kind of schizo whack job. "They? Who is they?"

It took her several seconds to respond. He sensed her move again, lean back against the wall beside the door. "I don't know their names, or even who they are except for being friends of the guys who went away for Kevin's murder."

Real enough. So far. "And you think they're after you?"

"They've been after me since the trial."

There were a dozen things he wanted to ask, all related to wondering why she was still living here in this part of the country when she had no ties? Why, if there was a legitimate threat, had she not found out who *they* were and filed a restraining order? Why wasn't she in witness protection?

But her fear was immediate, her need for a diversion urgent enough to bring her in here while he showered. He ended up asking, "And you think they're here? Now?"

"I don't know. It's just . . . When I looked out the window, I saw a truck idling behind yours, then rolling forward slowly and stopping as if searching for our room. Or searching for me."

He didn't want to discount what she was feeling, or ignore what she thought she'd seen. But he'd been the one driving, and nothing about the traffic around them had struck him as strange or hostile.

No, he hadn't been on the lookout for a tail or had any reason to be, but those early years behind bars had left him with a good pair of eyes in the back of his head.

As far as he knew, they were still working, and they hadn't seen a thing. "I'm sure it's nothing."

She bit off some not so nice words. "You're sure I'm hallucinating? Is that it?"

Women. Twist and turn everything a man said. "No, I'm sure you saw what you saw."

"But until you see it for yourself, then it doesn't count."

"I didn't say that either."

"You didn't have to. You don't believe me."

What he believed was that they weren't going to get anywhere with this barrier between them.

He shut off the water, grabbed his wet rag and held it with one hand in the most strategic of locations, then whipped the curtain out of the way and met her gaze.

The hooks clattered the length of the rod, and Cady jumped, her eyes going wide as she took him in in all of his Garden of Eden glory.

Then a smile teased one corner of her mouth upward, and a knowing brow followed suit. "Nice fig leaf."

He glared, moved his other hand to his hip to secure the terry cloth from both sides. "I can't talk to you when I'm naked and you're not."

"Are you saying you want me to take off my clothes?"

That hadn't been the response he was after, but now that she'd brought it up . . . "If you're not up for doing that, then I'm going to put mine on. You can stay and watch, or stay and help, or you can turn your back until I'm dried off and dressed. And we can pick up this conversation then."

She'd lost a bit of her smirk during his speech, and though she hadn't run screaming out of the bathroom, he wouldn't be surprised if she turned and did.

He wasn't much to look at as it was, but dripping wet and naked save for his terry cloth fig leaf—the rag itself growing wetter with all the dripping going on—he could scare the chocolate out of an M&M candy shell.

So it left him feeling strangely naked and vulnerable when she was slow to reach for the handle, and even slower to open the door, leaving him behind with an expression he swore was tinged with regret.

Ten

Cady prided herself on not being an innocent. Living in the city meant she'd seen a lot of things she wouldn't have living in the rural Midwest, or even living in the town she'd grown up in. She wasn't judging, just stating facts.

And the fact was, it took a lot to get her to bat an eye or turn her head and stare. And that included the male body in various states of undress.

Leaning back on her stacked hands on the safe side of the bathroom and listening to King's movements as he dressed, Cady felt as if she'd been cloistered away all of her life in that monastery she'd been threatening to run to.

She closed her eyes because it was easier to see him again with nothing pulling her gaze elsewhere. She didn't want to look elsewhere. She only wanted to look at him—a man who wasn't some young hard body of ambiguous sexual orientation who sold everything from boxer briefs to gym memberships.

He'd been fully clothed, in fact, in the photographs taken for the Ferrer Fragrance ads—a fact Cady now considered a damn shame, if not a waste of a once in a lifetime marketing opportunity.

Standing there the way he'd been in the bathroom, his hands low on his hips, fingers spread to hold what there was of his fig leaf in place . . . thinking about it now, she could hardly breathe.

He had body hair, and he had muscles, and he had scars, and on his right collarbone, a tattoo of a crown sitting on top of scattered doubloons and draped with strands of beads, all of it in Mardi Gras colors.

King. Kingdom. The name fit him, as did the idea of his being master of all he surveyed. She'd imposed herself upon him, and he'd taken charge the way he saw fit rather than doing what she, a mere peasant, his subject, his serf, wanted or suggested or told him to do.

Just her luck she'd stowed away with royalty—royalty whose fig leaf she wanted to blow out of the way. God, but he was beautiful, and so out of her league.

She pushed off the door before he could open it and catch her simultaneously drooling and kvetching, and returned to perch on the foot of her mattress to wait.

If he were a typical man, he'd be using this time holed up alone to prove her suspicions of being followed unfounded.

But he struck her as anything but typical, leaving her no clue what to expect when his highness emerged from his chambers and took to his throne—an image that had her smiling, a smile that was a welcome surprise.

And then he was there, fully dressed down to his boots. She tried not to gulp at the beads of water pooled in the hollow of his throat above his T-shirt's ribbed neckline. Or jump up and cup his freshly shaved face in her hands to see how soft his skin actually was.

But mostly she tried, and failed, not to remember what he looked like naked.

Since that was impossible, she tried for casual when she asked, "Going somewhere?" After her bathroom confessional, she didn't believe he'd walk out and leave her alone. But really, casual was the last thing she was feeling, and her question came out on a squeak.

He nodded, snagged his wallet from the desk. "Thought

I might walk through the parking lot. Make sure no one is lurking in the bushes under our window."

"Are you making fun of me again?"

"Again? When have I made fun of you ever?"

"You didn't believe me about the suspicious truck outside."

"Sure I believed you." He swung his key ring on one finger and palmed the clattering keys. "That's why I'm going out there now. Make sure all is well."

He believed her about the truck. Just not that whoever had been driving was necessarily looking for them. Or coming after her. "You sure you're not trying to get out of finishing our conversation?"

Actually, she wasn't so sure she wanted to revisit her past to the extent answering his questions would require. Curling up her battered body beneath the bed's blankets, and sinking into the cushy down pillows was a much more appealing option.

She chose it instead of choosing to talk.

"Never mind," she said, reaching for her backpack and the T-shirt and sweatpants she'd packed for sleeping, and then realizing he hadn't moved.

She looked up at him then, for the first time concentrating on his expression instead of his looks. "What?"

His eyes were those of a raptor, keen and piercing. "I'm not avoiding the conversation or running out on you."

She dipped her chin, pulled her laptop out of her bag, knew what a field mouse must feel like before a hawk swooped down. "I know—"

"No you don't," he said sharply. "But it's okay. It takes a lot to hurt my feelings."

She hated to admit that she hadn't considered his feelings at all. It was just that she was used to being on her own, used to having conversations avoided, used to seeing the backs of others running away from the cloud of bad karma that hung over her head like a shroud.

She shrugged what she hoped passed for an apology. "I'm going to see if the wireless is working. I need to log into my bank and figure out how I'm going to finance my escape from New York."

"You're a funny girl," he said, still staring at her, though with less of a hooded look.

"Thanks. Entertaining you is the least I can do." And then she realized what she'd said, and decided not to say anything else the rest of the night. Not so King.

"I'll be back in a few," he said. "Just sit tight," he told her. "Nothing bad's going to happen while I'm gone," he promised. "It'll be morning before you know it, and that's when everything looks brighter, right?"

All she could do was smile weakly while avoiding his gaze, and nod, because even if nothing bad happened, it was going to be a long time before there was anything resembling brightness lighting up her life.

Eleven

King shoved his hands in his pockets and hunched his shoulders, wishing for his jacket and dry hair. It wasn't that he'd been in too much of a hurry to grab his coat before leaving the room, but a case of not thinking straight.

If he had been, he wouldn't be here now, freezing his balls off, instead of huddled in toasty sheepskin.

It had taken him forever to finish up in the bathroom because he couldn't get the hungry look in Cady's eyes out of his head. Since she'd climbed into his passenger seat in the garage this morning, he hadn't once thought of her that way. At least not seriously. She'd been someone in trouble, someone needing help.

Even when she'd rubbed against him during that ridiculous Ferrer photo shoot, he hadn't considered messing with her any more seriously than he would've a Hooters' waitress leaning over him to serve up his order of hot wings and beer. Enjoying an eyeful of tits didn't mean a thing.

Except best he could tell, Cady's tits really weren't enough for an eyeful, and she'd never worn anything that exposed her cleavage to prove him wrong. Head to toe, she'd always been completely covered up when around him. Until standing there in the bathroom looking at him with bare, naked eyes.

What he'd seen of her then had scrambled everything he'd been thinking, as well as the plans he'd been making behind her back to ditch her and get on the road. Best he could do now was talk her out of wanting to come along, let her think it was in her best interest to get rid of him.

If anyone had been messing with his brand-new wheels and delayed him any longer, he was going to have their hide. But a quick look around the exterior of the SUV, made while he ran his hands up and down his goose-fleshed arms, didn't reveal slashed tires or smashed windows or siphoned fuel.

The electronics in his key fob had disengaged the locks, so he popped the hood, started her up, and listened to his horses whir. He knew engines—V6, V8, V10, V12, didn't matter—and this one was singing sweet. But he was cold and Cady was waiting, so he headed back to the room.

He didn't purposefully sneak in, but once inside was glad he hadn't made a lot of noise because Cady was fast asleep. And she was fast asleep in the bed that was supposed to be his for the night.

He sat on the foot of the one where she should've been sleeping—the one that was now covered with everything they'd brought inside, including his dirty clothes, and was missing the bedspread to boot.

It was as if she'd made sure he had no choice but to bunk on the floor—if not with her—or else wake her and ask, "What the hell?"

He didn't want to wake her. Not after the day she'd had. Her body needed recovery time and nothing beat sleep for healing.

But even though he'd said otherwise, there was no way on God's green earth he was going to spend the night on the floor knowing he'd be sitting behind the wheel most of tomorrow, and most likely the day that followed.

Spending the night propped up in one of the room's two wing chairs wasn't any more of an acceptable option . . .

though hitting the front desk for another room was. He'd just leave Cady a note first—

She interrupted him by clearing her throat. "You're trying to get out of sleeping with me, aren't you?"

He tossed the pen he'd found back to the desk. He hadn't even made it as far as finding something to write on. "Actually, I was trying to remember the last time I bailed on a woman who invited me to bed."

"It must be hard to be King."

He liked this girl. He liked her a lot. "In a manner of speaking."

She raised up on one elbow, tossed back the bedspread she was wearing like a cocoon. "I'm fully dressed. I'm under my own covers. There's no chance here for accidental physical contact. So come to bed. We both need sleep."

It had to be the shadows from the room's dim light making her face look so ghostly. Yeah, her hair was dark, as were the bruises marring her skin, plumping one side of her mouth into a fleshy pillow and sinking her eyes into her skull. But still. She looked like the waking dead.

He returned to the foot of the bed to tug off his boots, wondering if he'd ever slept with a zombie before. "You get your banking done?"

She burrowed deeper into the covers. "I couldn't get onto the hotel's network. I'll try again in the morning, if there's time before we leave."

"How much you think it's going to take to finance this escape of yours?" he asked, weighing the pros and cons of sleeping in all of his clothes or just some of them.

She didn't answer, and he left it alone, suddenly more tired than he had reason to be. Along with his boots, he pulled off his belt, then left the first bed for the second and slid beneath his sheet and blanket.

Cady's bulk was nothing at his side. There was no dip in the mattress from her weight causing him to roll toward her.

He could've been sleeping next to a pile of clean laundry for all he noticed her being there.

It took several minutes for him to relax, for his breathing to steady, his heartbeat to settle, and his goose flesh to disappear, before he realized he was feeling her body heat and not just that of the bedding.

Things got kinda weird then, what with the two of them being in bed there together, and her warming him so nicely the way she was, and him remembering the way she'd stared when confronted with his wash cloth and his body. He hadn't come up against that expression in a very long time. In fact, he wasn't sure he'd run into it ever.

It was a wanting kind of look, a hurting for something kind of look, a look that tore at something inside of him that even he didn't like knowing was there to be torn. He sure didn't like thinking that he'd disappointed her, left her unfulfilled, but that was exactly the sense that was eating at him now, and making it hard to get to sleep.

It had been awhile since he'd slept all night with a woman, since he'd gone to bed wrapped in one's arms and woke up with her wrapped in his, his dick at the ready, her pussy hot to trot. Because those were the only women he'd slept with. The same ones he'd fucked.

He'd never had a woman he had no plans to touch warming him the way Cady was now—with the heat of her skin seeping into the blankets, and her soft breathy snores, and the tiny sounds she made when she stretched and turned and rolled.

And this woman, who had no one in her corner and nowhere to go, was the woman who tomorrow he was going to have to find someplace to dump so he could hit the road for home. Yeah, that made him feel like a first place winner. More like a first class mother fu—

A window shattering explosion of fiery light and booming thunder cut off everything King had been thinking and sent him into survival mode. He knew Cady had bolted upright, and he dived toward her, taking the both of them and all the covers to the floor between the two beds.

She screamed, but she didn't fight. She ducked as completely beneath his body as she could, leaving him to the brunt of the raining glass and debris. He felt the scatter shot of detritus like bullets pummel the blanket where it draped him, felt shards strike his uncovered shoulders and head.

In seconds it was over, smoke billowing into the room through the frame where the window's panes had blown out. He tossed off the blankets and urged Cady to her feet, finding her shoes on the extra bed and his boots on the floor, then sprinting for the room's exit.

Coughing against the smoke, Cady grabbed her backpack and laptop and sweatshirt, following him into the hallway and the chaos of half-dressed people, strobing lights, and the hotel's blaring fire alarm.

"What happened?" she called over the panicked voices and crush of bodies.

Fearing their separation, he took her by the upper arm and pushed their way through the crowd. "Your guess is as good as mine."

Fuck orderly fashion. He wanted out of here and now, because there was something telling him he wasn't going to like what he was going to find outside, and the sooner he found it, the better.

They reached the end of the hallway in time to see the first fire engine blow into the parking lot. King shoved his way through the knot of hotel guests congregated there and pulled Cady behind him through the door and outside into his worst nightmare.

"Son of a fucking bitch!"

His Hummer was a burning shell. Orange fire licked through what was left of the vehicle. Black smoke rose in foul-smelling columns. The rest of it, including his supplies and all of Cady's possessions, was strewn around the parking lot in pieces, the result of the blast that had turned their room's window into similar shrapnel.

"King, you're bleeding."

"What?"

"You're bleeding. You've got a piece of glass sticking out of the back of your head."

Too bad it wasn't sticking out of his eyeballs so he wouldn't have to see this. He reached back and nudged the embedded shard. "Ouch. Shit. Ouch."

"Come on. Sit down." She led him to the sidewalk and forced him to sit, dropping her bag and computer in his lap before shrugging into her hoodie. "Hold my stuff. I'll see if there's an ambulance on the way, or if any of these guys are medics or whatever. Don't move until I get back."

He watched her go, knowing he wasn't going anywhere. Not anytime soon, and not under his own steam or in any vehicle he owned, goddamn Hummer garbage shit blown everywhere.

Soon enough he'd need a ride to the hospital for stitches. And then to the police station to find out who the fucking hell had blown up his truck. But for now, he'd do as she'd told him and sit.

Cady was right. It was hard being King.

Twelve

Her backpack hefted over her shoulder, her hands stuffed in the pockets of the hoodie she was so glad she'd grabbed from the room, Cady paced a rut in the speckled linoleum in front of the emergency room cubicle where King was being stitched up. She'd been checked out in the cubicle adjoining, and released, no damage or dangerous smoke inhalation.

King was the one who had taken the hardest part of the hit. King was the one who'd lost what looked like half of his blood. King was the one who'd protected her when all she could think to do was sit up and scream.

If she'd taken off on her own this morning, she couldn't imagine where she'd be now, if she'd be anywhere at all, or if she'd be dead. Because she knew without a doubt that what had happened to his SUV had nothing to do with King and everything to do with her.

And yet he'd saved her before saving himself.

She didn't know why she was sticking around. She knew he wouldn't want to see her. But she couldn't make herself go without knowing he was okay.

Then again, neither one of them would be leaving until they'd talked to the authorities. The doctor who'd looked her over had relayed that order from the investigator standing near the ER door.

She was doing her best to ignore him. She knew his type, had dealt with men cut from the same cocky cloth during the investigation into Kevin's murder. They knew it all, knew better than everyone around them, knew a lie when they heard one—even when the lie was the truth.

She was not looking forward to the grilling she knew was coming. She should've just stayed in New York, recovered from her beating, and moved on. Except moving on hadn't worked in all the years she'd been doing it. Why she thought things had changed . . .

But then she stopped thinking about the cop who was waiting, stopped wondering whether or not she'd ever be able to move on, because the curtain to King's cubicle opened and the doctor who'd been attending to him told him, "Good luck," and walked out.

Cady rushed into the small partitioned room and watched as the nurse finished dressing the back of King's head. When the other woman nodded, Cady came closer, leaning down close to King's ear. "Hey. It's me. Are you all right?"

"Sure," he mumbled from where he rested facedown on an inflatable donut-shaped pillow. A four-inch circle on the back of his head had been shaved to the scalp. "As all right as a bald man can be."

The nurse rolled her bright brown eyes, but couldn't stop from grinning, her teeth white in her dark chocolate face. Cady didn't even try. "You're not bald. Just looking like a mangy dog."

"Thanks. That helps." He reached out a seeking hand, and she took it. "What about you? Any damage to your jugular or carotid?"

"Not even to my hair," she said, laughing when he groaned.

"That'll do ya, Mr. Trahan," the nurse said, packing away

the rest of her supplies. "Your discharge papers have the doctor's orders on them. If you insist on traveling while on pain meds, you'll have to get your girl here to do your driving for you."

"Since my truck just blew up, that's going to take some doing on her part," King said, leaning more on Cady than on the nurse as they helped him to sit. "I think my face went to sleep while I was lying there. I can't feel a thing."

"Your face went to sleep because of the anesthetic the doctor injected before pulling that window out of your head." The perky nurse showed them both the shard of bloody glass in the bottom of an aluminum pan.

Cady gasped. "Wow. I had no idea."

"He's lucky it hit where it did," the nurse said, staring down at the huge projectile. "He jokes about your carotid and jugular. This thing could've sliced through either. Head wounds are big bleeders, though, so we gave up on trying to save his shirt."

Cady didn't know what to say. It was all she could do to meet King's eyes and mouth, "Thank you," without bursting into tears. But just as quickly she found herself telling him, "I'm so sorry," and then whirling to leave before he could say a word in response.

This was all her fault, and as soon as he realized that, he was going to send her packing—unless he did worse. Why give him the chance when she could leave under her own steam before he forced her out?

She was stopped from completing her mad dash by the cop who'd been waiting. "Miss Kowalski? Mr. Trahan?"

King had been frowning at the paper scrub top he'd been given to wear, his T-shirt having been cut away during his examination, and was still frowning when he looked up. "Who wants to know?"

Cady wanted to laugh and ask him if it wasn't obvious that they were about to be grilled and accused and covered by a blanket of suspicion and doubt.

Just because the man was wearing a designer suit, his silk tie barely askew, his white shirt gleaming, his leather shoes lacking a single scuff mark, and all of this in the middle of the night, was no reason to think otherwise.

But the cop surprised her by giving King a hand off the table and looking at her as he asked, "Are you two up for a very early breakfast?"

King gave the other man a thorough once-over. "Depends on who's buying and what you want in return. Oh, and whether or not you can rustle me up a shirt made out of something besides paper towels."

"I think I can do that," the cop said with a smile.

"Good," King said, pulling the disposable scrub top gingerly over his bandaged scalp. "Because everything I had with me just went up in flames."

"Wait a minute," Cady said. For King to be so compliant, his brain must've been deadened along with the rest of his head. Holding the strap of her bag, she demanded of the man not under the influence, "Who are you?"

His smile took on the look of molded plastic. Too shiny and fake to be worth anything. "I'll fill you in on all of that once we've got a pot of coffee in front of us."

Cady shook her head. "You'll fill me in now, or I'm not taking another step."

"Then let's do this in the cafeteria at least."

King finally came around. "Sounds like you don't want an audience for this conversation."

"If it is a conversation," Cady added. "He hasn't said a word about what he wants besides breakfast."

The cop's brown eyes darkened. His smile faded completely away. "You can't think you wouldn't have to answer questions about what just happened to your vehicle."

"I figured I would've been asked a lot more of them by now, come to think of it." King pushed by Cady and the cop, and looked up and down the ER corridor. "So where're the troops? Where's the bad cop to go with your good cop?"

"I'm not a cop," the man told them. "But you are going to talk to me or I'll bring them swarming down on this place to see that you do."

Cady stayed silent and where she was, holding tight to her heavy backpack should she need to it as a weapon. His gaze fixed on that of the man between them, King remained in the corridor unmoving—the corridor that she realized was unnaturally quiet and absent the hustle and bustle of only minutes before.

There were no patients calling out for help, no gurney wheels rattling, no rolling crash carts or orders shouted, or pounding feet. Even the nurse who'd been attending to King had vanished, as had the doctor from before.

And where were the other victims of the explosion? It wasn't like King had been the only one hurt, or Cady the only one who'd been transported to the ER to be seen to. Something was going on here, and she didn't like it one bit.

She took matters into her own hands, needing to do something before King's wooziness sent them down a path that ended in another trip to the ER—if not the morgue. "We'll go to the cafeteria. But we're not going anywhere else. Not without a whole lot of explanation and documentation and answers from you."

The man-who-wasn't-a-cop's smile came back. "That I can do."

"Fine. Just don't think this is going to be the start of a beautiful friendship or anything."

"Friendship? No. But we'll see about the anything," he said, then indicated she and King should go first.

She shook her head, gestured with her chin for him to get moving. "You lead. We'll follow. I prefer having someone behind me who's got my back, not someone waiting for a chance to stab it."

At that, the man laughed, a strangely chilling sound that had Cady wondering if she, the peasant, should've left things alone, and let the royalty call the shots.

Thirteen

"My name is Fitzwilliam McKie. You can call me Fitz, Will, or Liam," the man told them. "I answer to anything that gets close."

King, Cady, and the ridiculously named Fitzwilliam McKie were sitting in the corner of the cafeteria that was the farthest from the door and the food service line. McKie had insisted.

King had insisted the conversation not go beyond an exchange of names until he'd downed a sausage biscuit and two cups of coffee, strong and black.

It wasn't that he was hungry, but he was halfway to being stoned.

Thank God Cady'd had the sense to keep them inside the hospital's walls, else who knew where the hell they'd be by now, King going along for the ride because the bright lights and sirens made the trip in his head more fun.

"Okay . . . Fitz." King grabbed the first choice the other man had offered them. "Who are you? What do you want with us? And how did you manage to clear a busy hospital ER?"

"And can we see some ID?" Cady added. She'd ordered a cup of hot tea that had gone cold three times over, but had skipped ordering food. "Something that doesn't look like it came out of an arcade machine?"

That was Cady. Suspicious to the end. And obviously still stuffed with last evening's cheeseburgers and onion rings.

"The ER wasn't that busy so it wasn't hard to clear. Small town. Small emergencies." Fitz looked from King to Cady and back. Cradling his coffee mug in one big hand, he leaned into the forearm he'd braced on the table. "Most of the explosion victims were routed elsewhere."

"You mean *you* routed them elsewhere," King said as he lifted his drink and finished it off. Fitz didn't respond with a yay or a nay or a bite me, so King prodded. "You routed them elsewhere because you wanted to talk to me and Cady alone."

The other man still didn't acknowledge King's accusation. What he did was say, "I know who hit your truck."

The blow came out of nowhere and left King stunned. At his side, Cady gasped, nearly knocking over her tea, righting it with shaking hands. Fitz lifted his gaze slowly, taking in one of them then the other, as if how they responded would determine what he did or said next.

King recognized the power play, and he wasn't having any of this man's bullshit. He wanted to get home and gorge himself sick on crawfish. And this suit with too many names was not going to stand in his way, even if he did work for some X, Y, or Z Files government agency.

He glanced toward the empty food service line, hoping to steady his skyrocketing blood pressure, wondering if staff members used to grabbing muffins or fruit or cups of coffee on their breaks were being kept out at gunpoint, or maybe by an alien technology force field.

Then he glanced back at Fitz, pissed. "You know who hit my truck. And you're doing what about it?"

Fitz shook his head. "Nothing yet."

"Right. Because you're not a cop, and you're not sharing what you know with those running the real investigation."

McKie didn't say a word.

"Well, Fitz." King paused to make sure he had the other man's attention. "That's a load of shit."

"Especially because you still haven't told us who you work for," Cady put in, taking hold of King's hand where his fist rested on the table beside his empty plate. "Or what you want with us."

"Actually, Miss Kowalski, I want you."

King felt his hackles rise. He squeezed her fingers that had gone numbingly cold. "You want her for what?"

"Wait." She pulled her hand free, reached across the table, and grabbed McKie's wrist, as if she needed his truth more than King's protection. "Does this have something to do with Kevin? And the trial?"

Fitz nodded. "And the men who've been watching you since it ended."

Cady pulled away, brought both hands up to cover her face, and sobbed once. King kept his fists on the table, his gaze on the crumbs scattered over his ugly beige plate. He wanted to reach for her. He wanted to offer her something.

But he didn't do anything, because he didn't know what to do—or know her. She was a girl who'd stowed away in his truck. That was all.

"I can't believe it," she finally said, dropping her hands to her lap. Her eyes were red and wet, though no tears spilled free. "After all this time. I knew it was happening. But I didn't think anyone would ever be able to prove it. Or do anything to make it stop."

"I can prove it," Fitz said, and when he left it at that, turning his mug in a circle on the Formica tabletop, King picked up the gauntlet.

"But you're not going to make it stop." The words were hard to speak, and held the weight of very bad news.

Fitz didn't look at King, but glanced toward Cady instead. "Not immediately, no."

"Why not?" she cried, tears leaking at last from the corners of her eyes. "Do you know what it's like to look over your shoulder for eight years of your life?"

"That's why I'm here," Fitz said. "With your cooperation, I'm going to make sure those eight years pay off." His gaze remained locked on hers, as if he knew he had her on his hook, and was waiting to reel her in.

It was all King could do not to choke the man with his own ugly silk tie. "You're here to make sure she keeps looking? Is that it?"

And then it hit him. His fishing analogy was off. This guy wasn't baiting Cady with his words. He was here to use her as bait. He wanted whoever it was stalking her, and she was the easiest means to that end.

King pushed to his feet, knocking against the table hard enough that their dishes clattered. "Not happening, Fitz. Not in this lifetime. We'll be going now."

Cady reached for his arm, squeezed, and said, "Hang on a second. I want to hear more. I want him to tell me exactly why he's here, and what it has to do with me looking over my shoulder."

Spitting out a lot of nasty words, King sat. He wasn't the one who'd been looking over his shoulder and existing day to day. Well, he had, the first part while in prison, the second for a lot of years after.

But this wasn't about him. It was about Cady, and it was only right that she call the shots.

Hell, his only inconvenience was the loss of his ride that had been insured within an inch of its life. Good thing, since it was no longer living.

No, the only reason he was sticking around was to make sure Cady didn't get stranded, and had someone on her side. Once they heard what the government man had to say, King would be in a better position to know if he was needed, or if he was in Cady's way. If his being here meant extra grief.

"Does the name Nathan Tuzzi ring any bells?"

King shook his head in response to Fitz's question, then

turned his gaze on Cady to see that her face had blanched the color of bones—a pale deathly white that made her railroad track stitches seem to pull angrily at her skin, her black and blue bruises to growl.

"Who is he?" he finally asked, still watching her.

"He's the one who pulled the trigger," she said, her voice ringing hollow, her words flat. "The one who shot Kevin."

Fitz took over. "He denies it, of course. To this day, he claims he was convicted on nothing but circumstantial evidence. And that his cohort who turned snitch is lying."

King had gone to prison based on circumstantial evidence, and because the judge sitting his case wanted him there. That didn't mean he automatically sided with this Tuzzi.

But it did mean he'd keep his opinions to himself as he dug for the facts. "The snitch cut a deal?"

"He's serving a lesser term in another facility."

"And he's still alive?" King had seen more than one snitch eat the floor of the showers for his last meal.

Fitz gave him the point. "The other facility is minimum security and far far away."

"He's not getting out, is he?" Cady asked. "Are they? Tuzzi or Felwouk?"

"Felwouk the snitch?" King asked of Fitz.

The other man nodded. "Blake Felwouk." And then he told Cady, "Not a chance. Felwouk's got a number of years to go before he even comes up in front of the parole board. And Tuzzi never will. He'll be proudly wearing the state's colors for the rest of his life."

King let that sink in, but knew there was more to the story. He had the man with no badge across from him as proof—not to mention the woman at his side with a face that told the truth and what remained of his Hummer blown across half of New Jersey.

So he wasn't surprised when Cady filled in the blanks. "It's Malling, isn't it? He's out."

Fitz nodded. Cady hung her head. Since King was the only one who didn't know shit about anything here, he asked, "Who's Malling?"

"Jason Malling was charged as an accessory," Fitz told him, Cady adding, "He drove the getaway car."

"There were three of them then. Involved in the murder." King figured he needed to level the playing field if he was going to catch up.

Fitz held up four fingers. "There was a fourth. Ryland Combs. He was the one who broke out the window on the front door and was the first one inside. Tuzzi and Felwouk told that part of the story the same way."

Cady snorted. "Combs couldn't argue. He was dead."

"What happened?"

Fitz looked at Cady as if wanting her permission before he caused her to revisit the painful details of her brother's death. She hesitated a moment, then picked up her empty cup and got to her feet.

"I'm going to get some more tea," she said, and headed to the other side of the cafeteria and the station stocked with tea bags and sweetener packets.

It was only then, watching her walk away, her head hung low, King realized that beneath her unzipped hoodie, she was still wearing the T-shirt and sweatpants she'd put on to sleep in before wrapping up in her bedspread cocoon.

All those layers were supposed to keep her safe from him . . . yet because of her, he was sitting in a hospital cafeteria with a dozen stitches in his scalp and some government goon keeping him from his crawfish.

And now neither one of them had anything to wear but the clothes on their backs. They didn't even have a toothbrush or a comb. At least he had things at home. Cady had no things. And no home.

"I'm not going to hurt her," Fitz said, bringing King back to the moment.

He looked at the government man in his choice suit and

designer haircut, his build lacking anything in the way of fat, his eyes lacking the compassion to back up his words. Flat. That's what they were. Flat.

King was sure his own eyes were anything but. "The girl chose walking away over listening to you talk about her brother. How do you think that's not hurting her?"

"She's been through all of this. It's nothing new. It's nothing she doesn't know or hasn't heard."

"That doesn't mean she's not hurting. Or that anything about it is easy for her."

"And you're such a good friend you can speak for her about what's easy and what's hard?"

"Not such a good friend, no." Goddamn this man. "Just a fucking human being."

Fitz looked down, then cast a quick glance over his shoulder at Cady before telling King the truth. "That's one thing I can't afford to be. I have a job to do. It's not a pretty one. But what I'm doing is going to save lives.

"If reminding that girl over there of what happened to her brother helps me get what I need to do that, then maybe Kevin Kowalski won't have died in vain."

Fourteen

T*hen maybe Kevin Kowalski won't have died in vain.*

King let that sink in as he fought off the cold of the cafeteria and the tingling ice pricks in his face as feeling to his deadened nerves returned.

He wasn't investing his fortune in what this guy was selling, but the pitch had caught his attention. Now he needed details. "Whose life are you trying to save?"

"The stupid fucks who snort or shoot up what Nathan Tuzzi is putting on the streets."

"You just lost me, boo. I thought you wanted Cady because of the dick tied to her brother's murder being cut loose. The one I'm guessing is responsible somehow for me being on foot. I loved that Hummer, you know."

"Tuzzi's got a lot of puppets in his pockets, but his pulling Malling's strings is personal. They ran together in college, and went down for the same crime."

That helped, but King still wasn't quite there. "So Tuzzi's running drugs from the inside."

Fitz nodded. "He went in, set up shop, and no one's been able to plug his pipeline."

"And now he's got Malling on the outside to do his personal dirty work. Which is where Cady comes in."

Fitz nodded again. "Tuzzi's made no secret of the fact that he's coming for her."

"She said she's been looking over her shoulder for eight years. When did Malling get out? It had to be recently because Cady didn't know."

"Two days ago."

"Why didn't you tell her?"

"I don't work for the court system."

King was beginning to wonder if he worked for anyone but himself. "Meaning it's not your job to let her know to look over her shoulder for real. Even though that's the human thing to do."

"I'm here now. And I've had people following Malling since the moment he set foot outside."

"And the trial? Who's been looking out for her since then?"

Fitz shook his head. "I've only been working the case since last year."

Convenient, like so much of the rest of this circus. "The guy set up shop eight years ago, and he's just now on your radar?"

"Like I said—"

"Yeah, yeah. You and your people are new on the job. You're not responsible for who did what that far back. Who are your people, anyway? You never have said. Or produced any sort of ID," King reminded the other man.

Fitz reached into his suit coat's inside pocket and pulled out a leather badge holder that held no badge. Neither was it embossed with any government insignia.

Inside, there was nothing but a picture of Fitzwilliam McKie along with his name, the presidential seal, and the commander in chief's signature.

"Impressive, but that doesn't tell me much." Except that he'd probably been right about the X, Y, and Z files thing.

"It tells you all I can."

"Well, your 'all you can' doesn't explain what you want with Cady. I'm assuming you want to use her to get to Tuzzi somehow, but I just can't wrap my tiny Cajun brain around how that's supposed to happen."

Fitz twisted his seat to lean against the wall. "There's a reason Malling, who was relegated to do nothing but drive, got caught."

That one was easy. "He wasn't the brains of the operation."

"Exactly. And we're counting on him to be just as loyal to Tuzzi without giving any more thought to covering his tracks now than he did then."

"I'm still not making the connection to that girl over there." The one who'd settled in with her tea at a table the width of the room away, and hadn't once looked over to where King sat talking to the government man. He could've sworn the shard of glass had splintered into his gut.

Fitz took a deep breath. "We weren't sure until last night's explosion exactly what Malling was up to."

"But now you know."

"We have an idea," he said, giving King a bit of a nod as he palmed his mug. "We wouldn't have made the connection except Cady's name popped up on our radar when the locals plugged it into their system."

Huh. Interesting. "You were watching for it?"

"We watch for anything related to Nathan Tuzzi," McKie said, and brought his mug to his mouth.

And that anything included a black-haired waif from New Jersey. "Back to this Malling. He's after Cady?"

"Best we can figure he's supposed to make sure she knows that Tuzzi doesn't forget or ever forgive."

"But if Malling's been inside until recently, who's been giving her grief all this time? Never mind. You've only been working the case a year." King frowned, wished he had another cup of coffee because he was taking way too long to put this puzzle together. "What I don't get is why Tuzzi blames her for his conviction."

This time Fitz considered him more closely. "Has she told you any of what led up to the break-in?"

"Not much. Just that she holds herself responsible for her brother's death. Nothing about why Tuzzi or any of his bunch would blame her for their situation."

"It started out as a college prank. One Cady got caught up in without intending to, I'm quite sure."

"Why are you sure?"

Fitz cast a glance toward the third member of their strange little party before looking back at King. "She might like to tell you herself."

Or she might like not to, since this was the first he'd heard of any prank so far. "I've got a bald spot the size of Montana on the back of my head thanks to her. I think that buys me something."

"Nothing in the case files are sealed," Fitz said, after several moments spent studying the floor as if searching for permission to speak. "Everything's public record. So it's not like I'd be betraying a confidence."

And if he was, King wouldn't care. He didn't have time, energy, or the means to do a search through courthouse files right now.

Begged, borrowed, or stolen, he wanted the information so he and Cady could get out of here, and he could get some sleep. "Speak, man. I don't have all day."

Fitz gave him a look that reminded him his day was no longer his own. "A friend of Cady's had a beef with another girl at school. This girl belonged to a sorority that did a lot of charity work. They had a sculpture of their mascot, a Persian cat, in the sorority house's front hall. Cady's friend lifted it as a joke."

So far, all Cady seemed guilty of was a bad taste in friends. "That's it?"

"No, but it is where the story starts."

Patience, once his strong suit, no longer was. "Can we move on to the part where it gets good?"

"The friend knew Cady was going home for the week-end, and asked her to take the sculpture with her and keep it for a while."

"Did she know what it was? Cady?"

"She did, yes, but says she didn't think much about it. Figured the prank would play out like these things do."

"How did this one get so out of hand?"

"There was more to the figurine than met the eye."

"What was inside?" King asked, though he knew.

Fitz shook his head. "A kilo of smack."

"Shit," was all King could think of to say, though he was now keeping tally of all the things Cady hadn't told him that he would've liked to have known. "Dealing drugs was how the sorority funded their charity work?"

"The heroin belonged to the boyfriend of the sorority's president, the girl who got into it with Cady's friend."

Now things were cooking. "Let me guess. His name was Nathan Tuzzi."

"It was. And the stuff was ninety-two percent pure, just off the plane from Thailand with his number one mule, Ry-land Combs."

"A drug-dealing college boy murderer."

"That about covers it."

"Did the girlfriend know?"

"She denies that she did."

"She just sent him after her pussy."

Fitz nodded, fought a smile. Then he looked over at Cady and that hint of a smile faded away. He didn't have to fight it anymore.

King followed the direction of the other man's gaze, see-ing his stowaway in a whole new light, one that left him fighting an uncomfortable emotional battle of his own.

She'd been minding her own business when one wrong

road taken, one bad decision made, had put her on a collision course with another man's crime.

Her life had been turned upside down, the direction of her future taken out of her hands. An innocent, she'd been sentenced to eight years of looking over her shoulder.

The only difference between their situations was that he'd spent his time behind bars, a guest of the State of Louisiana, one who should never have been locked up at all.

He'd long since quit believing punishments ever fit the crime. Tuzzi should've been strung up by his balls.

"So, Tuzzi and his bunch take a trip to New Jersey to recover this cat. Combs is first through the door, itchy to get back his product, and bites it."

"Best we can make out, Kevin Kowalski was sleeping on the couch in the living room when Combs busted the pane out of the front door's window."

"He woke. They fought. He won that round, lost the next."

"Tuzzi wasn't leaving without the cat. Even if that meant going through Kowalski."

"What a fucked-up mess."

"That's putting it mildly."

"So rather than blaming Cady's friend who stole the statue in the first place, he decides to make Cady's life a living hell because her brother thwarted the recovery." King paused as another thought began to form. "Tuzzi was put away for the murder, but he didn't go down for the drugs?"

"If I'd been involved then, he would have."

"That's what you want to happen now, isn't it? You don't care about what's happening to Cady. You're only here because she hit that radar, and you need her." King didn't even bother to tone down the accusation. It was all cards on the table or nothing.

Fitz responded just as bluntly. "It's what I do. It's how I work."

And King had always thought himself cold. "What do you want with her? Besides to make her life even more miserable than it already is?"

"I don't want to make her miserable. I do want her to let Malling follow her, and do whatever it is Tuzzi wants. That flow of information will get me to the drugs."

King laughed so hard and so loud that Cady got up from where she was sitting and made her way back across the room. She took her seat again at King's side and asked, "What's so funny?"

King did his best to knock the snot out of the other man with nothing but a poisonous look. "Fitzwilliam here was just explaining how he wants to put you in a world of danger so he can get him some Tuzzi."

But it was King who was poleaxed when Cady said, "If it'll make this nightmare go away, I'm in."

Fifteen

"One room?" Cady asked, when King offered her the single card key to open the door. Not that she minded sharing again. In fact, being alone was the last thing she wanted.

And since her choices for company were limited—King on one hand, an anonymous afternoon crowd at a suburban shopping mall or city park or business district on the other, she preferred sticking with who she knew.

King would keep her safe.

"I can get Fitz to pony up for another," he said, taking a step in reverse, his expression torn, as if he didn't want to let her out of his sight, but neither did he want to be more of a burden than a help.

She shook her head, took the key, and opened the door. "This will be fine."

It would be more than fine. She wouldn't have it any other way—but that she kept to herself. Just as she did her plans for spending the night curled up beside him.

After everything they'd been through, after being reminded so graphically of Kevin's murder, she wanted to be able to scoot her toes across the mattress and find King there. She wanted his warmth, his scent, his weight on the mattress to remind her that she wasn't alone.

It was hard to process that she was finally letting her guard down because of someone she didn't even know.

She tossed her backpack to the bed nearest the door. King did the same with the bags of things they'd found waiting in Fitzwilliam McKie's car.

Who he'd sent shopping for them and when was as much a mystery as the man, but Cady wasn't going to worry about anything involving McKie or what he wanted of her.

At least not for the next eighteen hours.

He was due to deliver a replacement vehicle to King in the morning. Thinking about him could wait until then. It might be only noon, but she needed a good night's sleep.

She also needed a shower.

"I'm going to take a shower," King said before she could make a move toward the bathroom door.

She stood watching as he ripped off the paper scrub top and wadded it into a ball. "Feel better now?"

He glanced around the room. "No beer, no crawfish, no sunshine. Nope. Don't feel any better at all."

He was here because of her. He'd lost his way home, everything he had with him, and his plans because of her. Yet since driving away from Freehold Township, his complaints had been tempered by humor, couched in sarcasm.

Either he was all bark and no bite, or she hadn't yet felt his teeth.

The thought of his teeth brought to mind his mouth, and thinking about his mouth with him standing shirtless in front of her wasn't smart.

Especially when thinking about him in the shower had her thinking about his fig leaf, and oh, she did not need to go there when she was this incredibly tired.

"I can't do anything about the crawfish or the sunshine, but I can probably find you a beer." That would require making a trip to the hotel bar if they didn't have room service to deliver.

She wasn't thrilled about the idea, but she should be safe

enough. No doubt McKie had his minions lurking, ready to ride in and save the day.

King nipped off her worries. "I'll settle for a pain pill. And about ten hours of sleep."

Except for his taking the meds, they were on the same page. A long hot shower and plenty of shut-eye.

She'd be so glad to get out of these clothes and rid herself of the sooty grit from the fire and smoke and the sterile pine hospital smell that lingered.

"Go ahead, then. Take your shower." She pulled her laptop from the padded slot in her backpack. "I'll see if the wireless is working since I never did get into my bank yesterday. I may need to stop and wait tables for a month before getting on with the rest of my life."

King stopped at the door to the bathroom. "If you're going to be working with McKie, I'm sure he'll be seeing to your finances."

That was one way to put it. "You mean paying me for being bait? Do you think I'll get more than minimum wage? Or is bait a job grade at the bottom of the government pay scale?"

"I mean he'll see to your needs. Until you're back on your feet."

Back on her feet. Was that King's way of saying "out of my life"? Because that's what this was about, wasn't it? King handing her off to Agent McKie?

"I'd rather see to my own needs."

"Yeah. I figured you would, seeing how that's been working so well for you the past eight years," he said, then slammed the door behind him.

They were both tired and cranky and dealing with the sort of disaster aftermath very few people faced. She knew that. She knew better than to let his comment rile her.

But those words—"working so well for you the past eight years"—scooted and squirreled their way into her mind like an irritation too deep to scratch. And his presumptive gall started to drive her mad.

"One, two, three, four," she muttered aloud, continuing on to ten. And then she continued to twenty.

By that time, the shower was running, King singing, and her fury had taken on a life of its own. There was no one, absolutely no one, who could imagine what the last eight years had been like for her.

That included estranged family members who'd known her since birth, and the friends and coworkers who'd supported her—even if from the periphery—through a whole lot of ups and downs they didn't understand.

To have Kingdom Trahan smart off to her about how she had handled things, when he hadn't been there to know what she'd been through, was the breaking point at the end of a day she could just as well have done without.

She left the laptop plugged into the socket on the table lamp and booting up on the extra bed and headed for the bathroom. Telling him off through another shower curtain was not how she'd have chosen to say her piece, but she was in no mood to wait for the optimal time and place.

Unfortunately, her timing sucked. King wasn't yet in the shower. Oh, he was on his way, had the curtain pulled back, one foot lifted to step into the tub, but he was completely dry. And completely naked.

She quickly averted her eyes—just not quickly enough—from his muscled thighs and rump to his face, freshly shaved and still dotted with remnant blobs of shaving cream. "I'm sorry. I didn't mean—"

"Are you sure?" he taunted, laughing, before stepping beneath the spray and closing the curtain behind him.

Arrogant pig. Beast of a man.

And yet she stayed where she was, shutting the door, breathing in the steam as it began to smell of King.

"Was there something you wanted?" he asked her after sputtering out a mouthful of water. "Another look maybe? To share my hot water as part of your plan to fight global warming?"

The day she showered with him, they'd better pray for

global warming because hell would be freezing over. "What I wanted was to tell you to mind your own business. You don't know anything about the last eight years of my life, or whether or not the choices I've made worked for me."

"You've been working dead-end jobs and bunking with dead-end roommates. That's all I need to know."

She felt her blood pressure rising, her anger coming alive. "Sounds to me like you're an expert at dead ends, recognizing them so easily the way you do."

"I spent a few years with nothing but a prison yard to run in, chère. Coming up against razor wire and walls lap after lap taught me a lot about dead ends."

"Maybe so," she said, pushing away her chagrin. "But that doesn't make you an expert on me."

"I never claimed to be. Hell, how could I be?" He sputtered more water, his feet squeaking against the floor of the tub. "You haven't told me enough to give me a chance. Most of what I do know I learned from McKie."

She closed her eyes, powering up to being really pissed off. "That's why you're acting like a shit? Because I didn't tell you everything?"

"No, I'm acting like a shit because I am one. I thought you might have figured that out by now."

"I'm guessing it takes longer than twenty-four hours for the shit factor to fully manifest."

He jerked back the curtain, fuming, his eyes red and fiery, and this time he didn't even bother with the rag. "If you're not going to get in here and scrub me down the way I like, then get the hell out of my bathroom so I can do it myself. This conversation is over."

Cady couldn't speak. King's chest was heaving, his cock rising, his stitched-up head that he was supposed to keep dry soaking wet. This conversation was not over. He knew it as well as she did. But she wasn't going to fight him over the time and place now.

He arched a brow as if reminding her that he was waiting

for an answer. She was feeling just perverse enough to goad him in return, so took her time leaving, giving him a thorough once-over, and then a careless shrug as if to say she'd seen it all before.

She hadn't, of course. And he knew it. Knew she had never in her life seen a man so thick and hard, or come across one who presented this one's aggravating challenge to her ability to walk away.

Her body responded, her nipples tightening beneath her T-shirt and the sports bra she'd put on to sleep in and had been wearing ever since.

Their staring contest became a battle of wills, one she knew she could win by stripping down to her skin—a win that would become a loss when she joined him in the shower, which it was growing so tempting to do.

And so she exited the room, the string of curses King uttered at full volume her consolation prize.

She didn't want to be here when he came out, but she had nowhere to go, and nothing to do once she discovered the wireless wasn't working. She loathed daytime TV.

Going to sleep without showering would've been an option had she been able to stand the smells that had seeped into her pores. But she couldn't, and so she gathered the things she'd need to bathe.

She stood beside the bathroom door waiting, her toiletries and clean clothes clutched to her chest. As soon as King opened the door and took two steps into the room, she ducked into the steamy space and locked herself inside.

Outside, King howled with laughter. Even turning on the water didn't drown out the maniacal sound she feared would ring in her ears forever. But then closing her eyes didn't keep her from seeing him naked and fully aroused.

She groaned, stripped, climbed into the tub, and sat, letting the water beat down on her battered and bruised body—a stinging punishment for stowing away with the man in the first place.

Sixteen

In a repeat of how yesterday's bad evening began, King walked into the room to find Cady fast asleep in the bed they'd be sharing. He could only hope it wasn't an omen that today would be just as bad.

Just like last night, she'd stripped the spare bed of its bedspread, unloaded their crap on the sheets, and wrapped herself up safely to avoid any meeting of body parts in the middle of the night—or in this case, the day.

After their earlier encounter, King had to side with Cady on the two of them needing their own space even if they were in the same bed.

She'd pissed him off in a very big way.

He still couldn't believe he'd let her get to him, especially since it was what she hadn't done, hadn't said, rather than anything she had that infuriated him into nearly losing his temper.

Here he was trying to get her out of trouble and to where she wanted to go, and she couldn't be bothered to give him a map. Oh, she'd pointed out a landmark or two, had told him where to turn when it was time.

But the big picture gaps she'd avoided had left him flying blind. And the fact that Fitzwilliam McKie had been the one to fill them in . . .

King had been itching to light into Cady since hearing the details from the government man, but they'd ridden from the hospital to the hotel in silence, not talking until they'd reached the room.

Since they were both beat, and he in no mood to be civil, he'd taken himself off to the shower before their sniping got out of hand.

He'd never expected her to follow, which served to prove how tired he was, because if anything in life, he knew to expect the unexpected.

All well and good to remind himself of that in hindsight, he grumbled under his breath, sitting in one of the room's chairs to tug off his boots.

Even the midday beer he'd had in the hotel's restaurant bar while Cady showered had done nothing to douse the spark the fire in her eyes had lit in his gut.

He'd tried to forget that moment in the bathroom, the one when she'd looked him over as if thinking of eating him alive. Really, he'd tried.

He'd downed his beer, and tried. He'd thought about calling Simon and sharing the latest, and tried. He'd focused on the things McKie had told him, and tried.

He'd failed every time.

He'd never been one to say no to a woman who wanted him. And Cady would've had to be blind not to see that he was up for whatever she wanted.

But goddamn they did not need that sort of tension between them. Here they were, making a detour into the unknown at the request of a man with a ridiculous name and an ID that didn't prove much of anything.

Adding sex to the mix was about the worst idea ever.

So it figured that King couldn't get sex off his mind.

"I'm awake," Cady said out of the blue.

The room was dark, the heavy drapes drawn. He'd been able to see her form but not her eyes. Had she been watching him all this time? Listening to him mumble? Had she purposefully waited until his thoughts turned to sex to speak? And how had she known that they had?

"Sorry. I was trying to be quiet."

"No, I mean, you didn't wake me up. I wasn't asleep."

Did that mean she'd been waiting up? "I'd've brought you back a beer if I'd known."

"I thought you didn't want one."

"I changed my mind." And if they were going to start in again with the sniping, he was going back for another. He held onto his boot just in case.

"I thought that must be where you went."

A note would've been nice, dickhead. "Sorry. I should've told you."

"It's okay. Really. I'm hardly your keeper."

"Yeah, but we're rowing in the same crappy boat here, so . . . well . . . sorry." He wasn't big on apologies, but this one he meant.

Cady sat up, left the light off. "You can go home. Fitz said he'll figure out another way to do this if you want to check out. You're pretty much an innocent bystander."

"And you're not?" King dropped his boot to the floor. "Besides, how would it look to Malling at this point if you suddenly had wheels of your own? Not to mention he thinks we're traveling together, and if tomorrow we're not . . ."

He had an out. A way home. Sunshine and crawfish on the horizon. McKie had offered it. Cady was offering it. And King was arguing his way right back in.

He didn't know if it was the beer or the pills or going on thirty-two hours without sleep, but he was obviously off his ever-lovin' rocker.

"If you're sure."

"I am." The most sobering thing of all is that he was. Completely sure. "Of course, after a good night's sleep, I may not be, so if you want to bring out a Bible for me to swear on, now would be a good time."

The sound she made was part laugh and part sigh, and

had him feeling cozy all over. The fact that he let the word *cozy* enter his mind was almost as bad as imagining glass shards from the explosion embedded deep in his flesh.

At least that stopped him from thinking about sex.

"Did he tell you everything? McKie? Did he tell you about me getting Kevin killed?"

He started to tell her that she wasn't responsible for Kevin's death. That Combs had broken the window, that Tuzzi had pulled the trigger, that Felwouk had been there, as had Malling who'd driven them away.

Cady hadn't been there that night. Yes, she'd stashed the mascot filled with heroine in her bedroom on the second floor of the family's home. But that did not make her responsible for her brother's death.

King got out of his chair, walked between the two beds, and turned on the lamp farthest from Cady. "You didn't get Kevin killed. I understand you feeling that way—"

"Do you really? Or is that just one of those things that sound good when you say them?"

King braced his elbows on his knees, laced his hands, and hung his head. "I can't feel the same emotion, the pain, or the anger or the wishing for a chance to go back and tell your friend to hide the mascot herself. But I can understand why those things haunt you."

A sad smile teased the corners of her mouth. "Haunted. Yeah. That's exactly how it feels. It never goes away. Like a specter that's always hovering over me."

He certainly hadn't meant to make her put a name to her suffering. "Hopefully this plan of McKie's will double as an exorcism, and you can get your life back."

Cady pulled her knees to her chest, wrapped her arms around the bedspread that covered them, propped her chin on top. "I think starting fresh with a new one is a better plan. Even if I help Fitz plug Tuzzi's pipeline, it's not going to change the past. Kevin will still be dead. My parents will still blame me. Malling, now that he's out, and Felwouk's and Combs's friends will still make my life a living hell."

This was new. The fact that she was willing to put names and faces to her persecutors. She'd been vague, and reticent to do so thus far. "How're they making your life hell exactly? Who's doing it? Do you know?"

"Tyler, for one." When that didn't ring a bell and King frowned, she added, "Alice's boyfriend. The one who crawled into my bed."

It took several seconds for that to sink in, then . . . "Wait a minute." King shot to his feet. "This bunch of drug-dealing thugs is responsible for you getting beat to a pulp? And you didn't tell me?"

"I didn't know until today. When I got out of the shower and you weren't here, I tried the wireless again. It was working so I checked my bank balance, and there was a charge I'd forgotten about."

King returned to where he'd been sitting. His jumping to conclusions wasn't helping anything, and was going to cause Cady to clam up, leaving him scrambling for a flight plan again. "What was the charge?"

She cringed, as if embarrassed. "I'd ordered a bottle of piña colada massage oil from Renee, my other roommate, for her sorority's fund-raiser."

"Piña colada?"

This time she grinned. "It was either that, strawberry daiquiri, orange marmalade, or green apple martini."

Uh, no. He'd stick to things that didn't smell like a bar. "I'm more an unscented kinda guy myself."

"I'll keep that in mind," she said, and then fell silent, as if picturing the same thing he was, slick hands on bare bodies.

He cleared his throat and tried to get them back on track. "So the charge triggered a memory or something?"

"Not a memory, no. It just made a whole lot of things fall into place."

Patience, patience, patience. “How so?”

“I gave Renee my debit Visa number for the form, but never paid attention to the receipt and who would be billing me. But it was there online. The name of the sorority.”

“The same one with the Persian cat mascot,” King said, the conclusion drawing his stomach into an angry knot.

Cady nodded.

“Were you already living there when Alice hooked up with this Tyler?”

She nodded again. “And I’m pretty sure she came looking for me yesterday afternoon because he’d put an end to their hooking. No need for him to stick around. He’d done what he’d come there to do.”

“Screw you over,” King said, then got up to pace the room at the foot of both beds. “This is the kind of thing Tuzzi’s bunch has been putting you through? For eight years?”

“This is the first time I’ve gone to the ER, but yeah.” She shrugged, pulled the bedspread up to her shoulders, held it beneath her chin. “I stopped caring about the gossip and rumors a long time ago. I’d given up all my friends, or I’d given up those who hadn’t already disappeared, so what strangers thought of me really didn’t matter.”

She closed her eyes, rubbed at them gingerly, looked at him again. “I take that back. It mattered when it came to having job interviews sabotaged. Or the few dates I had ruined by graffiti appearing mysteriously on the guys’ cars. I sold my own a long time ago. I couldn’t afford to keep buying new tires, having it painted, the windshield replaced.”

If not for his current hate of all things glass, King would’ve put his fist into the room’s mirror.

He wasn’t a saint, and had left a long trail of people he’d treated like shit, but he was pretty damn sure he’d never been this type of asshole cruel.

If he hadn’t agreed to go along with Cady and McKie and

the plan to end Tuzzi's reign of terror, he'd be out securing his boarding pass now.

Cady deserved better than the life she'd been forced to live. He was going to see that it happened, even if it meant putting his sunshine and crawfish on the back burner until next year's crop was ready to boil.

Seventeen

"I'm going to go to sleep now," Cady said, dousing the light. The mattress squeaked as she settled deeper into the bed. "Or I'm going to give it a shot anyway. Knowing Malling's out there somewhere, I don't think sleep's going to come easy."

"McKie's out there, too," King reminded her. "Don't forget that."

She could see his silhouette as he tugged off his jeans and T-shirt. He was coming to bed in nothing but his boxers. She hadn't counted on that. "I know. If he wasn't, I wouldn't be sleeping at all."

King pulled back the sheet, blanket, and bedspread. The bed dipped as he sat on the edge, evened out as he pivoted and laid down. "You sure you don't want that beer? Or a pain pill? I've got enough to go around."

"And if you run out, you can step outside and have Malling put you in touch with Tuzzi for a refill," she said with no small amount of sarcasm, wanting to take the words back almost immediately because King didn't deserve to be connected to drug-dealing scum. "I'm sorry. That wasn't nice."

"It's called black humor, Cady," King said softly, crossing his arms beneath his head. "It's okay. If we can't laugh at ourselves or this fucked-up world, making it through in one piece is a crap shoot."

She smiled to herself. "Such a cynic. I never would've guessed."

"Ah, but a hopeful one. Which is a big improvement over the total dick I was for a lot of years."

Now that wouldn't surprise her at all. He had a very dick-like vibe, and he hadn't been the nicest man to stow away with. At the same time, he had done more for her—a veritable stranger—than anyone she'd ever called friend had done for her since the trial.

Part of that was her fault. She'd turned away when anyone had reached out, not wanting to answer questions about how she was doing, feeling, was there anything she might need.

She hadn't known how she was doing, feeling, and the only thing she needed—Kevin to come back—no one could give. Eventually the questions stopped, as did the hands in offering.

But once she was in a better place, she found herself alone. By then she wore the scarlet letter of blame for ruining so many young promising lives, and her parents' lives as well.

She supposed her accusers didn't consider hers ruined, or thought whatever she suffered, she deserved. It hadn't taken much to convince herself of the same.

At her side, King murmured, "You asleep?"

"No," she answered, barely a whisper.

"The thought of sleeping next to a dick keeping you awake?"

"I've slept next to dicks before. One just a couple of nights ago. Didn't even know he was there."

It took several seconds, as if he was deciding whether or not to move, but finally King rolled to his side, propped up on his elbow, and faced her. "I know we can't nail this guy for the shit he's put you through, but we can take away something that gives him power and makes him money, and it's going to hurt. Trust me on that. I know his type. I served time with his type. He loses this, he'll be nothing."

Cady was glad it was dark. It was only midafternoon, but the room's heavy drapes were drawn tight and blocked the light from outside. She was afraid she was going to cry. She did not want him to see her cry.

She was tired, and he was being so nice, and she'd been an emotional glacier for years. To have this bit of warmth was painful. Her chest ached, and she fought his attempt to thaw her with a strategy she knew well. Deflection.

"When were you in prison? How old were you?"

He didn't answer right away, and she didn't know if she'd crossed a line she should've honored, or if he was wise to her deflecting ways.

But finally she heard him breathe in, as if he'd only paused to corner his thoughts. When he spoke, it wasn't what she'd thought she'd hear.

"It was a long time ago. I went in at eighteen, came out at twenty-two."

She waited for more. When nothing came, she said, "You were so young."

He still didn't say anything, just flipped onto his back. She stared at the dark ceiling, thinking out loud, unable to drop a subject in which he obviously had no wish to participate.

"Those are the same years I was in college. I mean, not the same years, since you're older, but I moved onto campus when I was eighteen."

After another deep breath, King asked, "Did you ever finish? Get your degree?"

She nodded her head on her pillow. "Yeah, though my last year took two since I was paying my own way by then. I did most of it online."

"Your parents cut you off?"

"I thought I told you that."

"You did. The college funding thing just never registered."

"It was a complete break, King. All the way down to the emotional ties made at birth," she said, unable to hold back a snort.

"My folks were killed in a car wreck when I was a kid. My cousin and I had grown up as best friends, brothers really, so I lived with him and his folks after that."

She wondered if he thought telling her that would lessen her pain, or make her feel less alone in the ugliness she'd gone through. Then she wondered if the confession had sprung from a need to purge himself of the abandonment he'd suffered.

She did feel less alone, but that was because he was beside her and talking to her, and she'd been her only companion for so long. "I'm so sorry. That had to be hard."

She felt him shrug. "I got through it. Can't said I'm proud of every decision I made after that, where I went with my life, but it's been an interesting one for sure."

"Why did you go to prison?"

"To serve time for a fire I didn't set."

Her breath caught. "What?"

"Yep. Simon, my cousin, and I both, though Simon chose the military instead."

"What happened? The fire, I mean."

"We were celebrating the end of high school. Celebrating with more booze and dope than was good for us. And sharing an older woman to complete the trifecta of teenage male stupidity. Investigators ruled the fire that swept through my family's house arson. Since we were the only ones there . . ."

But they weren't. "What about the woman?"

"Lorna Savoy. She was sleeping with the judge. The Honorable Terrill Landry Sr."

Wow. Just wow. "I thought things like that only went on in fiction."

King gave a sharply bitter laugh. "This was twenty years ago in rural Louisiana, chère. And fiction doesn't hold a candle to the truth."

Cady turned to her side, rested her face on her stacked hands, and studied King's silhouette in the dark. He was a hard man. A crude man. A cynical man, and damaged just as she was.

Here they were, sharing the same bed, involving themselves willingly in more danger than she, for one, had ever known.

If they were successful in helping McKie take down Tuzzi's prison drug empire, she'd at least have the satisfaction of inflicting a great deal of misery on the man who'd stolen her brother's life and hers.

But King . . . "Why are you here?"

"In this city? Because this was where my ride was blown all to hell? In this hotel? Because McKie is paying. In this bed? Because you tossed all your crap on the other one and stole the bedspread to boot."

"That's not what I mean."

"Then you need to be a little more clear on what you do mean, Miss Kowalski, or I might come up with a reason I don't think you'll care for."

He was back to being the ass who'd challenged her naked in the bathroom. The one who thought he could scare her away with his cock.

"Why are you helping me, and don't say it's because McKie promised to upgrade your ride."

King huffed, then lowered his voice to a growl. "If you really want to know, come a little closer."

He didn't intimidate her at all. Yes, earlier he'd unnerved her, and she'd made a hasty escape. She hadn't been prepared for the threat of his words or his body.

Since then, she'd had time to think, to shore up her flagging self-confidence, to listen to him talk about the things that made him who he was. He was just a man, and if he hurt her, she would wisely blame only herself.

She moved closer, scooting toward him until she could feel his body heat, could touch his bare ankle with her bare toes.

He flinched. "What happened to your nice safe cocoon?"

She wanted to laugh, but settled for a private smile. "If you'd paid more attention, you would've seen the other bed's spread was on top of this one, not wrapped around me."

"How the hell am I supposed to see anything in the dark?" he grumbled back.

"Night vision?"

"You having a good time? Goading me?"

"I'm just answering your questions, and doing what I'm told to do."

"And since when has compliant been your middle name?"

"Since I decided it would be fun to try it on."

"Fun you say? You want fun?"

"Depends what you have in mind," she shot back, hearing his rising frustration in his voice.

"Well, chère. If you really want to find out, you're going to have to come a whole lot closer than that."

She wondered if he meant it. If he wanted to have sex with her. Or if he was baiting her because he didn't expect her to accept his offer. Because he thought he was safe. That she would say no.

Because he didn't think she'd do what she did, scrunch her way closer, roll onto her belly, raise up on her elbows, her face above his. "Close enough?"

She could see his eyes go wide, then narrow, but all he did was clear his throat.

"Do you need me closer? Like this?" She straddled her upper body over his, her hands on the mattress above his shoulders. "Can you answer my question now?"

"What question? I thought you were here to have fun." The words sounded like gravel beneath the heels of his boots.

"Is that why you're here?"

"Can you think of another reason?" he asked, his chest heaving beneath hers.

She felt his chest hair crackle against the thin fabric of her top. "I don't know. You tell me."

"Take off your shirt and I might."

It was going to be a battle all the way. He wasn't going to tell her why he was sticking around. Now she was more curious to find out why he wouldn't answer than she was to learn the truth.

But most of all she wanted to know what his hands would feel like, skimming down her back, how rough the pads of his fingers would be tiptoeing from her nape to the base of her spine.

She lifted one arm, ducked her head and her shoulders out of the shirt, then resumed her position above him. "Answer, please."

He sucked back a breath, moved his hands to her sides, and pulled her down so that her nipples teased his. "Can't. Not enough blood left in my brain."

"That so?" she asked, and he nodded, and she didn't object when he urged her with his hands to check his blood flow for herself.

Sliding the length of his body as he was helping her to do, it didn't take long to find the problem. His boxers were tented very nicely, and warm where they strained against her belly like a wildcat in a cage.

She tossed back the blankets and sheets and climbed on top, clamping his knees between hers. "I see what you mean."

"If you can fix that, I'll do what I can to answer your question."

Sure you will, she thought, searching for the opening in his shorts. "All of my questions?"

He groaned when she wrapped her fingers around his shaft. "Every last one."

"I'm going to hold you to that," she said, pulling him free.

"As long as you don't stop holding me now," he told her, just before she leaned down, breathed deeply of his scent, and took him into her mouth.

The head of his cock was already sticky with anticipation, and she licked the moisture away, ringing her fingers around the top of his shaft, slicking her thumb across his plum-ripe glans.

She sucked him there, drawing just that plump bulb between her lips, toying the slit in the tip with her tongue, then letting go and taking him in until he hit the back of her throat.

He reached for the elastic band of his boxers with a hurried desperation. She pulled away and slapped at his hands. "My fun, my way. The shorts stay on."

He spit out a string of words she wasn't sure she'd ever heard used as profanities. He was nothing if not creative with his epithets, but as quick as he was with most comebacks, that didn't surprise her at all. She liked smart men . . . though this one seemed to have some trouble playing by her rules.

"And stop trying to spread your legs," she said, bending over again and running her tongue along the seam on the underside of his cock's head. "Be still, or I'm moving to the other bed. Alone."

More grumbling, then, "If you come up a little farther, I can get to your tits."

"I don't want you to get to my tits."

"Well at least turn around here and let me get my fingers wet."

She couldn't help but grin. The man was persistent. But she was hardly cotton candy herself. "What makes you think I'm wet?"

"Christ, woman, I can smell you."

"Hmm," was her only verbal response because her mouth was too full for her to say more.

She slid down his shaft until her lips kissed his boxers, then began to ease away, keeping her tongue pressed to the thick ridge of veins running the length of the underside, finishing with nothing but his cock's head in her mouth.

And then she let him go. King was right. She was wet, and she wanted him. "Do you have a condom?"

More curses, these more creative than before and involving llamas. "I can't give you a baby. And I won't give you a disease. But it's your call on how we play this out."

She was curious why he couldn't give her a baby, but would ask him that question later. Right now all she cared about was having him inside of her, and while she peeled off her pants, he shucked away his boxers like the husk from corn.

When neither one of them was wearing more than their skin, she climbed up to his hips, lifted up to her knees, let him position himself there between her legs that were open, then slid down until she had no choice but to stop.

There was no more of him to put inside of her, and no more room inside of her even so. She shivered, shuddered, braced her hands behind her on his knees, and leaned back to catch her breath.

"That wasn't what I was expecting."

"Too much? We can switch positions. I'll go slow."

"Speed's not the issue. It's been awhile for me. And you're . . . not what I'm used to." Though that was a temporary situation. Getting used to this . . . to him . . . wouldn't take much effort at all.

He settled his hands at the crease where her hips met her thighs and slid his thumbs down to her sex. "Take your time. I'll just play here while you do."

He caught her clit, pinched it. She jumped, driving him deeper. "I'm afraid your playing is going to kill me."

"Should I stop?"

"Oh, hell no," she said, and he laughed like a wild man half out of his mind. "I hope you're laughing with me and not at me."

"Goddamn, woman. I'm laughing because it's the only thing keeping my cock from killing you."

"I'm good to go," she told him, and leaned forward,

threading her fingers through the hair on his chest and bracing her weight on his pecs. "Try to keep up."

She rode him then, up and down, grinding, gyrating, rubbing her clit against the base of his shaft where his wiry pubic hair tickled.

He held her hips and helped her, raising up to bite at her nipples, the flesh of her breasts, her neck, her shoulders, leaving bruises of his making to mark her like the rest, easing back when he finally reached her mouth.

There he was gentle, kissing her softly where he knew it was safe to kiss, nuzzling and petting as if to heal her. But the time for gentleness passed quickly, and he bucked his body upward.

She cried out, shushed him when he voiced his fear that he'd hurt her. "I want you to hurt me. I want your hurt to keep me walking bowlegged for days."

After that, he didn't seem to worry about causing her pain, or he hid it well if he still did. He surged up, his fingers digging into the muscles of her thighs as he held her where he wanted her.

She moved with him, against him, stopping and letting him be the only one in motion, rejoining him when her belly pulled taut and contracted.

She felt her orgasm in her mouth, her nipples, her rib cage, her cunt. She came apart like brittle glass, shattering, falling, crushed. Irreparable.

She knew that he'd followed; she could feel the warmth of his semen, could hear the guttural sounds he made, the pain of his pleasure, like raw wounds flayed open.

But the sensation of fracturing consumed her, and she couldn't let it go. Neither could she find where to start the cleanup, or how to put herself back together.

It was enough, she supposed, that she was finished. That there was nothing left of her to break.

Eighteen

There was a big part of King that wanted to stay in bed when he came awake the next morning, and that big part was making itself known between his legs.

The woman responsible for the state of his mind and body was snoring softly—and still naked—at his side.

Her nakedness and her softness made a damn compelling case for his not wanting to get up and get going. It didn't matter that they'd been in bed for fourteen, fifteen hours, maybe sleeping ten.

He liked lying here, remembering Cady riding him like a wild pony, reliving the way he'd flipped her over and showed her the stallion he was.

She was a hungry wench, and an agile wench for being so busted up. Not wanting to hurt her, he'd held back, gone easy, kept things toned down to gentle rather than the rough he enjoyed.

At least he'd done all that until she'd threatened to hurt him if he didn't treat her right.

Having sex with Cady sure wasn't what he'd expected to happen when she'd climbed into his truck in that Manhattan parking garage and refused to get out. Was that just yesterday morning?

Damn if he would ever complain about her stowing away again.

Neither was he going to complain about the pain slicing through the back of his head, down his neck, and into his shoulders. If not for looking at a long day of driving, he'd pop a pill.

He'd turn over and pop Cady if not for the sixth sense telling him McKie was on his way.

Reluctantly, King rolled out of bed, found the clothes he'd been wearing before rolling in, and pulled them on, grimacing when he reached up to run his fingers through his hair and hit his stitches.

A new bandage was probably in order, as was a shower, he realized, standing at the toilet for the morning's first pee, but he kinda liked smelling like Cady, and so he zipped up to hunt down coffee instead.

Three soft raps of knuckles on the door stopped him in the act of pulling on his first boot, and stirred Cady at the same time.

"Who is it?" she asked, drowsy, sitting up and switching on the bedside lamp. "Is it McKie?"

King glanced over, finished with boot number two. "If it's anyone else, they'll be stuck there till he shows up to play good guy."

"You're a good guy," she said, pouting.

"Maybe so, chère, but I am all out of ammo." Not an easy thing to admit, but there it was. The waif in the bed had fucked him worthless.

And at that emasculating thought, he went to answer the door.

It was McKie—he identified himself when King asked—and the government man came bearing not only coffee but breakfast. "I'm not too early, am I?"

"Guess that depends on who you're asking," King said, stepping back to let McKie step inside the room. "Except for needing a stitch or two tightened, I'm raring to get going again. But Cady? I imagine the girl could use another couple of days to recover from the assaults she didn't bother reporting to the police."

"Assaults?" A dark brow arched, McKie set the box of food and drink on the room's table, then handed one of the coffees to Cady. When she reached for it, King realized she was still jay bird nude under the covers she'd pulled to her chest and tucked beneath her armpits.

"Shit," he mumbled as she took the cup and asked for cream and sugar both. His own cup he drank straight black because black was the color of the cloud he was looking though. He didn't like the way McKie was watching the blanket slip and slide as Cady flavored her brew.

"How're you this morning, Miss Kowalski? Ready to get started? Or do you first want to tell me about these assaults?"

"Cady, please," she said, twirling a wooden stir stick in the cup. "No to the assaults, but yes to the other. Anything to wrap up this chapter of my life. I am so ready to move forward you can't even know."

McKie glanced from Cady to King then at the second bed covered with their belongings before his attention returned to the used one and the naked girl sitting there. "Sounds like you had a good night."

"I did, actually, yes." She paused, sipped her coffee, smiled like some sort of sex siren she-devil, and made it work—even with her black eyes and fat lip. "King and I boinked like bunnies, I'm still as naked as the day I was born, and I'd like to get dressed. So if you two could step into the hallway long enough for me to get to the bathroom . . ."

King felt his face heating from yet another blow to his manhood, and mouthed, "Me, too?"

"Yes, you. Both of you." She made a shooing motion with the hand not holding her coffee, which caused the blanket to slip, and King to groan as he watched more and more of her body being revealed. "Give me three minutes."

McKie was already at the door. He pulled it open, glanced both ways down the hall, then stood there waiting for King, leaving King no choice but to grab the key from the desk and do what Cady had told him.

Once outside, he shoved his hands to his hips and started counting the three hundred sixty seconds she'd said she needed. Then he stopped and looked at McKie. "I don't know why she told you that. The bunnies thing."

Fighting a grin, McKie leaned against the wall beside the door, his arms crossed over his chest. "Set everyone at ease. Keep me from wondering if you did, you from wondering how to hide it. Smart girl, that one."

"Hmph."

This time, McKie laughed, a short, sharp burst that said they'd been had. "Hey, she's in there, we're out here. She got her way. I'd say that qualifies as smart."

And qualified King, at least, for pussy-whipped. "Yeah, yeah."

"Hey, when you warned me off yesterday from hurting her, I figured there was something between you two."

There hadn't been then, but King wasn't about to weaken his position with more details when the man already knew more than he needed to know.

He turned toward the door. They'd been out here three minutes at least, and if it had only been two, tough shit. He was hungry. And he had a claim to stake.

McKie stepped forward and blocked him. "I need to know that it's not going to make a difference. This thing between you and Cady."

King considered the government agent who suddenly seemed more like an adversary than someone on his side. He felt a bad heat flaring up in his gut, one that stirred memories of being locked up. "You don't want our thing to mess up your thing, is that it?"

"Yeah," McKie said, his eyes dark and giving no quarter. "That's it."

It had been months since King had felt the urge to deck another man. He'd gone through most of his life with his hands in fists, waiting for a chance to swing.

Part of doing so had been self-defense. He'd grown up dirt poor, had learned to be tough to survive.

It was the same strategy that had given him eyes in the back of his head during his years behind bars. He wouldn't be alive today if he hadn't learned to live that way.

But another part of the urge that had him wanting to slam his knuckles into the other man's face, a very large part in fact, was about striking first, before he could lose, before something else was taken from him, his money, his family, his home, his life.

Now Cady.

He didn't like thinking this man was going to take her away, because that meant thinking about the fact that she wasn't really his, and that meant thinking about what life might be like if she was.

And so he didn't think it. Any of it.

He stuck the key card in the lock and said, "You heard the girl. She wants to get on with her life."

Nineteen

When Cady came out of the bathroom twenty minutes later, showered and shampooed and freshly shaved, she felt like a new woman. A new woman who was hobbling around like a much older one, true, and one still bruised to bits, but she wasn't going to complain.

She'd enjoyed last night beyond belief. Had sex with any other man ever been that much fun? Griping about the morning after soreness between her legs and rarely used muscles left quivering never crossed her mind. Even if it had, she could hardly do so in front of company.

Her telling Fitz that she and King had shared more than the hotel room's bed had, she imagined, been enough of a public revelation for one morning. If she said anything else about last night, King would no doubt throttle her.

The thought had her smiling as she used her fingers to pinch more spikes into her hair. She would never have pegged him for the shy type, or even the silent type—not that she'd expected him to brag about his conquest.

But it was rather sweet how he'd been struck speechless by what she'd said. She liked that he hadn't turned it into a joke and made their time together less than it was.

Fun and games aside, she'd done her best while going to sleep, while waking up, while showering, not to dwell on the unknown of what she and King had done. What it meant. Would they do it again. Were they going to talk about it or pretend nothing between them had changed.

She was changed. That much was a given. Whether the playful sex, the reflective sex, the near desperate sex, or the conversation they'd shared was responsible, something during the night had altered her sense of self.

Logical or not, there it was, though she wasn't going to examine it any closer. She didn't want to do anything to break what might be nothing but a spell. And so she tucked away everything but the moment and made for what remained of the breakfast Fitz had brought.

The two men sat huddled over her laptop studying a map of Pennsylvania. King looked up, and their gazes caught; she felt the tug of his like a magnet at her steely resolve not to look for more in what they'd done than she'd already found. She couldn't risk losing even the tiniest bit of that.

"Planning our itinerary?" she asked, then reached for a lukewarm sausage biscuit and bit in.

Fitz scooted his chair away from the small desk, looked her over before meeting her gaze with a probing one of his own. "King told me about one of your assaults, and the connection to Tuzzi you were able to make."

Cady stepped back until her knees hit the bed, then hopped up to sit there cross-legged. "It's a very weak connection, but after hearing what you said yesterday, it's hard to believe Tyler climbing into my bed was a coincidence. Still, Alice was the one who came after me, not Renee."

"Renee was the sorority member," King added. "Which makes her involvement a smoking gun just as dangerous as the Smith and Wesson I took from the psycho roommate."

Fitz glanced over, his gaze cutting into King. "You still have it? The handgun? I don't want this operation derailed on a technicality because you're unlicensed and carrying an unregistered piece."

"It's gone," King said convincingly enough that even Cady wasn't sure of the truth.

She knew that he'd taken the gun from Alice, but she'd been in such a panic that she didn't remember if he'd had it with him when he'd climbed behind the wheel of the Hummer and driven her away from that nightmare.

"Make sure it is," Fitz said to King, his voice containing a borderline threat which he didn't tamp down when he turned to Cady. "I want to know everything, no matter how weak you think it is."

Cady nodded, wondering if this was the time to assert herself and tell Fitz what was on her mind. "Anything that comes up, I'll let you know . . . assuming you're around for me to tell you."

"I'll always be close—"

"As close as the nearest satellite," King interrupted to add before biting into a muffin.

"I'll be close," Fitz reiterated strongly. "And I'll be checking in."

"So what is our plan, then?" Cady asked, hoping the change of subject would ease the strange tension between the two men, plus give her a chance to have her say. "And how is Malling sharing my day-to-day activities with Tuzzi going to help you stop the flow of his drugs?"

Fitz sat forward, leaning his elbows on his knees. "Those details are classified."

Yeah, that's what she'd expected to hear. But it was an answer she couldn't live with if she was going to be involved. "I'm just supposed to trust you, is that it? I have no idea who you work for, or if you're even one of the good guys. All I have is you telling me that doing what you say will get Tuzzi off my back."

"You don't have to do anything, Cady. But as far as trusting me . . ." He'd paused, focused on her more intently, made certain she couldn't look away.

"I'm the one who found you, remember? The one helping you out, keeping you from having to deal with red tape and official channels. Who would I be if not one of the good guys?" She started to shrug, was stopped when he added, "Besides, aren't you the one who said anything to help?"

"You found her by accident," King reminded the other man, giving Cady a chance to pull her thoughts together. "She popped up on your radar, remember? You didn't go looking for her. So that anything she's offering? It's qualified, boo. She's not giving you her services carte blanche."

Before Fitz could argue his point further, Cady launched into making hers. "Did you ever watch the show *Alias,* Fitz? Kick-ass government chick out to save the day? No? Well, the bad guys had the same equipment, if not better, than the good guys. They had moles inside the CIA. Hell, they convinced a lot of people that they were the CIA."

She took a breath, went on. "And before you give me some spiel about reality and make believe and telling the difference between the two, weren't you the one who said yesterday that truth is stranger than fiction?"

Cady met the agent's stony gaze directly, watched him shake his head, then glanced at King to find him wearing a cocky grin. She was in no mood for cocky. "What's so funny?"

"Nothing, chère. Not a goddamn thing. Except I was the one who said that about truth and fiction."

"Who said it isn't the point." Gah. Men. She took a deep breath and tried again. "The point is that I have to be sure I'm helping the right side. That I'm not indenturing myself to Tuzzi forever by working with someone who in some stranger than fiction reality is working for him."

Surely he could understand that. Surely wanting that one small assurance of who he was wasn't too much to ask, because frankly she didn't have it in her to go another round this morning, and she feared waiting until tomorrow to commit to McKie's plan would be too late. Malling, lacking the brains of Tuzzi, could screw everything up for good.

Fitz didn't respond right away, as if taking in and digesting what she'd said, and the conditions King had laid out. Finally, the agent leaned forward, rested his elbows on the arms, and laced his hands. His gaze traveled from Cady to King and back twice before he spoke.

"What Tuzzi has done to Cady indirectly, as cruel as it is . . ." Fitz paused for a breath, pressed his lips together and looked down.

Either he was a hell of an actor, or carrying a real burden, Cady mused, watching as he gathered his composure and went on.

"As cruel as he's been to Cady, he's perpetrated monstrous things against other inmates, as well as against those on the outside who cross him."

"Like I'm about to do," she heard herself muttering when she'd meant to keep the thought to herself.

"You've got me looking out for you. They didn't," Fitz assured her, but in the back of Cady's mind rang King's words, "the closest satellite away." Fitz continued, "I need to put a stop to all of it. To what he does on the inside. To what he gets others to do for him out here. And since I need your cooperation to make it happen, you can bet I'll have your back while we're getting it done."

"If you're the good guys, I suppose that helps. If you're not . . ." She let the thought trail, hoping to remind the agent that she had a name and a face, and she wasn't one of Tuzzi's others.

"Did you know him when you were at school?"

Cady shook her head at King's question. "I knew of him. Everyone knew of him. His name came up in gossip about his fraternity's pranks, and at the same time, he was written up in the campus paper for his community service."

"Volunteered or court ordered?"

This time, Fitz responded to King. "The Kowalski murder was the first time Tuzzi hit the system."

"Even though he'd been dealing drugs," King said, pushing out of his chair and crossing to the room's window.

"Even though," Fitz said, his gaze following King.

The Kowalski murder. God, she hated the sound of that. "Was Kevin the first person he killed? Did watching my brother die give him a taste for that? For taking life?"

"He was the first to die by Tuzzi's hand, yes. But then his taste . . . grew. Pulling a trigger was no longer enough."

And this Cady really didn't want to hear.

"He graduated to things like bloodbaths in the prison showers. Dismemberment. There was a fire in one cell where the inmate had been rendered unconscious."

Cady shuddered, and King stoically said, "Except you can't tie him to any of this. You can't prove he was involved."

"That's where Cady comes in."

Cady, who knew a guilt trip when she saw one unrolling at her feet like a long red carpet. Cady, who was no VIP. "How do I come in? That's the part that's still eluding me here. I want to help. You have no idea how badly I want to help. But I haven't heard details. I've only seen . . . gloss."

"You, Cady Kowalski, are Nathan Tuzzi's weakest link."

King dropped the drapes into place and came to sit on the bed beside her. "We running a game show here, McKie? Or are you going to give Cady what she wants?"

Cady ignored King's interruption and addressed what McKie had said. "I don't get it. Why am I a link of any kind? And why the weakest one if I am?"

"What you are, Cady, is Nathan Tuzzi's obsession. The one single person unrelated to his illegal activities who he's got it in for. You're not business. You're personal. And personal means getting careless, making mistakes."

Fitz paused as if he wanted to be sure both of them were listening, his face somber as his gaze swung from hers to

King's, then dropped to a spot on the bed between where they sat.

Her gaze followed the same direction, and she realized not only had she crumbled what was left of her biscuit all over the unmade bed, but that King was now holding her fingers, his thumb stroking the back of her hand.

"Wow. That's a mess," she said, not even sure if she was talking about the biscuit or being the center of a psychopath's attention. King didn't say anything, just continued rubbing her skin. Funny how she didn't seem to feel it.

Fitz reached for his coffee cup and dropped his gaze to the contents. "When it comes to business, no one is more exacting than Nathan Tuzzi. He guards his contacts and informants more jealously than I imagine he ever did that girlfriend who sent him after her cat."

"But he's not that careful when it comes to Cady," King said.

"He's gotten away with so much for so long that I'd be surprised to find he thinks he's anything but infallible. His information flow in and out of the prison never seems to hit a snag. And that's our biggest problem."

"You can't snag him," King said, pulling Cady's hand into his lap.

Fitz shook his head. "Not him, not his people. We have no timetable. His deals are too sporadic, and we haven't been able to catch a break intercepting his orders going out or the news coming back in. But if we know Malling is going to be reporting to Tuzzi, we can be ready."

Something had been bugging Cady and she finally spoke up. "What day was Malling paroled? What day did he get out exactly? It was yesterday, right? The same day Tyler finally crawled into bed with me?"

"Not yesterday, but the day before, yeah." Fitz tossed the cup he'd picked up earlier into the trash.

"I knew it! That's what he'd been waiting for. He wasn't there for Alice at all. He was there for me." She stopped, puffed out a breath as every fucking thing fell into place, and looked from Fitz to King and back as it did and as she realized that if not for Fitzwilliam McKie, she would never have been able to connect the pieces.

She bounded off the bed. She couldn't sit still. "He knew when Malling was getting out and that Tuzzi would be getting more aggressive. Tyler was planted there to make the first strike. To let me know the psychological war was over. That with Tuzzi's man back on the streets, the time had come to get physical."

She threaded her fingers into her hair and tugged as she paced, working it out, one puzzle piece tucking into a second, a third fitting tightly with a fourth, a fifth over there snapping precisely and turning a jumbled mess into a whole that was supposed to mean something . . .

That's when she stopped. When the picture began to come into view. It was so simple, she should've seen it before. "I don't have a choice, do I? I fight back, or I run for the rest of my life."

"You always have a choice," King told her, his voice gruff but soft, and Fitz nodded, both men on her side. She wasn't in this alone. And that made it easier to face the horizon, the unknown, and her personal Armageddon.

Even if she did have a choice, she wouldn't be able to live with herself if she said no. So ID or no ID, she gave McKie her yes—adding one caveat, and pinning him with a look that told him her terms were not negotiable.

"If I find out you're not who you say you are, what I'll do to you is nothing compared to what Tuzzi has done or plans to do to me."

Twenty

King had only been without his Hummer for thirty-six hours, but damn was it good to have it back. Yeah, yeah, *it* wasn't the same vehicle he'd been driving before, but if this upgraded version wasn't the sweetest thing he'd ever laid a hand on, then he'd never eat a crawfish again.

Uh, the sweetest thing besides Cady.

Fitz had taken care of the VIN change with the state and the insurance company who had no idea that they'd skated on a huge replacement payout. How he'd done it, what strings he'd had to pull . . . those things were part of the mystery that was Fitzwilliam McKie.

King was pretty damn sure there was more to the story of who McKie was, what he did, who he worked for, and who funded their gig, but there was no question that the man made things happen—and did so at a level that required either a lot of connections or a lot of cash.

Having fallen into a fortune of Civil War gold this last year, King was well aware of the strings money could pull, the people it could buy, the things it could provide, and how it kept machines well oiled and running. McKie could be using it to do all of the above, hoping to deprive Nathan Tuzzi of being able to do the same.

The thought of Tuzzi had King glancing at the woman

tucked into his passenger seat, looking out her window at the Pennsylvania landscape rolling by. They'd crossed the state line and left New Jersey only a few minutes ago. He'd pointed it out, but she hadn't said a thing.

Then again, she hadn't said much of anything since taking on McKie over breakfast. She'd been particularly silent while loading up the replacement Hummer after Fitz had run them through the plan. The government man's plan wasn't much of one, to King's way of thinking, and was no doubt giving Cady an assload of grief.

Hell, he was only an ancillary target, the bull's-eye on his back small in comparison to hers, and he wasn't happy. He couldn't imagine what Cady was going through, knowing she was wearing a big red circle like a crosshair, pointing her out to the thugs.

Since Fitz was certain that Tuzzi had sent Malling to hurt Cady over and over again, the plan was simply to let it happen—or at least to let Malling get close enough to try.

For that, she and King had to be available, on the move, and in the open. McKie would then follow Malling's reports back to Tuzzi, looking for the hub of his information flow in order to plug it up.

It seemed simple enough on the surface—as long as Malling didn't succeed and as long as McKie had his plugging mechanism ready to rock and roll.

King admitted he was curious. What exactly was McKie's mechanism? How was it activated? Who did the activating? What would happen to Tuzzi when he realized he was constipated and had nowhere to go?

What would happen to Cady when all was said and done?

Though he wouldn't wish any of this crap to befall anyone, King grudgingly admitted he was glad he was here to help her through. That didn't make a spit lick of sense; he might know her situation and her very fine body, but he didn't know more than a few piddly things about her.

During the photo shoot for Ferrer, she'd dusted his

Cajun country sun-baked skin with makeup, and foofed his hair this way and that so that he looked less like himself and more like the metrosexual population of Manhattan.

They'd talked. He'd enjoyed her tits pressed against him, her hands in his hair. He'd also enjoyed her fiery spunk without realizing how much of it was anger.

She was mad at the world, and with every right. She'd played an innocuously small part in a practical joke gone sour, and had lost everything including her freedom.

It left a damn bad taste in his mouth, and the more he thought about it, the tighter his grip on the steering wheel grew, the stiffer his thighs and his spine. At this rate and another ten miles, he'd be in no shape to drive.

Time to break the seal of silence.

"You look better. Your face. Your lip."

She turned her head, rolling it from right to left on the seat, meeting his gaze with eyes that appeared tired. "I still ache, and everything twinges if I move the wrong way, but your ice packs helped."

"I didn't hurt you last night, did I? Or make anything worse?" After the fact and way too late, but better than never. He hoped.

"Are we going to talk about it? The sex?"

Damn, but if that didn't feel like he'd been put in his place. Might help if he knew where his place was. "Do you want to?"

"Not really," she said, her lower lip protruding as she shook her head. "Tell me about your tattoo."

Hmph. So that was that. They could have sex, they just couldn't talk about having sex. Fine-o-dandy with him. "What about it?"

She sat up straighter, shifting her whole body so that she faced him instead of the road. She looked comfortable in the seat, and way too good in the Hummer. He was afraid he was going to get used to having her there then miss her when she was gone. A dog. He'd have to get a dog.

"I get what it is." She reached over and popped the snaps of his chambray shirt, pulling the fabric aside to get a better look at his ink. "The Mardi Gras colors, the beads, and doubloons. And the crown is obvious, you being King and all. But it's not faded, so it has to be fairly new."

He nodded, liking the way she didn't ask but took what she wanted. Liking, too, the feel of her fingers on his skin, and liking that part too much. "It is. I got it last year."

She traced the lower edge of the crown, lingering and staring for an eternal moment, before sitting back. "After finding the treasure?"

He'd told her about the treasure one day at Ferrer. How he and his cousin had been sitting on the buried gold their whole lives and never had a clue.

She'd wondered how it had felt, to have that luxury, to realize he could do anything with his life, go anywhere, never want for money again—unless he was a stupid shit and blew it all.

She'd said that. A stupid shit. He remembered frowning at her, wondering who the hell she thought she was to be giving him a financial responsibility lecture.

He had a much better understanding of the root of her name calling now than he'd had then. "I had the old ugly ass prison tats lasered away, and this one inked in their place. When I see it in the mirror every morning, I'm reminded about my good fortune. And I'm not talking about the gold."

"What was it like?"

"Prison?" When she nodded, he considered how much of the hell to reveal, how much to keep back, how much he wanted to revisit. How much he wanted her to know. "It was prison. You sit with your back to the wall to eat. You sleep with your eyes open. You stay to yourself, and stay in shape in case doing the first becomes a problem."

"And you did that for four years?"

"Four years inside, then a lot of years after. Old habits are hard to break." There were a lot he still battled, chalking up his losses to being a dick at heart. Whether or not it was true didn't matter.

Blaming nature was easier than being a failure, and continuing to fuck up. He'd fathered a kid and not known it until the boy was on his deathbed.

He'd remained estranged from Simon, his only family, for nearly twenty years. He hadn't known what a good woman he'd had in Chelle Sonnier until he'd let her go.

Money might not buy happiness, but it had certainly bought him a new perspective, which in turn had done a lot for his state of mind.

He supposed that was why he was here now with Cady. Not for the sex, not for her company, but to stop himself from another fuck up and failing someone who needed him.

Then again, that was the question of the hour, wasn't it? Did Cady need him?

"You don't sleep with your eyes open now."

He cut her a quick look. "You said you didn't want to talk about the sex."

"How was that talking about sex? I said you don't sleep with your eyes open. That was all." She huffed, sputtered. "I swear. Men. Everything for you is about sex."

"Well, yeah," he said, and she slapped the shit out of his shoulder. "Ow."

"I'd say I'm sorry, but I'm not. Though I should have asked how your head is feeling, and I am sorry about that."

He reached back with one hand to find the bald spot and the stitches, found her hand there doing the same thing. "Tender, but bearable. My vanity, on the other hand, not so good. I was hoping to keep my hair for ten years at least."

She laughed. Not just a giggle or a snicker, but a laugh that filled the cabin of the SUV with a lightness that lifted his spirits.

Surprising, because he hadn't known they'd been down. Or maybe it was hearing Cady sounding so carefree that did it. Whichever it was, he smiled.

"You goon," she said, still laughing. "Your hair will grow back. If anything, I'd worry that some of your brains escaped when the doctor pulled out the glass."

He liked hearing her laugh. Even if it was at his expense, he admitted grimly, yelping when her probing fingers got too close to his wound. "Get me a bottle of juice or a soft drink, will ya? All this heat I'm takin's dryin' out my throat."

Cady snorted, but popped her seat belt and squirreled around, digging in the cooler behind them and giving King the pleasure of seeing her ass up close as she did.

"I still can't believe all the supplies Fitz laid in back here. Malling could follow us all the way to Alaska and we wouldn't have to restock."

Driving to Alaska with Cady Kowalski. Funny the appeal the idea held, though making a sharp south turn and taking her to Louisiana held even more.

And that thought he cut off right there.

"Did he ever show you any ID?" she asked, handing him the bottle of orange juice she'd come up with, and twisting off the top of her own once she'd belted herself back into her seat. "Or is he still holding out on proving who he is?"

"He showed me something, but it didn't say a lot, or look like any government badge I've ever seen," he said, then brought his bottle to his mouth.

He'd downed half of the contents and driven several more miles before Cady spoke. And this time, she spoke softly, her earlier spunk squashed flat. "Do you think he's who he says he is?"

"McKie?" King shrugged. "I don't know, chère. I really don't know. Whoever he is, he makes things happen. Not a lot of people have the connections that can."

"What if the ID is fake? What if he's part of Tuzzi's gang?"

"I'm not going to say that either possibility isn't viable, but my gut tells me that whoever he is, he's okay." It was an eyes in the back of his head thing. Something he wasn't sure she could understand even if he could explain.

Holding her bottle against her bottom lip, she caught his gaze, then asked, "Is this the same gut that got you out of prison in one piece except for those ugly ass tats?"

"They really were ugly," was all he could come up with to say. Oh, he tried. He tried to figure out when he'd become an open book, or when his mind had become so simple that any waif off the street could read it.

But there was nothing there, nothing left to do but assure her when he wasn't sure of anything at all. "The ID being fake doesn't bother me—"

"But McKie being part of Tuzzi's gang does."

"It would if it made any sense, but it doesn't." And now that he'd said that, he was going to have to come up with a platform she couldn't refute. And sound like he knew something about Nathan Tuzzi while doing so.

Couldn't be too hard. All he had to do was sub one of the prison thugs he'd known for the one hounding Cady to hell. "What reason would Tuzzi have for coming after you this way? Through someone posing as a Fed?"

"Why not?"

"For one thing, I can't see him having a soft spot for government agents, so to get at you through someone posing as one, well, there's a dastardly twist of irony there, yeah, but I still think his pride would call foul."

"He's never struck me as someone to let his pride go before a fall."

Now she was getting biblical on him, and other than taking the name of the Lord God in vain on a regular basis, religion was not his arena. "He's had you looking over your shoulder for years. If his goal's been to see you suffer, I'd say he's been damn successful.

"And from everything you've told me," he went on, pausing because he realized there was a very good chance she had not told him everything, that she'd kept something from him and Fitz both, something vital to keeping her safe.

"What if he has a new goal?" she asked before he could grill her about the secrets she wasn't telling. "What if seeing me suffer isn't enough anymore?"

He steeled himself before finishing her thought. "What if he wants you dead, you mean?"

"What else could he want? What else is there?" she asked, her voice rising with each question. "I don't have anything for him to take away. I suppose he could set me up somehow, make sure I take the fall for something that would put me behind bars, but where would the fun be in that? I wouldn't be as easy for him to reach. Then again, he may have a gang of butch inmates on call."

King waited several moments to make sure she'd spilled everything she was thinking and worn herself out. There was no way for him to disprove her theory, or to prove his own. But she was borrowing trouble her mental health—her physical, too—could do without.

"Tuzzi doesn't want you dead, Cady. He's been put away for life. If you were in prison, his brand of torture wouldn't be half as effective. You'd be looking over your shoulder for reasons a whole lot bigger. And if you were dead, you wouldn't be there for him to torture at all."

She was quiet after that, as if letting King's hypothesis sink in and get comfy enough to settle. A lot of road passed without a response. He couldn't know what she was thinking; her mind wasn't quite as simple for him to read as she'd apparently found his.

But her stress level didn't seem to be rising. She'd slumped in the corner of the seat, pulled her feet up so that she sat cross-legged. Her seat belt crossed between her breasts, and when he realized that's where he was staring, he turned back to the road.

Then he took a deep breath and said, "Until we know differently, Fitz is a good guy, okay?"

Cady huffed, capped her empty juice bottle. "A good guy in that he's on our side, you mean."

"That works." Because she was right. That was the only thing King was going to count on, and he was only going to do that until Fitz screwed up and stepped in it. "Now that we've got that out of the way . . . you going to come back over here and snap up my shirt?"

He wasn't sure why he'd said it. Okay, that was a lie. He'd said it because he wanted her hands on him again, and he had no idea if their stop tonight would have them sharing one room or bunking in two.

Knowing Fitz was looking out for them took away the fear factor that had sent Cady into King's bed. He'd like to think she'd come back for a repeat of last night's fun. She'd said she didn't want to talk about the sex. Well, he could do without the words, as long as he had her body.

He spared her no more than a cursory glance, one assuring him that he had her attention. What he got was way, way more, and set his blood on fire. Her eyes weren't wide and shocked, but smoky, her lashes sweeping up and down as she considered him, where he sat, where she had him, caught behind the wheel of a machine running seventy miles per hour.

"Sorry about that," she said, clicking free of her seat belt and climbing onto her knees in her seat. She leaned across the center console, a forearm braced on his shoulder as she pulled together the plackets of his shirt and snapped. Slowly. Taking her time covering his tattoo. "I wasn't thinking."

She may not have been thinking then, but he was definitely not thinking now, what with that blood rush thing, most of it leaving his brain, settling in a place that needed attention and made it uncomfortable to drive.

He swallowed hard; his throat working to clear all that drool kept him from sounding off about what she could do with her hands once she'd finished with his shirt, or fuck the shirt, what she could be doing now.

She got to the top, the snap at his neck, the very last one before she'd have no reason to stick around, and she leaned close, her mouth at his ear where she whispered, "Tell me something, King."

He would if he could find his voice. "Anything, chère. What do you want to know?"

"Why can't you have babies?"

His gaze whipped up to her reflection in the rearview mirror. He'd later swear that was the only thing that saved them from roasting inside Hummer fireball number two.

He'd barely wrapped his head around the picture of the car running up on his backside at goddamn way too many miles an hour before it was there.

He slammed his right arm across Cady's backside, flattening her against the center console, half in the backseat, half in the front.

She screamed, a sound that was nothing compared with the banshee obscenities shrieking in his head as he watched the car barreling down on his tail.

He was blocked in on the left and the front both, had nowhere to go but right and off the road. It was either that, or take one up the ass.

He flung the steering wheel to the side and yelled at Cady, "Hold on!"

Twenty-one

Cady could not believe this was happening. It was what was supposed to happen, what Fitz wanted to happen. But she and King had only been on the road long enough to see a few miles of Pennsylvania.

And now here they were on the side of the road, the wheels of King's new SUV buried halfway up the rims in mud, the grill cracked where a broken tree limb half the size of a telephone pole had punctured who knew what in the engine compartment before piercing the hood and stopping short of the windshield on the driver's side.

That potentially lethal threat was one they hadn't seen until climbing out from behind the deployed airbags. With the way she'd been flung over the console between the two seats, Cady's had only popped against her ass. It was for the best. It was the only part of her not bruised.

Fitzwilliam McKie was nowhere to be found, a realization that had Cady backing away from King who was cursing imaginatively again as he circled the Hummer. She watched him a minute, then looked up at the sky and waved.

When King noticed, he stopped pacing and grumbled, "What the hell are you doing?"

"Hoping to attract the nearest satellite," she said, the hiss of steam from the radiator and the windy blast of cars whizzing by nearly masking the sound of wheels on gravel as a truck and two cars—one of them a Pennsylvania State Police cruiser with lights flashing—pulled to a stop.

Cady glanced at King as he turned toward the new arrivals. "I guess we treat this as a one-vehicle accident and leave out Malling's possible involvement?"

"Since we don't know that it was Malling, that's probably best, though another call to that satellite might be in order." King cast a quick look skyward. "Hear that McKie?"

Since we don't know that it was Malling? What the hell? Had he really just said that?

Did he think their accident had been an accident? That some newly licensed punk with a hot car and no brains had been out for a joy ride and decided to take on King's massive H3 for fun?

"You folks okay?" called the Statie walking toward them, his question forcing Cady to put a hold on that train of thought. "Do we need an ambulance out here? Ma'am? Is that busted lip from the airbag?"

Cady knew she still looked a mess, and knew from the way the cop was eyeballing King that he wasn't thinking the airbag had anything to do with her mouth. "No, I'm fine. My roommate gave me this when she caught her boyfriend in my bed. The black eyes, too. I was leaning over to get something out of the backseat, so the airbag actually spanked me."

The Statie nodded, looked from her to King who she heard grumbling under his breath about the llamas again.

"No ambulance," King told the officer, slamming his hand into the H3's back fender hard enough to make the metal ring. "But a tow truck for sure. Even if I could rock my way out of the mud in this ditch, I'd need a new radiator and who knows what else to do it."

"You might want to start with a chainsaw, though what that trash is doing out here . . . fell off a truck doing tree trimming, my best bet. You two are damn lucky, from the looks of things," the Statie said, before making his way around the vehicle.

King started to follow the other man while he checked out the damage and radioed for a tow truck, but Cady grabbed his arm to stop him. "What do you mean, we don't know it was Malling? Are you kidding me?"

"My first instinct is yes, Tuzzi was involved," he said, keeping his voice low, his words directed solely at her, his gaze fierce as he stared down, part insistence that he was serious, part ire that she'd chosen another really bad time to run her mouth. "My second—"

"Hey-ho!" The driver of the pickup approached, pulling his ball cap from his head and smoothing back his thinning hair before the cap went back in place. "I don't know where that guy thought he was going, damn stupid kid. He nearly clipped my front bumper when he cut in front of me."

"You saw what happened, then?" the officer asked, pulling a pen and notebook from his uniform pocket as he circled back to where King and Cady stood. "And the driver, too?"

"I saw the car and the kid both," said the second driver who'd stopped, a middle-aged woman, slightly hefty, wearing a loose floral thermal over navy sweats. "The car had no plates. Not on the front, or on the back."

"What about the make and model?"

Since Cady had been snapping King's shirt and wondering if they could stop somewhere so that she could climb into his lap for a quickie, she hadn't seen anything of either one, so she listened to the three who had described the vehicle and the man behind the wheel.

She hadn't seen Malling since his trial. A lot of years had come and gone. People changed. Hair color and style. Weight was lost, muscles gained. Or weight was gained, and muscles turned to flab.

Men grew sideburns or beards or mustaches. And at a distance, colored contacts weren't easy to spot. But the one thing no one could change was skin color.

And Jason Malling wasn't black.

She backed away from the group as they talked, hugging herself tightly and wondering whether to be relieved or more worried than before. King had said his first instinct was that Tuzzi was involved.

Did that mean his second was that someone else had planned this? Or did he think they'd simply been in the wrong place at the same time that some brainless punk black kid had taken his hot car for a ride?

And where the hell was Fitzwilliam McKie, she asked herself since no one else was around, adding a few choice words under her breath.

"Did you just say something about llamas?"

She turned to face King, noticing the Statie still talking to the man and woman who'd stopped. It had been nice of them to stop. It surprised her that anyone had.

"I might have." She nodded toward the group of three who'd come to their rescue. Unlike Fitz. "What's going on?"

"Mr. Lawman is taking their statements so they can be on their way, then he'll wait with us until the tow truck gets here."

"And then what? What are we supposed to do?"

"We'll go with the driver to his shop, and see what it's going to take to get back on the road."

"No government agent clearing the decks and producing another truck out of thin air? Considering he couldn't even produce himself . . . "King?"

"Yes, Cady?"

"Do you think Fitz wants us back on the road?"

"The thought has occurred to me that he may not. That he's changed his mind. That he wants to keep us close rather than having us get too far away."

Too far away for what? was the question that came to mind. "Then he might've done this? Seriously?"

"If he did, I don't think he was counting on the tree limb

putting us out of commission. We're looking at needing a new radiator, new airbags, and whatever else went south when we did. Plus, now I've got insurance to deal with. We're going to be stuck with a rental for at least a week. And I'm not taking a rental to Louisiana."

His last comment took several seconds to register. Somewhere along the way, Cady had forgotten that King's time with her was temporary. That Louisiana, his true love, was calling him home.

She couldn't think about that now, about him leaving her alone when she was finally fighting back. "If he wanted to keep us close, wouldn't it have been easier for him to reach you on your phone?"

"When has the government ever done anything the easy way? Assuming he is government, and knowing that assuming anything is going to make an ass out of one of us. Though better an ass than a llama, I guess," he said, and Cady laughed.

He laughed with her, hooking his elbow around her neck and pulling her close. It was almost as if he knew she needed nothing more right then than to burrow into his chest.

She didn't stay long. It would be weak to stay long. It didn't matter that he was solid and warm and smelled good, like the night they'd shared and safety. She couldn't go back to being weak.

And so she eased away, tilted her head, and called toward the clouds, "Got anything to say to us, Fitzwilliam McKie? What about anything to say for yourself?"

At her side, King chuckled. "C'mon, chère. Tow truck's here. The man in the satellite will keep. This one won't."

Twenty-two

The driver chatted all the way to the shop from where he'd been dispatched. Cady chatted back, leaving King free to brood. He didn't like to brood. He was a brooding master, but he'd gotten over finding it useful.

Whether or not it would turn out to be useful now, it fit his state of mind. Plus, his style of brooding did a great job of putting off both the driver and Cady, thus allowing him to think.

Problem was, he didn't know what he should be thinking about. Tuzzi and Malling causing the accident. McKie causing the accident. The accident being an accident, and how much worse it could've been. Or having sex with Cady.

Thinking about sex with Cady was what had gotten the two of them into this trouble, so common sense would have him thinking about anything else.

But his uncommon sense—or would that be his common nonsense?—said that if he mulled over, firmed up, and put away his thoughts of sex and Cady, he could move on to the business of keeping her alive.

Unfortunately, knowing what he needed to do didn't guarantee his success in making it happen. Especially when she was sitting crushed against his side in the cab of the overcrowded, standard transmission tow truck, and the only thing he could smell was her skin.

He should be smelling diesel fumes and oil and hand cleaner, the musty dirt coating everything, even the driver who was not the cleanest thing he'd ever seen, but he didn't. It was Cady's scent filling his nostrils, making him sweat, making him ache with wanting to strip her down and breathe her in.

When she'd been leaning over him just before the wreck, keeping his eyes on the road or his mind on navigating it had been next to impossible—proving that he had to get a grip on this sex thing before he got one of them killed. He'd come too damn close to doing just that already.

"You may have to get a room at May Wind's B and B," the driver was telling Cady. "Not much else in the way of lodging in Cushing Township. Oh, there's a couple of pay by the hour joints outside of town a ways, but you good folks don't want to be staying there."

Until then, King hadn't paid much attention to Cady's conversation with the man behind the wheel, but he perked up at the mention of accommodations, and Cady's snicker at the mention of an hourly rate. "This a small place? Your Cushing Township?"

The driver nodded, rolled down his window, and spit a dark stream of tobacco juice into the wind, causing Cady to wince and turn her face into King's shoulder. "Depends on your idea of small, but I can't think of but one or two boroughs in the county with less folks callin' 'em home."

Great. They were stuck in a nowheresville that King doubted rated more than a pinprick on the map. His home in Cajun country? Not much better when it came to progress moving beyond a snail's speed, which justified the bad feeling he had about them getting out of here anytime soon.

"What about the mechanic there? Or the body shop guy?

Any clue how hard it's going to be to get parts?" Or how long it's going to take to get them ordered, shipped, and his wheels back on the road?

"You're looking at the mechanic. Jarrell Bradley's the name. My brother-in-law's your body guy. Delton Dreyer. I also drive this truck and do some hot shot deliveries. I'll be the one picking up the parts once me and Delton figure out what exactly we're going to need."

King wanted to suggest they keep going until they hit Reading and found a shop with parts in stock and a mechanic that worked full time.

And if they continued on to Reading, he and Cady wouldn't be forced to rent a room in close quarters where their business could too easily become a power source for the local gossip mill.

But he kept silent, figuring if McKie wanted them to hole up in the middle of Bumfuck, he had his reasons. And if he wanted them to be somewhere besides Cushing Township, he'd make it happen.

"Here we are," Jarrell Bradley said, slowing the tow truck as they passed the township marker and the speed limit sign posted just beyond.

Cady straightened to peer out the windshield. "Is there anything we should see while we're here, Jarrell? Any historic landmarks or nature trails or museums to tour? Any restaurants we shouldn't miss?"

King rolled his eyes. The girl was deluded if she thought he was going to pack a picnic and take a hike, or treat this stop like a vacation.

And he damn sure had no intention of letting her wander the township like a sightseeing tourist when Malling could be anywhere around.

"Well, you're gonna want to sample May's breakfast buffet. She puts on the kind of spread that'll see ya through most of the day." The beefy man leaned across them to point out King's window. "There's her place, the B and B.

I'll give you a ride back down here once I unhook at the shop.

"Oh, and there's the McCluskey's." He pointed again, this time to a squat brick building with a hand-painted sign above the door that said RESTAURANT. "You want fresh fish with home fries? That's your best bet. May will have some brochures about what's close by for folks to see.

"Here's the shop," he said, turning off the main street and almost immediately into a parking lot of cars King assumed were there for repair. A lot of cars. Pickups, tractors, ATVs. More than he would've expected to see in a place that was a pinprick on the map.

"Looks like you keep busy."

"That and then some," Jarrell said, pulling into the only open bay, then stopping in the yard on the other side once the SUV was situated inside the building. "Delton and me have built up a clientele to go with our reputation. But you don't have to worry about waiting for us to fit you in."

Jarrell opened his door and climbed down. King did the same on his side of the truck, helping Cady out after him. When she gave him a questioning look, he shrugged, and called over the noise of the towing mechanism, "Why's that?"

"The Statie. He told me this was a priority job with a bonus that depended on how fast and how good the job got done. We appreciate that a lot, Mr. Trahan. Extra money always comes in handy around here."

King had no idea what Jarrell Bradley was talking about, but he wasn't going to share that with the other man. "We don't want to put anyone out."

"You won't be. No one else is in the same kind of hurry. We'll be moving you to the front of the line, as soon as Delton finishes up with the new water pump on Buster Wind's F150. Why don't you two grab what you're going to need from your things to hold you until tomorrow?"

Cady looked like she was about to explode from all the

questions piling up inside. King acted like nothing was wrong and headed to the back of his truck. "You said you can give us a ride to the bed and breakfast?"

"Oh, sure. It's not far, but it could be quite a walk if you've got a lot of luggage."

"Not a lot, no, but I think we're both a bit sore. We hit that ditch pretty hard."

"I'd say you're damn lucky you didn't hit it any harder, else that limb would've kept going and we'd be needing a hearse alongside the tow truck."

And that was enough to send King back to brooding again.

Twenty-three

"What was that about a bonus for getting your truck done fast and done right?" Cady asked, sitting across the table from King in a booth at McCluskey's.

They'd left the garage three hours ago after Jarrell had unhooked the Hummer, returned five phone calls, and introduced them to everyone who just happened by after seeing King's H3 roll through town.

As promised, Jarrell had eventually driven them the few blocks to May Wind's Bed & Breakfast.

If not for needing their luggage and having no idea what McKie had packed—not to mention having no idea where anything was since things had gone flying when they'd sailed off the road—they would've walked the few blocks and enjoyed the early afternoon sun.

They had walked to McCluskey's after they'd checked into their room. Neither one of them had eaten much at breakfast, and what they had managed to get down hadn't stuck through the morning. Plus, the adrenaline from the accident and its aftermath had Cady starving.

Though the restaurant's exterior was lacking in, well, anything inviting, the inside reminded her of the working-class homes of her childhood friends—and of her own before her parents forgot they weren't the ones who had died.

The paneled walls were hung with framed photographs of children and parents, sporting events and picnics. Ribbons and certificates hung beside them, between them, on top and below. Trophies—baseball, gymnastics, soccer, debate—stood proudly inside the glass case beneath the check-out counter.

The decorative oil lamps on the tables sat on red and white doilies. The glass panels in the hanging lamps above were painted with scenes of country life. The tables and chairs were blocky, and glossy white, the booths covered with a vinyl fabric in the same red print as the tablecloths.

The whole place smelled like sugar cookies and hot rolls. The sense of nostalgia made her homesick, but Cady blamed the ache in her midsection on hunger. She opted out of the fresh fish and home fries Jarrell had recommended and ordered meatloaf and mashed potatoes instead.

She loved meatloaf. She loved mashed potatoes. If she never had to eat peanut butter crackers again, it would be too soon, and she hoped she never had to replace the case she'd lost in the explosion.

That thought brought her back to why they were here. "King? The bonus?"

"I don't know anything more than you do. I sure as hell didn't make that promise, and I can't imagine the insurance company doing so." King forked up a huge bite of pan-fried trout from the biggest serving of headless, tailless fish Cady had ever seen slapped on a plate.

He swallowed the food before going on. "Hell, I haven't even called them yet. I was kinda waiting to see if Fitz had anything to say first. Then I figured I'd do it from the shop. Jarrell's comment put a stop to those plans."

It had put a stop to Cady's certainty that Malling was behind the wreck, too. "You think Fitz talked to the Statie? Do you think he wasn't a Statie at all? Maybe a fake Statie

Fitz sent in to make sure we ended up where he wanted us to be, though why he'd want us here . . ."

King took a long draft from the longneck beer bottle he'd insisted he preferred over a mug. "At this point, your guess is as good as mine."

She didn't answer right away because she needed another bite of meatloaf. And of potatoes. Then potatoes again. Oh, and her roll. "Whoever he was, he must've been right behind us to show up that fast. We're practically in the middle of nowheresville here . . . what's so funny?"

"Nothing, chère. Just . . . nothing." He nodded at her plate, then asked, "All that food giving you the energy to figure things out?"

"I'd say bite me but knowing you . . ." The look in his eyes reminded her that sex was a subject it wasn't even safe for her to tease about.

She propped both wrists on the table's edge, her fork in one hand, her buttered bread in the other. "You know, I almost feel like I'm living an episode of *Alias* instead of watching one."

He stabbed up a fork full of home fries. "Better than living an episode of really bad *Friends* like you were doing in the city?"

"You goon. I don't think there's a show called Really Bad Friends," she said, smothering a laugh with another bite of food. She was trying to be serious here, and he was too damn cute for his—or her—own good. "Though there should be one called Really Bad Sex and the City."

He arched a brow, the look on his face nothing if not censorious. "Had a lot of that did you?"

"A lot of sex, no. A lot of bad sex, yes. Though I didn't know how bad until . . ." She stuffed her roll in her mouth to shut herself up. Why was she going here? To that sex place? After telling herself how many times that it was not a good idea? And who was he to censor?

"Until me?"

The man was too cocky for his own good, making that a question best left unanswered. But, she admitted as she swallowed, she did owe him for what had happened. "I'm sorry about coming onto you in the truck. I'm pretty sure if I hadn't been all over you then, we wouldn't be here now."

He shook his head, reached for the ketchup, and shot another pool on his plate for his fries. "We were blocked in, front and left both. The only place to go was off the road. But, yeah. If I hadn't been so distracted, I might've found a way around the tree limb."

So he didn't blame her completely? But he did blame her? Or was he playing with her again? "Was it me climbing around that distracted you, or my question?"

He snapped the top to the ketchup, avoided her gaze. "I forgot I told you that."

"The heat of passion. It fries the memory."

"And," he went on, brow arched, "I *tried* to forget that you asked me about it."

"Ignoring things doesn't make them go away. Trust me on that."

"But you ignoring and me forgetting means I win and don't have to answer."

That didn't make any sense at all. "Says who?"

"Says the man who is King."

"The fact that it says Kingdom on your birth certificate does not make you royalty. Or in charge," she added, remembering how she'd thought about being his serf. "We're in no hurry, and I want more meatloaf, so you've got plenty of time to tell me all about your sperm."

He sputtered beer everywhere. "Christ and a half on a llama, woman. The things that come out of your mouth."

"Almost as good as the things I put into it," she shot back, stuffing said orifice full of a hot roll slathered in real butter. "Now spill."

He wagged his head as if accepting he was stuck, that he

had no way out, that she was not letting him off this hook ever. "I found out a few years ago that I have a son, Calvin. Cal. He's fourteen now. I probably would never have known except his mother needed money for his medical expenses and had exhausted every other avenue of help."

"She came to you."

"I don't know why she did," he said with a shrug. "We'd been lovers, obviously, but never in a relationship. I'd been pretty much a bum when Gina knew me, and things hadn't changed since. If I made enough money to pay my electric bill and buy a six pack a day, I was doing good."

Cady didn't know why, but King's self-portrait didn't surprise her. It was very similar to how she'd imagined his former life. She knew he was a hard man, one for whom things had never been easy, part of that by circumstances, part by his own making.

But it was still hard to hear. "What did you do? Did you give her money?"

He nodded. "I borrowed a small fortune from my cousin. Told him it was for a workover of the well on the property. The one our fathers worked when we were kids."

"An oil well?"

"It never produced a lot, which we learned a whole lotta years later was because our neighborly neighbor had slant drilled from his property to ours and was sucking us dry. But you should see that baby puttin' out now."

"First gold, and now oil. I'm impressed."

"Like I said. It's good to be King."

"Do you see him? Your son?"

King shook his head. "I keep up with what he's doing, but I don't play Disneyland dad, if that's what you're asking."

"I was just asking. That's all."

"He's a hell of a baseball player. Cracker jack shortstop with a batting average that'll get him some notice if he keeps at it, stays in school, and doesn't fuck up like his old man. But, no. I don't send him birthday presents or Christmas cards or drop in with a new video game or crap like that. He had, he *has*, a good life. A good family. He doesn't need a money bags 'uncle' hanging around."

And King wouldn't settle for being that. "He's healthy then. Your money helped."

"I guess."

"Yes or no. No guessing."

"Yeah. It helped. Kept me in hot water for years with my cousin, though."

"Because you didn't tell him the real reason you needed it?"

"I didn't want him to find out that I'd had a kid all those years and didn't even know."

"How could you if Cal's mother didn't tell you? If you weren't in a relationship and she didn't bother to involve you, there's no way you could've known."

"Yeah, but it felt like one more mark on the loser board. That I couldn't even bother with a condom."

Ah. Things were coming into focus. "And that's why you can't have babies now."

He held up an index and middle finger and made a snipping motion.

"A rather drastic reaction, wasn't it?"

"Why? You thinking about a little Trahan prince? An heir to the throne?"

To his fortune, he meant. She ignored her gut reaction to carrying his child. "You're afraid of gold diggers."

"I was snipped long before I found the gold, chère."

"Then I stand by what I said," she lifted her chin and told him. "It was a drastic reaction."

"Drastic revelations call for drastic reactions."

"Sounds like your six pack a day was doing your thinking for you."

"Back then? You bet it was."

Was he angry? At her? For digging into his past? Or because her doing so had made him visit a place he'd put behind him? "Do you regret having that done? Now that your situation isn't so dire?"

"Money changes everything." That was all he said, leaving Cady to wonder if he meant the three words as a yes. But before she could figure him out, he added, "I'm too old to start a family. If I had a kid now, I'd be dead before he finished high school. And having my own folks die before I was out? I wouldn't put any kid through that."

He wasn't that old, and they both knew it, but pressing him further wouldn't get her anywhere, so she dropped the subject, sitting back while their server delivered her second plate of meatloaf.

"Is this going to be all? You sure you don't want more potatoes?" the young girl asked.

"She'd have to put 'em in her pocket," King answered, causing Cady—who preferred to think for herself—to spitefully respond, "Potatoes, no, but I'd love another hot roll. And more butter."

After the girl had walked away, King gave Cady the eye. "You trying to die before *your* kids are out of school?"

"Kids, no. I'm just trying to get in all my last meals before Malling goes too far."

"Cady," King began, but she cut him off.

"I know what you're going to say, so just stop. I heard you earlier. Tuzzi doesn't want me dead. I got it. Truly, I do. But Malling is not Tuzzi. He's following Nathan's orders, but he's still dumb as a stump."

"Following Nathan's orders means keeping you alive. He likes playing cat to your mouse. As obsessed with you as McKie says he is? You can bet Malling goes too far, he's dead. He knows that. He's not going to make a mistake that gets him killed."

"That tree limb was a mistake. It could've easily happened. Accidents do easily happen."

"That tree limb was my fault."

No, that tree limb was her fault. And King could've been the one killed. "If I asked you for money, would you give it to me? I started to say lend, but I have no way of paying you back. Not now, anyway."

"I might, if I knew why you wanted it."

"So I can rent a car. You can wait here for the repairs to your truck, and I can rent a car and go . . . somewhere. I don't know. I'll figure it out. Let Malling follow me. Let McKie get the information he needs."

"You're ditching me?"

"I don't want you to die because of being with me." Gah, she was going to choke up. She did not want to choke up.

She wanted to get this out without crying. "You could've died in the explosion. Malling couldn't know that you wouldn't decide to make a burger run at the same time his timer was due to go off? See, dumb as a stump.

"And if that tree limb had been any longer, it could've pierced more than your hood." When he started to speak, she waved a hand and stopped him. She had to finish first. While she still had the breath.

While she could still look at him without tears clouding her eyes. "So, yes. If you'll give me the money to rent a car, I'm ditching you. You have a cousin, and even if you don't see him, you have a son. I don't have anyone, and I don't want you to die."

"You're wrong, Cady," he told her, his voice ragged and cracked. "You have me, chère. You have me."

Twenty-four

Cushing Township wasn't more than a mile from end to end, and King doubted it was any wider side to side. He and Cady had walked to McCluskey's from May Wind's B&B, and with Cady now full of meatloaf, they set out to walk back.

It was a slower trip than the first.

They were both carrying a lot more weight than earlier.

The idea of Cady wanting to strike out on her own hit King a lot harder than he would've thought possible. Especially the reason she wanted to go. That, in fact, even more so than her actually going.

Here he was wanting to make sure she stayed safe, and she was more concerned about him getting hurt in the crossfire of her war with the man who had killed her brother.

That wasn't how it was supposed to be. Her caring about him. Her putting him first. Her ditching him and his help to make sure he wasn't harmed.

He didn't know if it was the fish not sitting well on his stomach, or if the knot of rubber bands twisting his insides was tied into this other tangled mess and needed sorting out. Whatever it was, he felt like shit.

"You never did answer me, you know."

He hadn't answered her because their server had returned to refresh their drinks, and he'd asked for the ticket which he'd then taken to the counter near the door to pay while Cady finished her meal.

He couldn't sit there with her fearing she would lose him. Or his fearing there was nothing he wouldn't do to keep from losing her. Hell, all she'd had to do was ask and he'd spilled his guts like a cow strung up in a slaughterhouse.

Things between them had gone too far too fast, and he didn't know what to do to stop the forward motion. Or if he wanted to. If he wanted Cady Kowalski more than he wanted to send her away.

"No," he said, shading his eyes and wishing he knew what had happened to his sunglasses.

She stopped in front of him, looked up. "No? You won't give me the money? Or even lend me the money?"

"It's not about the money, boo," he said, taking off down the sidewalk again, stepping down to negotiate the cross street, stepping up onto the sidewalk on the next block. "I'll give you as much as you want, but I'm not going to let you go off to deal with Malling on your own."

"You say that like you have any control over what I do."

"I say it like I mean it."

"I'm your favorite charity now, is that it? We had sex and now you—"

He spun and grabbed both of her arms, squeezing harder than he'd intended. He relaxed his grip when she winced. "We had sex, and it was amazing, and I hope we have it again. But this is about doing the right thing, the human thing, and keeping you out of harm's way."

"They teach you that in prison?" she shot back. "Being human? Or is that something you learned when drinking a six pack a day?"

She was trying to piss him off, trying to get him to change his mind and send her on her way. That was what he'd learned in prison. How to hear meaning, not just what people said.

He did his best to disarm her with a smile. "I'm old, chère. So old I can't remember when I learned anything. Or how much of it I've already forgot."

"You're not old," she finally said, socking him in the chest, then slipping her arm through his as they walked back to their room.

He didn't for a minute think that was the end of the subject, but letting it go with an uneasy truce made for much better digestion.

Since they were her only guests, Mrs. Wind had given them her largest room, a suite on the third floor of the hundred-year-old Victorian that took up a whole block of the township.

They had a bedroom, a private bath, and a sitting room with a sofa and a Murphy bed stored in the wall.

It was all very cozy. That word again.

And then Cady said. "You take the bed. I'll sleep in here."

She cut him off. Just like that. "If we're not sharing, then no. I'll sleep in here."

"Don't be silly. You're twice as big as me. You saw the bed I was sleeping on in the city. I don't need as much room as you do."

Especially when you don't want anyone else with you, eh?

He shrugged, walked into the bedroom, pushed open both of the windows to let in the cool spring air. It would be a whole lot better to breathe whatever came in from outside than to breathe the air that smelled like Cady.

"You're not mad, are you?" she asked from behind him.

He didn't turn. "Why would I be mad?"

"Because we slept together last night, and now we're not."

"This is your party, boo. You call the shots."

"We didn't sleep much. If we share a bed, I don't think anything about that will change. And after all that food, not to mention, oh, being run off the road and slapped in the ass by an airbag, I want to sleep."

"Then sleep. I'm not going to stop you."

"King?"

"Cady?"

"I'm not going to be able to sleep if you're mad."

He was being a bastard. A horny bastard. "I'm not mad."

"Then look at me?"

Hands at his hips, he dropped his head, took a deep breath of the fresh air, then did exactly what she wanted because he wasn't able to tell her no. And open windows or not, the room smelled like her anyway. He was doomed.

"Thank you."

"N'cest pas."

"Okay. I guess I'll see you in the morning? For breakfast?" she asked, her eyes wide and bright above her bruises.

This woman. He swore. She was a black and blue bottomless pit. "You think you'll have room on top of all that meatloaf by then?"

"Are you kidding me? I have room now." And then she blew him a kiss and whirled on her toes, leaving him aching like he'd taken a blow to the chest.

Twenty-five

"You're not asleep, are you?"

He'd been in bed for what felt like two hours at least, not tossing, not turning, but neither had he been sleeping. Instead, he'd been thinking too much . . . about the accident, the sex, prison, the sex, his son, the sex, his cousin, the sex, McKie, the sex.

The sex he wasn't getting. But yeah.

The sex they'd had, and how he was still reeling. As taut and wired and pained as his body was, it was his head aching like the morning after Mardi Gras on Bourbon Street that was keeping him from getting to sleep.

Cady being a room away didn't help. He imagined her long legs tangled in the sheets instead of with his, her breasts pressed against the mattress instead of against his, her hands tucked beneath her cheek on the pillow when her fingers could be tugging at the hair on his belly if she were here.

And now she was here.

He didn't answer, just watched as she climbed up to kneel at the opposite side and end of the bed from where he'd already planned to lie awake until morning.

The bed springs squeaked. The mattress dipped. The two dormer windows on the opposite wall let in just enough light for him to see her. She grew still as if fearing that her whisper had stirred him awake.

Her whisper *had* stirred him, but he kept that to himself. Until he knew what she had come for, he didn't want to scare her away with his reaction to having her near. But he did decide to answer her.

"I'm awake."

She sighed, her whole body rising up then deflating. "Good. I was afraid I was too late."

Curious, he propped his arms beneath his head where it lay on the pillow. She hadn't been interested in being with him when she'd turned in for the night. Had something changed? "Too late for what?"

She dipped her head, toyed with the hem of her sleeping shirt. He noticed then that she wasn't wearing the sweatpants she slept in. He wondered if she'd taken them off before coming in here, a temptation, a tease, or if this time she hadn't worn them to bed.

She scooted farther onto the bed. "Will you do something for me?"

"Will I give you money?" That had to be what she was doing here, partially dressed, coming close.

"No, King. Money's not what I want."

If not money . . . he pushed onto one elbow, his interest and other things piqued. "Ask me, chère. As hard as I've tried, I can't read your mind."

"I didn't know you'd tried."

"Since you seem to read mine so easily, I thought it would put us on a more equal footing."

"I didn't know that I'd been reading yours."

He shut his mouth then, not wanting to dig this hole any deeper for fear he'd never be able to claw his way out. So rather than talking, he waited.

Something had brought her here. Something she was going to have to cowboy up and admit, and the sooner she got around to doing it—

"Will you please make me feel better?" she asked in a rush of words that zapped his heart.

He hoped it didn't short out right then and there, because he wanted to hear the rest.

"Will you make me stop hurting? Make the fear go away? I'm so tired of being scared."

King had no idea if he could deliver what she was asking. He could give her physical relief, sexual satisfaction, but taking care of her emotions . . . he was no miracle worker, spiritual healer, Zen master.

He was only a man, one no better than most broken-in secondhand models available from sleazy dealers on corner lots. But she'd come to him, not to any other. She wanted him to make her feel better? He'd die before he gave up trying.

"Stay there," he instructed her, rolling out of his side of the bed and coming around to hers.

He wore nothing but his boxers. She wore the same T-shirt that she'd slept in last night. He found the hem where it grazed her hips and pulled the garment over her head.

Standing pressed to her back, he lifted her arms, placed her hands around his neck, and told her to, "Hold on."

He started at her wrists, moved down her forearms to her elbows, savoring the softness of her skin against his palms that were work hard and callused.

The skin between her elbows and her armpits was even softer, but none of it compared to her breasts.

He cupped them, measured their weight in his palms, the fit of their curving shape to his hands. They were small, but he didn't expect them to be anything but a match to the rest of her waiflike body.

He brushed his thumbs up and felt her nipples pucker, felt the discs of her areolas pebble around them. He pinched and tugged, and her hands looped around his neck tightened as if telling him he'd better not even think of stopping, or of letting her go.

He wondered if she had any idea how much pleasure he

got from hers, how something as insignificant as the urging of her hands stirred his blood. He was hard and he was ready, and by the time they got to the act most people called sex, he'd be long past ready to come.

But this was sex, too, and making sure Cady knew that it was, that she knew he felt that way mattered as much—or more—as making his dick happy did.

He leaned down, nuzzled the spot where her shoulder met her neck, kissed her there, bit her there, licked the spot to soothe it. She moaned, raised up on her knees, tried to pull him down to the bed. His dick would be getting happy way too soon if he let that happen, so he put her off, moving his hands to hold hers and keep her where she was.

He continued to kiss and nibble, running his hands up and down her sides, skimming his fingertips along the elastic band of her bikini panties. She shivered, gooseflesh changing the texture of her skin. He leaned into her, his chest against her back, and again he was reminded of her size, how easily he covered her, how slender her body was.

He'd loved a lot of women, and he'd never measured a one by her size, but the match he and Cady made in bed left him hurting, wanting, spring-loaded, and taut. She may have come to him softly, feeling vulnerable, even afraid, but he could take her away from all that.

He wasn't going to see her disappointed. Holding her breasts with one forearm, he nipped at the lobe of one ear and slid his free hand into her panties where she was already wet. He used his middle finger to spread her wetness around, toying with her clit and the rim of her hole.

She pushed her mound against him, whimpering, and as easy as it would be to give her that quick release, he was selfish. He wanted to give her more, something she would remember, something that would be there to help her with the monsters, because he might not be around to drive them into their closets and back under their beds.

He reached up, pulled her hands from around his neck,

pushed her onto all fours, and tugged her panties to her knees. He palmed both cheeks of her bare ass, then moved lower, stroking the soft flesh between, teasing her with his thumbs that spread her open.

Her whimper became a groan, and she lowered her face to the bed, the position giving him full access to her pussy and her ass, her surrender giving him the right to take her any way that he wanted.

He was a kid in a candy store.

He didn't know where to start.

The first thing he did was lose his boxers. The second thing he did was smell her. He leaned close, he breathed deep, he sighed with the pleasure of knowing she was his for as long as he wanted to use her.

His hands on the mattress on either side of her legs, he leaned down and put his mouth to the inside of her thigh, and he kissed her there, licked her there, sucked on her skin and made his mark.

He moved to the other leg, bit down and drew another bruise. Then he probed through her folds with his tongue, finding her center, and spearing her.

She rolled her hips, and he pulled away to kiss her again, to tease her, to promise her things she had no idea were coming, things that done with her would be new even to him, he realized, climbing onto the bed behind her.

He used his weight to lay both of them down, his front to her back, and angled them to the right, their arms on that side stretched above their heads and their joined hands hanging off the mattress.

His left leg he cocked up beneath hers, a position that allowed him to ease his erection between her thighs and up against her pussy. She wiggled, letting him know she wanted him inside of her. For now he did no more than part her plumped up lips with his girth.

"You're making me feel worse, you know. Not better. Not better at all."

A laugh rumbled deep inside of him and vibrated loose. "You're an impatient one, chère. Don't you know that good things come to those who wait?"

"But I've been waiting for this forever. I've never known any of it before."

He liked that. Liked knowing he was giving her a new experience, teaching her new things. It was a gift he hadn't given often during his life, and he found her left hand with his to show her more, sliding their fingers low on her belly and into her sex.

This time, he was the one impatient, sucking back a sharp breath as she toyed with the head of his cock. "If you don't stop doing that, you're not going to have to wait long for something good to come."

She laughed, less of a rumble, more a sound of girly conquest. "Oh, you think it's good, do you?"

"No question," he said, grabbing her fingers and moving them from his juicy goodness to hers, and using both of their hands to masturbate her.

He rubbed her clit, made her rub her clit, then pressed and pulled and rolled it around until her breath came in gasping pants, and her hips rocked rhythmically against the tangle of their hands.

She came silently, the arm above her head straightening, her fingers stretching, before closing once more around his. She shuddered, stiffened, pushed his index fingers against the side of her clit, and shuddered again.

She tucked her pelvis forward, pressing it into the bed. When she moved back against him, his cock slipped to her pussy's entrance, and he did what she wanted, pushing inside.

She was tight and wet and hot, and she closed around him like a greedy fist. Her hand continued to work her clit, but she played with him, too, teasing him with her fingers as he stroked. He moved his hand to her hip, then slipped it down to tease the tight bud of her ass.

Her back arched. Her muscles contracted, squeezing,

milking, tugging him deeper inside. She squirmed there beneath him, dug her fingers into the thick quilt as if needing something to ground her, then pushed back to increase the pressure from his hand, and groaned.

"I can't stand this," she grumbled, the bedclothes swallowing half of the sound. "If I don't come, I'm going to melt all over the sheets, and you'll never explain all that girl goo to the maid."

The mess they were making? He wouldn't doubt that they'd be the last people to ever sleep on these sheets. "Tell me, chère. What can't you stand?"

"Feeling all melty and gooey. Like I'm dissolving. Like I'm not even here." A shiver ran the length of her body and pricked his skin where he lay against her.

"Would you rather have your feet on the ground?" he asked, catching the skin beneath her ear with his lips, tongue, and teeth, marking her again.

"God, no. Never again."

"Then I'd say I've made you feel better. And that would mean my job here is done."

"Like hell," she said, pulling away, crawling to the pillows and lying down, inviting him between her spread legs. "You're just getting started."

He grinned because he knew this woman was going to give him a hell of a sleepless night, and he couldn't think of any way he'd rather spend it.

He pushed onto his hands and knees and climbed on top of her, lowering himself slowly, fully, sinking into her until he had nothing left to sink but his balls.

Cady wrapped her legs around his, dug her heels into his thighs, her fingers into the cheeks of his ass, pulling him against her, into her, as far up her body as he could get without slipping inside of her skin.

Her need left him breathless, left his heartbeat stunted. His skin beneath her hands tingled when she cupped his face and brought his mouth to hers.

Her lip was still swollen, and it had to hurt her to press her mouth to his, but he wouldn't have known it from the way that she kissed him, from the way she made their mouths one.

She slanted away from the damage and opened enough to slide her tongue against his, making love to him with slow slick thrusts that matched those of his cock, fucking his mouth while he did the same to her cunt.

With his weight braced on his forearms on either side of her head, he rolled his body in and out and over her, and she mirrored every motion, going deep, shallow, hovering at the barrier of his teeth as he hovered between the lips of her pussy, plunging home when he did the same.

He couldn't take it anymore. He groaned, pulled away, and buried his face in her pillow as he came, his balls drawing tight in their sac, his thighs clenching, his calves burning, the small of his back rock hard.

She followed quickly, grinding against him and crying out, a copycat to the end. He felt a burst of laughter rising in his chest, and he couldn't hold it back, collapsing on top of her as he finished.

She was barely breathing when she growled and asked him, "What's so funny?"

He couldn't tell her that he had a new appreciation for what it meant to be fucked, so he just shook his head and nuzzled his cheek close to hers. "Nothing's funny. I was just tickled."

"Tickled? Like this?" And then she went after his ribs, gouging him right where it hurt.

He scrambled away before she got more out of him than a yelp, then rolled back and pinned her down. There was something he needed to know. "Why did you change your mind?"

"Change my mind?"

He nodded. "About spending the night with me?"

"That's easy," she said, reaching up to brush his hair from

his forehead, her eyes glistening with as much moisture as emotion. “I said that I didn’t have anyone. You said I had you.”

And just like that she broke his heart. He didn’t know what he was going to do about mending it. Or if there was anything at all to be done.

Twenty-six

"Do you think we're ever going to see Fitz again?"

King didn't respond, so Cady asked the second thing she'd been thinking.

"He stopped us almost as soon as he got us started. I don't know if Cushing Township was where he wanted us holed up. I mean, he had to know it would take a day or two at least to replace the airbags, and that rental or not, we wouldn't be going far." Not that they'd done anything about a rental. So far they'd stuck to using their feet. "Why do you think he stranded us in the middle of nowhere?"

"Why do you talk so much when I'm trying to sleep?"

He was sprawled on his stomach, taking up most of the bed, leaving her a small corner near her pillow to sit cross-legged, the sheet draped over her lap, her top half whisker-scraped and bare. Either McKie had skimped on the razors, or King hadn't cared enough to shave.

He looked totally debauched. Unshaven. Uncombed. Sweetly slovenly. Only one leg was covered by the wrinkled sheet, and the one beneath him was a maid's worst nightmare. She couldn't help herself. She leaned forward and bit him, right where his thigh met his ass. Then she kissed him. Then she bit him again just because she could.

He, of course, hadn't been asleep at all. And while her ass

was up in the air and she was bending over playing with his, he planted his mouth similarly and bit at hers.

Only his bite went on forever, and he used his tongue and his fingers as well as his teeth, and then—just as he'd done last night—the weight of his body, too, lowering himself on top of her, penetrating her, and nibbling on her ear.

"Good morning, chère. And that's from both of us," he added as he thrust.

She closed her eyes and gave herself up because she couldn't focus on conversation, or even remember what she'd wanted to know with him filling her, and moving inside of her the way she loved him to do.

He drove forward again, rocking her into the bed, back and forth in a slow lazy motion that made her think of hammocks and mint juleps and the Mississippi River. Her, a Jersey girl, who'd never crossed that Civil War line.

And the way he called her chère when she wanted to hear it most . . . it just did her in. She was in so much trouble here, a trouble that was as good as the one stalking her was bad, yet trouble she needed to ditch before she lost her edge and King distracted her to death.

But then he moved and the distraction consumed her body. Her nerve endings sizzled, her skin burned, her womb tensed, then released and relaxed. Sensation washed over her, sending her soaring, a stalk of grass caught up on the wind, her limbs loose, her body weightless.

King followed, grunting and rutting like an animal while she slipped into a spiritual coma of bliss. Moments later she returned to earth, and the man beast collapsed on top of her, rolled off and looked at her, his eyes drowsy and sexy and satisfied, as was the smile that pulled up one corner of his bad boy mouth.

Even his voice was all aged Scotch whisky and rich smoky Cubans when he said, "People get one look at your neck, chère? They're going to know all the nasty you've been up to in this room."

The next thing she knew, he was snoring.

She rolled her eyes, rolled herself out of bed, and set off to the sitting room to find clothes for the day. She showered while he got in the rest of his good night's sleep; when she looked in the mirror, she realized he'd been right about her neck. Ugh.

She couldn't remember the last time she'd had a hickey—though with the rest of her bruises, these at least wouldn't stand out any worse than the others.

While she was dressing and doing spiky things to her hair, King grumbled and stomped past to clean himself up, and she spent that time packing up their things in case Fitz called with a change of plans.

Oh, yeah. That was the reason she'd woke King up! To talk about Fitz, and why the hell he'd stranded them here. If that's what he'd done, or allowed Malling to do . . . whichever one it was, there had to be a reason.

As she was loading her laptop into its slot in her backpack, King came out of the bathroom wearing his towel around his shoulders and nothing else. The drowsiness was gone. As was the satisfaction. The only thing she saw in his eyes now was sex.

"You like being naked, don't you?"

"I like being naked around you."

"Well, get dressed. I'm hungry."

He snorted. "Like that's any kind of surprise."

"I'm hungry and feeling a lot like a sitting duck. Not to mention more than a little bit gullible." She zipped her backpack, set it by the door. "I thought Fitz would've made contact by now, and I don't like not knowing if the wreck was part of his plan or Malling's."

She glanced over to see King standing there, eyes closed as he towel dried his hair. Now he was wearing an unbuttoned denim shirt. That was it. "You're not listening to me. You're not even getting dressed." The ring of the room's phone cut her off. "Can you answer that at least?"

"Sure thing, chère. Anything to stop you railing like a fish wife."

"Hello?" he said, and she stared at him, her face heating as the echo of her words and tone pinged back. Ugh. She was railing. She did sound like a fish wife. She was just so ready to move forward that she'd forgotten about patience, much less remembered perspective.

"That's fine. Send him up," King said, grabbing for his boxers and jeans the second he hung up the phone.

"Mrs. Wind?"

He nodded, found socks and his boots. "A courier's bringing up a package. She'd heard the shower so knew we were awake, but wanted our okay before she let him interrupt. Guess she thought we'd be all fresh and clean, and ready to go at it again. You know. Like bunnies."

Cady ignored the dig. "The courier. He couldn't leave the package with her?"

"Guess not."

"You think it's from McKie?"

"She said the insurance company."

"Addressed to you?"

"It's got this address, but all the driver knew was that it was for the people who'd been in the wreck."

So it was from someone who knew they were here. McKie knew they were here. Did Tuzzi's people? Did King's insurance company? "Did you ever call them?"

"Nope."

"Then how could it be—"

"My thoughts exactly," he said, and went to meet the delivery at the door.

The older man, nearly Jarrell's twin but for a hundred pounds and a pair of glasses, handed King the letter-size file box and a clipboard.

He was wheezing from the three-story climb as he told him, "Sign here."

King did, scrawling his signature. Cady came close

enough to look over his shoulder at the name on the bill of lading, a hot shot service out of Reading. The insignia on his shirt pocket matched.

She took their copy of the receipt, folded it, and tucked it into her back pocket. Later, she'd give the number a call, or check the URL online and see if the place really existed. She did not like the idea of them being caught up in someone's elaborate hoax.

King handed her the box while he dug for his wallet to tip the driver. Cady was tempted to shake the contents, see if they rattled, or if they sounded like something more than a bunch of insurance paperwork.

The return address was, indeed, that of a national agency, complete with their red and white logo, and the address of a branch in Reading. She would Google that office, too, because it was obvious someone was sparing no expense or skimping on the set or the costumes.

After closing the door behind the driver, King nodded at the box. "You going to open that?"

"I don't know," she said, bringing it up to her ear and gently jiggling it, laughing as she added, "Do you think it's safe?"

And then she stopped laughing. "King?"

He took it from her hands, leaned close, and listened. "Goddamnit. Cady. Get the hell out of here."

She was at the door before he could push her toward it, grabbing her backpack and heading for the stairs as he called from behind her, "Mrs. Wind!"

The stout older woman met them at the bottom of the staircase. Cady opened the front door and waited. Mrs. Wind frowned, twisting a dish cloth in her hands as she looked from Cady to King. "What is it, dear? Was the package bad news? Is there anything I can do to help?"

"Is anyone else in the house?" King asked, holding her by the shoulders so that he had her attention. "Anyone other than you and me and Cady?"

"No, dear." Her dish towel was now a ball of cotton threads. "You're my only guests, and Mr. Wind—"

"Then run, Mrs. Wind." King turned her toward the door. "We've got to get outside. Now."

Cady didn't hear anything else after that, leaving the B&B's proprietress to King as she bolted through the door and onto the wraparound porch, forgoing the stairs, leaping, and sailing over Mrs. Wind's bed of tulips.

She hit the ground running, and didn't stop until she was half a block up the street. She'd seen the damage rent by Jason Malling's explosives. And she didn't for a moment think Fitzwilliam McKie had sent either one of them a watch.

King caught up moments later, one arm around Mrs. Wind's shoulders, his other hand holding her nearest elbow to keep her close. Once the three of them were safely away, King pulled his cell phone from his waistband, and asked, "Is there a way to reach the closest cops rather than through 911?"

"Jarrell or Delton can raise them on the radio as fast as they can be dispatched." Mrs. Wind was frightened, but made of sturdy stuff, and didn't panic. "Will one of you please tell me what's going on?"

Cady took the other woman aside as King dug for Jarrell's card and made the call. "The package, Mrs. Wind. It was ticking."

"Ticking? Like a bomb?"

"We don't know if it's a bomb," she said, feeling like she might as well be telling the older woman a lie. "We just want to be safe."

"But you were just in an accident. And now this?" Mrs. Wind had obviously dropped her dish towel, so reached for her apron, and worried the hem. "Is someone trying to hurt you? Jarrell didn't mention that someone was trying to hurt you. It might have been a better idea for you to stay someplace else. Mr. Wind has a bad heart . . ."

Cady didn't know what to say—she obviously had no reassurance to offer—and was glad when King finished with his call and joined them. "Jarrell's putting out the word, and evacuating the adjoining blocks."

"He can do that?" Cady looked from the top floor of the B&B toward King.

His gaze, grim and bitter, was focused on the three-story Victorian, where white smoke had started pouring from the windows of their room. "It's a small town. I have a feeling Jarrell can get just about anything done."

"Oh, he can," said Mrs. Wind. "He and Delton, too. I hope it's nothing big. The volunteers have to come from all over. I just wish Mr. Wind hadn't gone to Pittsburgh this week. Oh, look at the smoke!"

Cady wanted to reach for King, but she held Mrs. Wind's hand instead, standing beside Tuzzi's newest victim as others joined them. Everyone in the small crowd kept their eyes on the house. Sirens sounded in the distance, and Cady heard an engine rumbling toward them from behind.

She turned, looking for the flashing colored lights of a police cruiser or fire truck as the vehicle drew close, seeing instead the overly bright headlights of a car bearing down—a car that matched the description of the one that had run King's Hummer off the road.

"King!" she screamed, her heart exploding from her chest into her throat.

With King right behind her, she grabbed Mrs. Wind, pulling the older woman across the street and onto the raised sidewalk, ducking into the doorway of the nearest shop and huddling beneath the block-long awning. The others who'd gathered scattered and scrambled, too.

The driver whipped his wheel, turned toward where Cady stood, revved his engine even higher, and hit the gas—all as Jarrell's tow truck roared off the side street and into the car's path.

The bulk of the bigger vehicle blocked the smaller one

from view. Only the rooster tails of smoke, dust, and gravel thrown up by the tires were visible.

No one but Jarrell had a chance to react. Cady watched him dive across the tow truck's front seat seconds before the car rammed into the driver's side. The truck jolted, rocked. Metal screeched, rending.

People screamed, jumped, and dashed away, some toward their friend in the truck, others heading for the car, its engine now steaming on the far side.

Cady couldn't move. Her knees were locked, her whole body shaking, her stomach lying somewhere at her feet. The car had been coming for her, the second time that it had.

If not for Jarrell Bradley . . .

She looked at King, reached up to wipe away the trail of tears stinging her skin like rubber tire tracks burned on the road. "You still think someone doesn't want me dead?"

Twenty-seven

No. King didn't think that at all. Not any longer. He wouldn't think it ever again.

But the smoke bomb—and that had to be what was set off by the timer ticking in the box—had already fizzled out into cloudy white wisps and just wasn't enough to make that happen.

Neither was the accident on the state road that had brought them to Cushing Township. Both of those were more of Tuzzi's psychological assaults on Cady.

The driver doing the wild thing, however. . . . King tried to cough out a sharp curse, one that stuck in his closed-up throat. Yeah, that could've done the job, he mused, hardly happy to make the admission, to realize how close the threat to Cady's life had come.

Thanks to Jarrell Bradley, whoever had been behind that wheel wasn't going to be doing anything anymore. More than a few people here owed the burly mechanic their lives.

And King, well, he wasn't sure his heart would ever find its rhythm again.

He held Cady hugged to his chest, stroked her head while shaking his and trying to breathe. Goddamn but his chest hurt. His chest and his gut, and even his head as he tried to make sense of what was happening.

Someone had wanted them out of that room . . . so another someone could run them down with a car? Why something so complicated? Why a bomb that did nothing but smoke up the place instead of one that laid them out, did some damage?

Was Tuzzi trying to silence Cady permanently? And why would he, if her role in what had gone down eight years ago was as small as she claimed? More than any of those questions, however, there was one that wouldn't let go.

What the *hell* had McKie gotten them into?

At King's side, Mrs. Wind doubled over, whether crying or coughing or choking King couldn't be sure. He kept one arm around Cady as he bent to assist the other woman. "Mrs. Wind? Are you okay?"

"The driver. Did he survive?" She straightened, her chest heaving, one hand pressed there. "I lost my son Allen in a car accident when he was only ten. I can't bear the thought of anyone dying that way."

King looked up and down the township's main street. He was unfamiliar with everything here but Jarrell and Delton's garage, the Winds' B&B, and McCluskey's.

The state trooper who'd responded to Jarrell's call and arrived to cordon off Mrs. Wind's home had left two locals guarding the block and moved to the accident. He'd also radioed for help.

King knew things would be busting out like a downed beehive here soon, and that he and Cady were going to be the honeycomb, the prize right in the middle that everyone was going to come after.

He turned to Cady. Cady, who'd been abandoned by so many people. Cady, who'd been paying for a bad choice with more personal currency than was reasonably due. Cady, who'd been expecting him to keep her safe.

He shoved a hand through his hair, glanced toward the accident, back to Mrs. Wind, then to the woman who was becoming his whole world. Asking Cady to see to the older woman while he stayed at the scene. . . .

"I want to be here. I need to be here." Her face was pale, drawn. Her voice cracked. "This is about me. You know that."

He did know, but as soon as law enforcement descended, the information free flow would be cut off. These minutes, even these seconds they were wasting were crucial. Goddamnit! He needed to get to that car now!

"May, oh May!"

Hearing her name called, May Wind looked up, and before either King or Cady could react, their hostess rushed toward the taller woman of about the same age waving a handkerchief to flag her down.

The two of them embraced, and then hands were waving and flapping as they gathered with a gaggle of other friends to cluck and peck at the goings-on.

That left King free to grab Cady's hand. "Let's go."

He led her the length of the sidewalk toward the tow truck. They descended the steps at the end of the block and made their way onto the edge of the side street.

Her fingers tightened around his as they circled the back end of Jarrell's vehicle, stopping when met with the wreckage. Cady choked back a gasp.

Steam hissed from under the crumpled hood. The grill dangled in two pieces. The left front tire was blown and that fender peeled back toward the driver's side door.

The accident wasn't any worse than what King had seen on the side of many a road down in bayou country, and was sure Cady had driven by the same in the past. But knowing this car had been gunning for her . . .

The driver had obviously braked when Jarrell had rolled into view. Braked, fishtailed, overcorrected, and spun out of control. The front of the car on the driver's side had slammed into the tow truck.

And the shattered windshield made it pretty clear the driver hadn't been buckled in.

If King had been the compassionate sort, he would've said no one deserved to be taken out by such a blow. But he wasn't, and this guy had been after Cady, so he deserved exactly what he'd been given—if not worse.

That didn't mean King wanted her to see what happened when a hard head met windshield glass. "You can stay here, but I want to see if the driver was the same one who ran us off the road yesterday."

"Who else would it be?"

"Have you forgotten who we're dealing with here?"

"I haven't forgotten anything." She hooked her arm through his, her hands shaking. "I'm coming with you."

He covered her fingers with his palm, looked into her eyes. "Cady—"

"I'm coming with you," she said again, stressing each syllable of every word.

He stared at her long and hard, and she stared right back, talking him out of talking her out of joining him. "No passing out, puking, or screaming."

"I'm not a screamer."

"Oh yeah, chère," he leaned close to tell her, to tease her and raise her spirits. "You are."

She smacked his shoulder and stuck close.

Soon enough, King picked up the chatter and realized the driver was indeed DOA. That put the accident ball back into Tuzzi's court.

King couldn't see McKie working with anyone but a pro, and a pro would've been aware of what was coming at him instead of being too singularly focused to avoid head-butting Jarrell's truck.

The single trooper on scene had pulled the driver's wallet from his pocket, and the name Deshon Coral whispered through the growing crowd. King tried to move in to hear more, but Cady held him fast in his tracks.

The second he looked at her he knew something had soured. "What's wrong?"

"Deshon Coral. I know that name. I'm pretty sure he was at school when I was."

That would put him at school with Tuzzi and Malling and the rest. It would also hammer the final nail in the coffin of who King was going to hold responsible for Cady suffering through today's hell.

Just then, the tone of the chatter changed, growing louder, more agitated. Heads began to turn, attention shifting from the accident to him and Cady.

"Uh-oh," he heard her say, and quickly told her, "Don't mention recognizing Deshon Coral's name," and she came back with, "Yeah, I'd already decided that for myself."

Notebook in hand, the Statie left the body to be guarded by another local and walked toward them. King steeled himself and got a good grip on Cady's hand. "Morning, folks. I hear you may have seen this car before."

King nodded. "It looks like the one that ran us off the state road yesterday. A couple of miles back. That's why we're here. My SUV's in Jarrell Bradley's shop."

"Cushing Township isn't used to this activity, and here we have the same problem twice in two days? Not to mention the issue of a ticking package that seems to have produced a whole lot of smoke but no fire?" the trooper added, glancing toward the B&B and back. "Anything you have to tell me about what's going on?"

"If we knew anything, we'd be happy to."

"Then you have no reason to believe someone's got it in for you or your girl here?"

King's first response had been half truth, half lie. He wouldn't be happy about revealing anything. But getting around this second question was going to be trickier. His experience with the judicial and penal systems had taught him to watch every word coming out of his mouth.

"Until today, I wouldn't have thought anyone was out to get us, but even if that's the case, I can't give you a reason." Not without Fitz giving him the okay.

At the sound of sirens, the three of them turned to see

three state police vehicles, two cars, and a Jeep speeding toward them. The Jeep continued on to the B&B, a crime scene van following, while the cars stopped just outside the circle of accident onlookers.

While the newly arrived state troopers herded the crowd away and barricaded the immediate area, a dark, unmarked sedan pulled to a stop behind them, looking as government issue as the man who climbed from behind the wheel.

"It's about time," Cady muttered under her breath as King watched Fitzwilliam McKie walk toward them.

The trooper who'd been taking King's statement, held up his pen and said, "Don't go far. Either of you. I'm not done with you two yet."

"No problem, sir," King said, figuring what sticking there was to be done was out of his hands.

Fitz flashed that same impressive badge for the Staties, which got him inside the barricades. He was decked out in better than government threads, the long tails of his greatcoat flapping behind him and giving him an authoritative edge. Must be what they meant by clothes making the man . . .

"You two okay?" he asked, his gaze furiously intense and flicking back and forth between them. "Is there somewhere we can go to talk?"

This man had left them hanging for twenty-four hours during which two attempts had been made on Cady's life. King could give him lessons in furiously intense. "Talk? You drop in and out of our lives on your schedule, fuck what we're going through, and that's all we get? No explanation as to where the hell you've been?"

"I couldn't get here yesterday. An unavoidable delay. I did make the necessary calls to be sure you were taken care of. And if there's somewhere we can go to talk, we'll get things sorted out."

"Did you send the package?" Cady asked before King could mention it.

"Package? No. I haven't sent you anything. And just to be clear? I won't."

King gave the other man a look that conveyed a whole lot of the fury he was feeling. "That's what I was thinking. Besides, smoke bombs don't seem your style."

"Smoke bombs? Not the real thing?" Cady and King both nodded, and Fitz glanced down the street to where the crime scene team was at work at the B&B. "Did it say who it was from? The package? Or who delivered it?"

"A courier service out of Reading brought it. The return address on the label had the logo of my insurance company. A local branch," King told him, watching with interest as the troopers with real guns and real uniforms and real badges continued to give Fitz deference.

It was definitely an unexpected scenario, and left King even more uncertain about who he was dealing with—though the seal and signature on the agent's badge were obviously good enough for government work—an irony that he mused on with no small amount of derision.

"Since someone did call the body shop, we weren't sure if the delivery from the insurance people was legit or bogus. In fact, we're having a lot of trouble figuring out what's legit and what's bogus. Care to help?"

"That's why I'm here, King. You find us a place to talk," Fitz said, "and I'll see what I can do."

Twenty-eight

"So what you're saying is that you had nothing to do with the accidents or the smoke bomb. That the trooper who stopped yesterday was the real deal. That this was all directed by Tuzzi and executed by Malling, who did a really piss poor job hiring a competent driver."

Fitz nodded at Cady's rambling and inquisitive statement while pouring cream from a tiny stoneware pitcher into his coffee, adding sugar from a matching bowl.

He continued to stir long after the mixture was a creamy tan. "The troopers today were the real deal, too. The only thing I've done was call the garage after getting word of where the Hummer had been taken."

"That's some network you're running there," King said, pulling his cell from his waistband, and tapping the touch screen. "Jarrell barely had the Hummer unhooked when he got the call. Strange that I didn't get one. This thing seems to be working okay."

The three of them were camped around a table in the far corner of McCluskey's dining room. It was, Cady mused, much like a reenactment of the morning they'd huddled over tea and coffee in the hospital cafeteria after King had lost his first Hummer in the explosion.

His new one wasn't lost, only out of commission, and the

restaurant, opened for breakfast, was much more inviting than the cafeteria had been. But none of that made Cady feel any better now than she had then.

If anything was lost, it was her faith in McKie. He hadn't contacted them following the accident. Yes, he'd called the mechanic to make sure King's vehicle was put to the front of the repair line, but that didn't do diddly-squat to soothe the two human beings involved.

All she'd wanted was some small reassurance, a word, a quick phone call to let her and King know that Fitz was aware of what they were going through.

Was that too much to ask from the man who'd asked her to risk her life? The fact that he hadn't shown an inkling of human compassion made it harder to trust him now.

It also made continuing to put her life in his hands next to impossible. "That's all we wanted, Fitz. A word, you know? We can't do this for you if you're not willing to understand what it's like in our shoes."

Fitz set his fists on either side of his coffee mug, clenched and unclenched them, and stared down between them instead of looking up. His words, when they came, were glacial, and almost cruel. "I thought you were here because you were tired of being hunted like a dog."

Cady swore King was going to come out of his chair. He was sitting beside her, and the blocky legs scraped as he scooted back on the hardwood floor. She laid a hand on his wrist to keep him in place. Or at least to ask him to stay. She wasn't strong enough to keep him anywhere.

Then she leaned across the table toward Fitz, forcing his gaze up to hers with nothing but her will. "I can handle being hunted like a dog as long as I know you're just as aggressively dogging the heels of these creeps. If I die, they die. That I can accept."

This time, King wouldn't stay put. He jerked away from where she held him, and with what sounded to Cady like a feral growl, surged from his seat and headed for the restaurant's front door. She watched him go, felt a knot of sadness grow in her chest, her heartache choking off her words.

She returned to her own coffee and cinnamon roll, digging her fork into the latter and not looking up until there was nothing left but crumbs and ribbons of sugary cinnamon glaze on the plate. Then she set the fork beside it, and finished off her coffee.

Once there was nothing left for her to eat or drink and no reason to avoid the man she was sitting with, she folded her hands in her lap, sniffed, and looked up. "This wasn't what was supposed to happen, McKie."

"I know that—" was all he got out before she cut him off.

"Malling was supposed to scare me or haunt me or whatever, and report back to Tuzzi on whether or not I was sufficiently freaked. You were supposed to follow that information, follow Malling, listen in on his calls with your satellite or whatever, and find out how he's getting his information into prison without making a personal visit."

"I know that, Cady," he said, though he still hadn't moved his fists.

"Well then, Fitzwilliam. In case you didn't notice, the guy dead behind the wheel of that car? He was not Jason Malling."

Fitz finally moved, sat back in his chair. "But he was someone Malling knows. Someone you know."

Had he been using his satellite to listen in on her conversations with King, too? "I don't know him. I know of him. Or *knew* of him. But just his name, that was all. And that was a long time ago."

"You may have known him then, but he came after you twice in two days," he said, as if she needed the reminder. "He came after you now, not a long time ago. Don't you want to know why?"

"I know why. Don't I?" Deshon had been connected to

Malling. What else was there to know? And then it occurred to her . . . "Wait. You have no idea who Deshon Coral is, do you?"

Fitz's gaze returned to his coffee mug. "He wasn't on our radar, no."

Oh, this was perfect. Just perfect. She wasn't just bait, she was a guinea pig, a lab rat whose cage had no walls, but a lab rat all the same. Next thing she knew, he'd be injecting her with some sort of transmitting virus. . . .

Crap. He'd been at the hospital. He'd been in their hotel room. What if he'd bugged her, the bastard? What if he wasn't using a satellite at all, but a transmitter?

There could easily be more than the onboard GPS in the Hummer he'd provided, and then there were all those supplies, so many places to plant bugs . . .

"If you've got such a flaky *radar*, maybe you should stick to your satellite," she said, and shoved out of her chair. She was going after King. "If you don't even know who Malling has doing his dirty work, then you and I obviously have a different concept of what aggressively dogging means."

Twenty-nine

King was still leaning against the front of McCluskey's building when Cady flew out the front door. He'd meant to be a lot farther away than he'd made it by the time she came after him. He hadn't intended to be there for her to find.

He'd thought about hitching a ride toward New York and having Simon meet him halfway. Then he'd considered pony-ing up the bucks for a low slung sports car with a herd of wild horses under the hood and making his wild west way to Louisiana pronto.

He'd be just peachy keen happy for the rest of his life if he never laid eyes on another Hummer.

It was the idea of never seeing Cady again that had stopped him outside the restaurant's door. And it was know-ing that she could accept dying over this fucked-up shit that had kept him there.

Her relief at finding him was palpable. Not only was her sigh loud and heavy, the tension draining from her body vis-ible in the way her shoulders drooped, she seemed, too, to shed the skin she'd been wearing, the protective shell shielding her from the prospect of finding him gone.

She came to him, leaned into him. He wrapped his arms around her, backpack and all, and pretended his heart wasn't aching. Pretended, too, that his life today was the same as it had been yesterday. Pretended, finally, that he wasn't a changed man.

"I thought you'd left me."

"I'm not going to leave you, chère." He kissed the top of her head. "But I don't want you talking about dying. Nothing here is worth you dying for. McKie can find another way to get what he needs without you giving up your life."

"But Kevin—"

He cut her off. He wasn't going to let her guilt over her brother's death claim another minute. "You dying won't bring your brother back. You staying alive means you can make sure no one forgets him."

She hugged him tightly, her cheek damp against his shirt, her hands skating up and down the muscles of his back. She played his spine like piano keys; he was so tense, she had to feel it. But she didn't say anything, just melted into him as if she never wanted to let go.

If the group still huddled around the accident two blocks away hadn't begun to stir, he would've gladly stood there as long as it took her to finish her song. But they were stirring, looking, turning, waiting. Things were going to get itchy if he and Cady didn't move.

Just then, Fitz exited the restaurant. "We need to go. Now."

Now was cutting it close to too late. "Whisking us out of here, are you?"

He hadn't waited for them to follow, but kept walking. "I am. Unless you'd rather deal with all the questions local law enforcement is going to have. And by now I imagine Homeland Security's been alerted to the ticking package, so they'll have some things to say, too."

The Pennsylvania Staties King wasn't so worried about. But the threat of *Federales* with official badges? That spurred him into motion, and he spurred Cady in turn.

Once Fitz had herded them past the cluster of law enforcement vehicles clogging Cushing Township's main drag and opened the back door of his car for Cady, King asked, "What about the Hummer in Jarrell's shop? You planning to leave that here?"

Fitz nodded.

"With my name on the title and registration? And my insurance company footing the bill?"

"Your name's no longer connected to either that vehicle or the first. And your insurance company has never been involved," he said, closing the door behind Cady and circling to the driver's side. "Get in. Now."

King glanced over his shoulder just long enough to see two state troopers walking toward them. Fitz started the car and hit the gas the minute King's butt was in his seat, leaving nothing but rooster tails of gravel and King's toothbrush behind.

Five miles later, he was still mulling over the issue of vehicle ownership when Fitz pulled into the parking lot of an abandoned gas station and stopped his sedan next to an H3 identical to the two that had come before.

King didn't even look at Fitz. He stared instead at the man in black with the sunglasses and jarhead haircut climbing down from the SUV. "And this one? Am I connected to it? Or does it belong to Mr. Ray-Ban there?"

"This one's yours." Fitz pushed open his door, got out and headed around to Cady's.

King beat him to it. "Now what? Since you're the man with the plan?"

Fitz ignored him and turned to Cady. "Do you know how to get to your grandmother Josephine's farm from here?"

She nodded, her frown one of concentration rather than the confusion King felt. "I think so."

"If you have any trouble, it's programmed into the Hummer's GPS."

"Wait a minute." Forget Cady having a relative nearby who she hadn't bothered to mention and didn't seem set on avoiding. "You want us to be sitting ducks on some farm?"

"You'll be safe there."

"Can I take that to mean that we weren't safe on the road." When Fitz lifted a brow, King realized the absurdity of what he'd said. "Scratch that."

As if they needed reminding, Fitz told them, "For some reason, Tuzzi has escalated his attacks."

King blew out a snort. "Yeah. Attempted murder's a lot higher up the scale than psychological terror."

"This is all happening in real time, King," Fitz said, waving one arm expansively. "While we stand here? The clock is ticking. Malling will be on the way to report to Tuzzi. I need to be there to follow that. But I need to know you and Cady are safe before I do anything."

"I can get us to the farm," Cady said.

King broached the subject of family no one had mentioned. "What will your grandmother say about us barging in? Is she on your side, or your parents'?"

"She passed away years ago, before Kevin died. My parents take two weeks of vacation every summer and spend it there fishing. They keep water and canned foods stocked. We should be fine for a few days." She turned to Fitz. "That's all you need, right? A few days?"

Fitz nodded. "If we can get Tuzzi on the accidents and the bomb, then it's over and you can get back to living your life."

King didn't say anything. He just headed for the driver's seat, started the SUV, and put it into gear, waiting for Cady to ditch the government man and join him.

Thirty

Cady and King had been on the road in his newest Hummer for nearly an hour when she was poleaxed by a paralyzing hunger pang and a sudden idea. She glanced at his profile and asked, "Do you think we can find a spot for breakfast where we can pick up free WiFi?"

King frowned, whether at the idea of her eating more food or her question about WiFi, she couldn't know, but he answered quickly enough. "If you don't mind a side trip out of the boonies and into civilization, I'll see what I can do. Why the WiFi? More banking to do?"

"I want to look up the courier service. See if it's a legitimate company. And the insurance agency's office, too." She turned her attention back to the road. "If I use a free network, the search can't be traced. And, yeah, I know what McKie said, but a lot of things are still bothering me."

"You're not the only one who's bothered. This whole thing stinks worse than that smoke bomb."

"I don't get that either." Though she wouldn't doubt King having suspected as much, she kept her suspicion that she'd been bugged to herself. Fitz was probably helping himself to the Hummer's GPS broadcast even now, so whether he'd been tracking her individually was moot.

"The smoke bomb doesn't make sense," she said, continuing her thoughts aloud. "If I'm being watched, it would be easy to come after me the second I step onto the street. Are they on some kind of schedule? And they knew the ticking package would get us out of the room at a certain time?"

King reached for the sunglasses he found tucked in the visor. "Best guess? This Coral kid didn't want to hang out all day waiting to finish what he started. He wanted you out of the way ASAP."

And if not for Jarrell Bradley . . .

Cady shuddered, pushed free from that thought and the others she didn't have time to deal with. No doubt everything that had happened the last few days would rush in and devour her the moment she let her guard down.

But she couldn't do that now. She had to keep her mind clear to think. "Since Fitz didn't know anything about the package, it had to be Coral or Malling who sent it. It just seems way too sophisticated a plan for those bozos to put together. Especially on such short notice."

"It wasn't so short. Think about it," he said, adjusting the rearview and side mirrors. "We were out of commission before noon yesterday. That gave them a good twenty hours to rig the bomb, fake a delivery receipt and uniform, and hire some guy with a van to drop off the package."

She supposed he was right. "You don't think the courier service was real?"

"The service, maybe. The driver, maybe not." He inclined his head toward a parking lot packed with tractor trailer rigs. "You want to give this place a try?"

It was a truck stop, but it advertised free WiFi and blueberry waffles. It was enough to make her heart—and her stomach—go pitter patter. "Works for me."

"You remember enough of the details for your search?" he asked, as they parked and headed inside.

She'd handed the delivery receipt to the first Statie on the scene, but she remembered enough.

"I want to call the courier before the cops do," she said

once they'd settled into a booth and King had signaled for two coffees. "As soon as law enforcement's involved, the service will clam up. But as the consignees, they should give us some details, yes? If they really did send it?"

"Find me a number. I'll call them."

When the coffee arrived, King ordered waffles and bacon for both of them, then waited patiently while she booted the computer and reconfigured the wireless permissions per the instructions they'd been given.

"Yay, I'm in," she said two minutes later, bringing up a browser window and typing her search terms into Google.

King rolled his eyes. "You and that machine."

"Trust me. If I had the money, I'd have a cell with a data plan. I'm lucky to have this. Even luckier that a lot of people don't password protect their networks," she said seconds later, adding with a wink, "Got a pen?"

She found the courier's Web site, gave him the phone number, went searching for information on the insurance company while he doodled with the numbers he'd jotted on his napkin. Once she came up with the second set of contact details, he went to use the pay phone outside the truck stop's front door.

The call to the delivery service and insurance agency's office netted him the same information. Both were legitimate outfits—but neither one had any record of a package being sent to Cushing Township, Pennsylvania.

It was clear that someone out there had contacts they could tap at a moment's notice—or at least within twenty hours' time. That description fit Tuzzi and McKie both. Did they trust McKie that he'd had nothing to do with the bomb? That he would never send them a package?

"Well, that sucks the big one," King said, shredding the napkin he'd carried with him.

"Does it mean that McKie was telling the truth? That he didn't send the package? Or does it mean he buried his lie in all sorts of red tape and bribes?"

King stacked the strips of torn paper one on top of the other around the rim of his plate. "I'm going to go with the package being Coral's way of getting you out of the house."

"Okay. Now explain how he pulled it off."

"He found the shirt at Goodwill, printed up the delivery receipt and manifest at Kinko's, bought the clipboard at Office Max, and paid the guy with the van by the hour. He told him what time to drop off the box, and here's a hundred bucks not to worry about what might sound like a clock. It's just a joke between friends."

It made too much sense to blow off. "And that means we do what?"

"The only thing we can. Pack up the laptop and hit the road. There's a farm out there with your name on it."

She laughed. "You have no idea how true that is."

"Let me guess. Cady Jo?"

"Cady Josephine," she corrected him, sliding the laptop into its padded compartment and securing the backpack's buckles and straps. "Don't forget either, because there *will* be a quiz."

He dropped several bills on the table to cover their check and the tip, gave her a wink. "You mean you're the answer to a test as well as the answer to my prayers?"

She wanted to grin, to think he meant it, to hold close the feeling that he did. But she'd been stupid enough for this lifetime already, so she said, "If I've been sent down as an answer, you've been praying to the wrong gods."

Thirty-one

Cady hadn't been to her grandmother's farm in years. As kids, she and Kevin had come here with their parents for summer vacation. They'd traipsed through the nearby woods after Redcoats. They'd prayed their tiny fishing hooks would hold should they snag any of the human bones rotting at the bottom of their grandmother's five-acre lake.

They'd romped through the pastures where cows plopped patties the size of baseball diamonds. They'd ripped the skin off their knees, shins, and elbows climbing trees. That had all stopped, of course, when they'd become teenagers with concerts, friends, and parties calling their names.

Cady had been eighteen when Josephine Kowalski had died, two summers after her last vacation here. Thinking back now, she regretted not choosing family over material things, but hindsight was always twenty-twenty, and even more acute when looking back with matured eyes.

Though the house was empty and the property unused save for that one time each year, a caretaker checked in regularly, keeping the yard mowed, clearing away storm debris of downed limbs, repairing broken windows, deterring vandalism by local kids with nothing better to do.

Squatting to lift the heavy iron flower pot that sat beneath the front window looking out over the porch, Cady slid her hand along the damp and dirty board, searching for the key. She gave it to King when she found it, and eased the pot back into place.

He hadn't left her side since they'd parked. It was cute, really, his attentiveness, his protectiveness, but there was nothing out here she needed protection from. No footprints but their own marred the dirt on the porch or the front steps, and there were no recent tire tracks on the road leading in.

More than likely they'd been seen driving onto the property, and the caretaker would be over before Cady had time to find sheets and make the bed. Or beds, if King decided he really did need a good night's sleep since he and she both were going on two days now without one.

The door squeaked on its hinges as he forced it open, the noise and the stickiness two more of her memories, as were the family pictures on the fireplace mantel and the rack of hunting rifles hanging above. The smells, on the other hand, weren't quite the same.

She was used to food being cooked at all hours, from bacon and maple syrup to toasted cheese sandwiches to fried chicken to her grandmother's never-ending supply of cookies—chocolate chip, peanut butter, frosted sugar, and oatmeal raisin.

Her stomach growled, and King looked back. "Don't even say it. We ate two hours ago. You cannot be hungry."

"Wanna bet?" she said, and pushed past him. She tossed her backpack to the sofa and headed for the kitchen.

The refrigerator, of course, was empty, and would stay that way until they got the power turned on and cooled it down. They needed the electricity, too, to get the well pumping water to the house, to cook, heat water, even to see after dark. There had always been oil lamps around, but she had no clue where they were now.

She pulled open the curtains over the window and peered out. The shed that served as a garage sat directly behind the house. When she felt King at her shoulder, she pointed it out. "You can pull the truck in there if you want to keep it out of the elements."

"The way things have been going, I won't have it long enough for the elements to do any damage."

Still facing the window, she smiled to herself. "Well, if you want to keep it out of sight, then. I don't know if that matters or not. If we were followed, it's too late. But if we weren't . . ."

She let the sentence trail, thinking King would pick it up and offer some reassurance. He went in another direction instead. "I know you said this place is stocked, but we need food that doesn't come out of a can."

She wondered if he wanted to forget about McKie and Tuzzi and Malling for now, or if he just preferred not to borrow trouble or speculate on who might or might not have been trailing after them—not hard to understand since she was worn out from doing too much of both.

And though he hadn't yet looked in the pantry, he had no trouble making a shopping list. "Eggs, milk, bacon. Steaks, potatoes, sour cream, cheese."

She liked that they were on the same food wavelength. "The last part of that sounds like someone else is hungry, even though he just got through eating, too."

"You're right about two hours being nothing," he leaned close to her ear and admitted, trapping her between his arms, his hands braced on the lip of the sink. "I could eat a horse and a cow."

This time she turned, looked up at him, and shared her laughter. "Let's check the breaker box and see about getting the electricity going. I'd like a hot bath later if I can get one. The water heater's ancient, and will have to be drained before doing its thing."

His brows drew together as he met her gaze. "Roughing it doesn't bother you? You don't miss having a bodega on every corner and three meals delivered a day?"

She blew him a raspberry. "You're obviously thinking about another stowaway. I've never had three meals delivered a day. And this sort of roughing it is a whole lot better than what I've been doing, having nothing of my own but a bedroom."

She turned around again and looked out the window. "Here when I look over my shoulder, I can see for miles. I have acres of land and trees and ponds surrounding me, not to mention the lake. And best of all, I can breathe."

"You'd probably like Le Hasard. Different climate. Different geography. Definitely different trees. Cypress. Spanish moss. Magnolia. And being in the Mississippi River Delta, most of our ponds are swamps."

"Le Hasard?"

"My place in Vermilion Parish."

"Oh, right. Louisiana."

She wasn't sure why he was telling her this. Did he want her to see his home? Did *he* want to see his home? Was homesickness causing him to regret being here?

After all, he was doing a favor for a stranger—a dangerous favor at that, and look at what it had cost him. In exchange for what? He wasn't getting anything out of it—except for the sex.

She would never believe the sex was keeping him here. Kingdom Trahan would have no trouble getting sex in any of the fifty states. As much as she would've enjoyed the ego stroke, his sticking with her in Pennsylvania or New Jersey or New York was not about her body.

"King?"

"Cady?"

"Why are you here?"

"Because every man's life could use a little adventure."

She swung her elbow backward, connected with his gut, got a lot of satisfaction out of his, "Oomph." "I want a real answer. You could've told me to bugger off in the parking lot after the explosion. Or at the hospital when you realized you were collateral damage in Tuzzi's hunt for me."

"What's a Hummer or two between friends?"

She elbowed him again.

"Hey. I need those ribs."

"And I need an answer." She did not enjoy feeling as if she'd been thrust into the role of damsel in distress, tied to the tracks by some dastardly villain, and had to be saved by a knight on a white horse or a lawman with a badge.

She was used to saving herself. Yeah, she hadn't done the best job in the world, but relying on someone else hadn't worked out for her at all. Better her half-assed self-reliance than being dropped on her head by others. "Please?"

King moved his hands from the sink and wrapped them around her midsection, pulling her back into his body. He tucked her head against his neck, rubbed his chin at her temple. She listened to the scratch of his whiskers against her hair stiff with product.

"I want to be here. Isn't that enough?"

It should be, but she needed more because this was no cake walk for him either. "No. You have to have a reason."

"You mean *you* have to have a reason."

"Semantics. Whatever." She closed her eyes, enjoyed his strength. It was so damn easy, so damn tempting to let her own seep away. "I'm not your responsibility, King. I stowed away with you, yes, but all you had to do was drop me at the bus station like I asked. You didn't have to come this far, or go through so much. You didn't have to do anything. I have to know why you have."

"Why?" he asked, after a moment's hesitation that was pregnant with emotion. "Are you thinking you're going to repay me? That I want you to repay me?"

"I can never repay you," she said, shaking her head. "You've done so much."

"You must have me confused with some other Good Samaritan, chère. I gave you a ride. That's all."

Why could he not answer this one simple question? "That's not all, and you know it. For one thing, you stuck around. If not for me, you would be home by now instead of playing farm boy."

"I happen to like playing farm boy. And I happen to like playing it with you. Yeah, I thought early on about dumping you at the bus station, or buying you a one-way ticket to Anchorage to get you out of my hair. And if all this shit had gone down a year ago, I'd've done just that.

"But I'm not the same man now I was then. I'd like to think I'm a better man, but maybe I'm just old. So if you need me to sum all that up, well, I'm here because you're here, and because not being here isn't an option. And then there's the fact that my dick hasn't been this happy in years."

She would've elbowed him again, but she was crying now. She didn't want him to know, and it was getting hard not to give in and sob, to sniff back her tears. And then she thought, to hell with it.

With her voice quavering, she asked, "Who do you get to write your speeches, because you're definitely not paying him enough?"

"Hey, what's with the disrespecting? That was one of my finer moments."

"I loved your finer moment," she said, turning in his arms and fighting her heart that was telling her she loved so much more. She clutched the front of his shirt in both hands. "I just feel like I have ruined your life."

"Oh, Cady, chère. My life was ruined a long time before I met you," he said, and she laughed. Then she cried. She couldn't hold in the emotion a moment longer, and the dam broke to an exhausting flood.

He cupped the back of her head and kept her there in the circle of his arms, rocking her gently while she sobbed like a heartbroken baby. Her shoulders shook. Her throat swelled. Her lungs felt on the verge of collapse. She ached from head to toe, and she wanted to stop, but she couldn't.

A groan rumbled through King's chest. He bent and

scooped her up as if she weighed as much as a pillow, and carried her through the house until he found a bed. The mattress was bare, but he laid her on top of it, then curled up behind her and held her while she cried.

"I'm sorry," she finally got out, amazed she had the energy or the breath left for any words at all. "I'm just so tired. I'm so tired."

"I know, chère. I know," he told her, stroking her arm from shoulder to elbow until she fell asleep.

Thirty-two

Once he was certain Cady wouldn't miss him, King eased off the bed. He'd seen a linen closet in the hallway, and found pillows, sheets, blankets, and quilts stored there in protective plastic bags.

He chose a well worn and soft as cotton balls quilt, and tucked it around Cady as best he could without moving her. He then pulled the curtains closed, shut the bedroom door, and went in search of the breaker box.

His plan was to get as much done as he could while she slept, and for her to sleep as long as her mind and body would let her. She'd been going strong for two days, going up against shit that could easily wear good men to nubs, going like that battery bunny that never stopped.

If she didn't stop, her body was going to slam her to the ground and keep her there until she ran out of breath to cry uncle. He wasn't unsympathetic; he knew what it was like, needing to unwind and being unable, all efforts to force muscles to relax making them tighten further, the fight for sleep more often lost than won.

The fact that she hadn't broken down already during the last two days was a surprise. The fact that she'd finally done so in a place she felt safe wasn't. The fact that he'd spilled as much of his guts as he had did not make him happy. Nor did her insistence on knowing why he was here.

Her insistence put him in the position of having to dig for an answer, and he'd been avoiding anything that looked like work, telling himself he was sticking around because he had nothing better to do with his time. Telling himself, too, that what he'd felt when he thought of losing her was nothing but a heat of the moment response.

It wasn't exactly a lie. At least the part about his time. He had no pressing engagements other than a date with his sunshine and crawfish. But the truth went a lot deeper, and he'd didn't think Fitz had packed a big enough shovel in the back of his truck.

Besides, he mused, finding the breaker box at the back of the house and switching the electricity on, if he did go digging for more, he might not like what he found and take off. And his running away from what was feeling like more than sexual involvement wasn't going to keep Cady safe.

Once the electricity was humming, and he'd checked the level of propane in the tank, he returned to the utility room and set about draining the water heater. Then he headed into the kitchen, lighting the oven's pilot and turning on the fridge so it would cool before they loaded it down.

Depending on how long it took to get fresh water pumped from the well to the tank for heating, and how soon Cady wanted that bath, he might have to haul water to the tub from pots warmed up on the stove. He'd roughed it himself a lot of years. The thought wasn't the least bit daunting.

What was daunting was the prospect of waiting for her to wake up so they could do something about shopping for food. He was damn near close to expiring. The protein in the bacon and the caffeine in the coffee was losing out to the overload of carbs in the syrup-drenched waffles he'd downed.

He'd unloaded the Hummer, looked through Fitz's latest stock of supplies, and done all he could think of to get the house ready for their stay. It was either pop open a can of Vienna sausages or pry his way into one of Spam, or starve while he sat out her nap.

Since he'd never been one to sit for anything, he went exploring instead, starting in the garage shed combo that hunkered behind the house. On a hook in the utility room, he found the key to the padlock securing the building.

Inside the building, he found a riding lawn mower, a fully stocked peg board and workbench, and room to park the H3. He'd move the SUV in here after they made the trip to the small grocery store Cady had pointed out before they'd turned off the main road from Rosingsville.

And then he decided this would be a good place to hide the gun neither one of them were registered to own.

He'd tucked both his piece and Alice's into the zip-away bottom of Cady's backpack that first night they'd shared a room when he still had his original Hummer and all of his hair.

Considering she hauled that bag everywhere the way most women would a purse, he couldn't imagine she hadn't noticed the extra weight, but she hadn't said a word or even hinted that she knew she was packing.

The backpack was on the front room's worn floral couch where she'd left it. He retrieved both guns, put his with the rest of his things still stored in the back of the Hummer, and the other in a coffee can of ten penny nails he found on top of a shelf in the shed.

He was busy checking out the tools—some rusted all to hell, some legitimate antiques—hanging on the pegboard when Cady finished her two-hour nap and joined him, driving all thoughts of shopping for food from his mind.

He heard her coming, her steps on the gravel of the driveway, and then he caught her scent, a mix of something warm and earthy and something else that he could only say was Cady. It was a harsh jolt to realize that he was so familiar with her after knowing her for just a few days.

Harsh, because it meant she was going to stay with him for longer than was good for him, long after they'd finished this detour, after he'd told her good-bye, after they'd both ridden off into their own sunsets. Yeah. He didn't like how much he was going to hate doing that.

For someone who hadn't had much sleep, she shouldn't look as good as she did. There was actually color in her face besides green, purple, and blue. And there was more. An expression of serenity, of being comfortable here. And just a hint of joy that she'd found him.

"Thank you for letting me sleep," she said, her hands in her jeans pockets, a shoulder propped against the open door. Her bangs hung into her eyes, her hair flatter on one side than the other and pointing this way and that on top.

It was a pretentiously affected look that he knew people with no fashion sense paid good money for. On Cady, it was cute. Even when she looked like she'd just run a balloon all over her head, it was who she was. Just like everything about her—the jeans, the sneakers, the T-shirts with logos for bands he didn't know existed.

Christ Almighty. He sounded like the fashion police.

"No problem," he said, looking down at the awl he held because looking at her was going to be his downfall. She was soft and sexy and he wanted to climb inside her clothes, a tight fit he wasn't sure she was ready for.

Rubbing at the back of his neck, he said, "If I hadn't been afraid I'd wake you up with my snoring, I probably would've stayed and done the same."

"You do not snore."

"Hmm. Must be you then," he told her, and she stepped inside the building and slapped him.

He caught her hand and laughed. "If this is how you treat all your men, no wonder you spend so much time looking over your shoulder."

"All my men?" She jerked, her eyes flashing when he pulled her closer and held her there. "You think I put up with this abuse from anyone else?"

"See? I knew I was special." And then he couldn't help himself. He kissed her. He tugged her between his body and the workbench and kissed her.

He wasn't gentle as he ground his mouth against hers. He knew he might be hurting her, but he couldn't stop. His need was too great. His heart too hungry. His mind unable to wrap around conscious thought.

She parted her lips, and he accepted the invitation, pushing his tongue inside to find hers. They played there together, sliding, loving, a parry and thrust that had his sword rising, had him moving Cady's hands to his fly.

She cupped him in her palm, pressed against him until he moaned into her mouth. Her hands were sweet, but not nearly enough. He moved his legs to straddle her thigh and ground his crotch against her, his hips bucking, his cock straining as it grew to mammoth size.

He found the hem of her shirt and pulled the garment over her head, but lost patience with the hooks of her bra and tore them out of their moorings. Her laughter spilled into his mouth. "You owe me a bra, mister."

"Fuck your bra. I'm about to owe myself a pair of boxers and jeans," he said, too caught up in his ache to snag her when she ducked away. She didn't go far.

For that he was grateful, because he was in no condition to chase her down. And when he realized what she was up to—unbuttoning, unzipping, pulling her pants to her knees, sliding her panties down to bunch on top of the denim, turning, bending over, bracing her hands on the lawn mower seat—he was afraid he was rooted to the spot for good.

All it took to set his feet in motion was Cady wiggling her ass. He made quick work of his belt and button fly, shucked his pants and boxers to the top of his boots. And then he spat into his hand, wet the head of his cock, and pushed inside of her all the way to his balls.

She groaned. He groaned. She cursed under her breath. He cursed out loud. And then he held her hips and began to move, thrusting, driving, pumping, in and out and in. Goddamn, but he liked to be in.

She was tight, so tight, like a fist, like his own skin, scraping him, sucking him, slicking him with her juices until he was dripping with her.

He reached around and found her clit, pressed against it the way she liked, rubbing, pinching, wishing his mouth was there so he could bite.

She shuddered, moaned, ground against his hand and his shaft. Then she shifted her weight on the mower seat so that she was leaning on one forearm, freeing up one of her hands to slip down and join his.

Her fingers were everywhere, playing with herself, with his shaft, with his balls, with the head of his cock when he withdrew to tease her, fucking through her folds and then into the cup she made of her hand.

He stayed there as long as he could stand it, pumping, clenching, closing his eyes and throwing back his head. Sweat beaded in the hollow of his throat and rolled down his chest. His thighs burned. His chest ached, and he pushed against the emotion building there, struggling to breathe as he moved his hands back to her hips.

Digging in and holding, he shoved his cock inside of her again. She gasped, and shoved back, meeting him stroke for stroke as things got wild, both of them giving and taking, hurting and easing, searching and coming apart.

His completion ripped through him like a knife to the gut. He jerked once, twice, unloading as Cady cried out and contracted, tightening around him like a cinch.

He held her while she shook, stayed with her until she calmed, waiting until he was empty to pull free, and then he slipped out and collapsed, draping himself over her and leaning against the lawn mower seat.

Cady finally pushed him away, mumbling something about her aching back. He wanted to laugh, but his lungs weren't working, and so he reached out and spanked her. She yelped, jumped, turned around and glared.

He looked her up and down as he went about pulling up his boxers and jeans. "You know, chère. It's hard to take that evil eye of yours seriously when your pants are bagging at your knees."

"I didn't ask you to take me seriously," she said, rubbing her bare bottom. "Only to take me."

"I'd say I did that."

"Proud of yourself, are you?"

If she kept standing there like that, her lower half naked and not the least bit inhibited, he was going to be proud of himself all over her again. "If you've got it, no need to be shy, my grandmother would say."

"Well, my grandmother would be rolling over in her grave if she knew someone, but me especially, was having sex in the shed."

"You've never had sex in this shed?"

"I've never even spoken the word sex in this shed until now. And the only place on this farm that I've ever dropped my panties is behind the closed bathroom door."

He wanted to see her naked outside. He wanted to fuck her naked outside. "So drop them the rest of the way."

"What?"

"Take them off. Take everything off. Your shirt. Your pants." He popped open the snaps of his shirt. "I'll get a blanket. We'll do it out in the open like animals."

It took her a minute to respond, her gaze measuring his intent, her head cocked to the side as she studied him. The next thing he knew she was slipping her feet—sneakers and all—through the skinny legs of her jeans.

Balling up her clothes—her jeans, her panties, her torn bra and top—she took off running, calling over her shoulder, "I don't think animals use blankets."

Thirty-three

Cady had been teasing King about animals and blankets before she'd run butt naked out of the shed, but she was glad when he'd followed her up the front steps, through the house, and out the back, that he'd stopped and grabbed the quilt off the bed where she'd napped.

The quilt had kept them from having to worry about dirt and sunburn and things with six legs coming close. Yet as much physical pleasure as they'd shared, she'd had a great time getting to know him better.

Not that doing so had come easy.

Prying answers out of him—serious answers—was worse than prying herself into panty hose, and even at the end of the day, she wasn't sure her success rate outweighed the work it had taken to get there.

"King?" she asked, curled up against him, her head on his shoulder.

"Cady?" he answered, his arm draped down her back, his hand playing with her bottom.

She wiggled. "Do you think we're compatible?"

"We seem to fit," he said, stretching out his fingers as if measuring her width. "You've got the round hole, and my peg ain't so square."

Men and sex. Always with the size. "That's not what I mean."

"You're going to have to be a little more clear then, chère, because except for you being the target of a psycho drug kingpin, we seem to be getting along."

She ignored his dig and rolled onto her back, staring at the sky that was turning indigo. "If we had checked each other out on a dating Web site, do you think we would've hooked up?"

"Wait," he said, a frown in his voice. "Are we dating?"

If she wasn't so lazy, she would've smacked him. "We skipped a lot of normal relationship steps on our way to intense."

"Wait," he said, the frown giving way to good humor. "Is this a relationship?"

"I'm afraid I'm going to have to hurt you now," she said, and pinched his nipple.

He pinched hers back. "And I'm afraid I'm going to have to like it."

"Can you be serious for five minutes?" she asked, squirming when he lingered longer than required by a retaliatory pinch. "Or for five questions at least?"

"What five questions?"

"Five questions you'd have to fill out for your profile on a dating Web site."

He huffed. "You fill out a lot of those?"

She wasn't going to tell him that she'd worked for a dating service and had been assigned to design them. She just started feeling him out by asking the ones that came to mind.

"Would you rather read *Sports Illustrated*, *The New Yorker*, *The Wall Street Journal*, *Paste*, or *Time*?"

"You're assuming I can read," he told her, turning onto his side and replacing his fingers on her nipple with his mouth.

She clenched her thighs that were tingling. "Would you rather visit the UK, China, Australia, Italy, or Tanzania?"

"The last three I could probably handle—" He paused, licked her, sucked her, blew a breath across her damp skin. "As long as you take me there in the middle of summer."

He wanted her to take him there. He didn't want to go alone. She closed her eyes, the thought even more than his tongue causing her nipples to tighten, and she found her hand sliding down to her clit that tingled in response.

It was getting really hard to remember what she was saying. Or why they were talking at all. "Would you rather eat seafood, barbeque, Tex-Mex, steaks, or lasagna?"

"I'd rather eat crawfish, but I won't say no to any of them." He opened his mouth over her belly, nipped her skin, moved lower, and sucked on her fingers wet with her flavor. "I'm like you that way. I love eating."

As long as he kept her on his menu . . . "Would you rather spend a day off fishing, playing golf, skydiving, hiking, or building houses for charity?"

"I think my best days off involve screwing and you," he said, moving his body to cover hers.

She closed her eyes and parted her knees. "Would you rather watch a horror movie, a Seinfeld rerun, a Broadway musical, a meteor shower, or an air show?"

"Porn. Isn't that one of the choices?" he asked, sliding into her with a slow, steady, never-ending stroke.

She was done being able to think. "Your turn."

"For what?"

"To ask me five questions."

"How about I just ask you one, but give you five answers to choose from?"

"Okay." That she could probably stay conscious for.

He leaned close to her ear, and on a gruff whisper asked, "Would you rather I make love to you on your back, on your stomach, bending over, standing up, or from beneath?"

"That is not an appropriate dating profile question," she said, then it was a very long time before she had the strength to say anything again.

Shifting his body weight from her to the ground, King stayed inside of her until he grew soft, and even then he didn't move, just slipped free to lay against her. "So you *are* familiar with those services."

"I never said I wasn't," she said, enjoying the intimacy and his comfort in letting her feel him.

"They work out for you any better than finding roommates online?"

She ignored the dig, concentrating on his naked body. "I met some people."

"People? Or penises?"

"Does everything have to be about sex with you?"

"It has something to do with my present company." He kissed the tip of her nose, her chin, her closest ear. "And my present lack of pants."

He tickled her, and she found herself charmed. "Ask me something real."

"Dogs or cats?"

"Goldfish. They don't require any work."

"Frank Sinatra or Frank Zappa?"

"Frankly, my dear, I don't give a damn for either one. I'd have to go with John Mayer."

"I don't even know who that is."

That didn't surprise her at all. "We're looking less and less compatible."

"If you found a buried fortune in gold coins, what would you do first? Build a new house, buy a shrimping trawler, or drill an oil well?"

"What did you do first?"

"I'm asking the questions here, boo."

Fine. "D. Other. I'd buy a vineyard in California and forget the East Coast exists."

"I've seen you drink coffee and tea. I've seen you drink water, juice. Maybe a soft drink. I have not seen you drink wine."

"I gave up alcohol after getting drunk and punched," she told him.

His expression grew protective and fierce. "Then why buy a vineyard?"

"Because it's the farthest thing from where I live, who I am, and what I know."

King rolled up onto one elbow and looked down at her, stroking his thumb over her undamaged cheekbone, his touch nearly making her cry. "This is all make-believe, Cady. You don't have to run when it's not real."

His words did make her cry. "That's the thing. I stopped believing in make-believe. I'll be running for the rest of my life."

Thirty-four

By the time they'd come back inside, having spent the remaining hours of daylight wearing themselves out, their bodies bared to the great outdoors and who knew how many prying creaturely eyes and satellites, she'd been freezing.

Temperatures dropped quickly in the city, yes, but the steel and concrete and millions of bodies held onto that warmth long after dusk. Out here in the middle of God's green nowhere they weren't so lucky.

When the sun set, it took the heat with it. The only way to generate more was with physical exertion and the friction of their skin. She would've loved it if they could've kept making love forever, wrapped up in the quilt like bugs in a rug, toasty and close and less two people than one, but by that time they resembled the walking wounded.

Her thigh muscles had never been so sore. Even the hot bubble bath she'd just climbed out of had barely eased the ache. Wrapping up in her grandmother's old terry robe that smelled of green fields and the sky and lavender, helped ease more than her physical pain.

She piled herself and the yards of worn pink fabric into one of the chairs at the kitchen table, counting the smorgasbord of soup cans lined up near the sink, and the pots heating on every burner of the stove. She and King never had made it to the store, so soup it was.

As cute as he looked stirring the pots' contents and checking the flames beneath, she wouldn't have traded this meal for one cooked by any of the hundreds of specialty chefs in Manhattan who prided themselves on their ratings and stars. "I never did thank you for getting the house ready."

"Not a problem," he said, bringing spoons and two mismatched crockery bowls to the table, adding two bottles of water he'd fetched from the truck, and dish towels to serve as hot mats.

And then he leaned close, as if to kiss her, saying instead, "No sex for you tomorrow until we shop. A grown man cannot recharge on soup alone."

"Hmm. Sounds like an old wives' tale to me."

"And they got to be old wives because they saved the soup for when their husbands had colds. You need to pay attention when they speak. Feed a cold, starve a fever. Or is it the other way around?"

That made her laugh. "When we'd come here for vacation, we couldn't do anything, not eat, not go to the bathroom, definitely not run off to play until the car was unloaded, the groceries put away, the electricity and water working again. My dad made sure to time our trips and bathroom breaks so that we flew through getting everything done."

"Must've been hard for you, the not eating part," he said, setting a pot of tomato soup on one towel, a pot of vegetable beef on another, adding serving spoons to both, then returning to the stove.

She breathed in the aromas of the veggies and salty broth, and her stomach growled its impatience. "I don't know when I became such a pig, seriously. I don't remember eating much at all as a kid."

"You're doing a good job of making up for it now." A pot

of cream of chicken completed their meal. "I found a tin of crackers, but they weren't good for anything but sticking together with mortar to build a house."

"I'm done with crackers, thanks, but I could go for a thick grilled cheese sandwich," she said, ladling tomato soup into her bowl and inhaling again. "Mmm. This smells so good. My grandmother was a big believer in soup for lunch."

"With the grilled cheese sandwich," he said, finishing her thought as he sat.

"Or fried bologna and onions. Or tuna." She sipped a spoonful of soup. "Was there tuna in the pantry?"

"Enough to populate the seven seas. But tuna's on my hit list. I lived on the stuff for years. Tuna and chips. Tuna and crackers. Tuna and tuna." Forgoing the serving spoon and then forgoing his bowl, he ate vegetable beef out of the yellow club aluminum pot.

"Was this before . . ." she left the question unfinished for a reason she didn't understand. Bringing up his history seemed an intrusion she had no right to make. One she didn't think she wanted to make when things here finally seemed so . . . normal.

"Before prison? Before my parents died?" He caught her gaze, held it, deepening her chagrin that she hadn't just blurted out her whole question. "It's okay to talk about it, chère. You're not going to hurt my feelings."

"It's so . . . personal."

"And having my cock in your mouth isn't?" he asked, shaking his head. "Sorry, sorry. I know. Grandmother Josephine would be turning in her grave to hear cock talk at her table. Bad enough to have one poking around in the shed."

Cady sputtered, blowing her soup off her spoon and back into the bowl. "Not to mention in the backyard."

"Guess it's a good thing cocks were allowed in the bedroom, or else Edgar would have never been born, eh?" He reached for his water bottle, uncapped it. "And I wouldn't be here eating soup with you now."

"Hey, at least it's not tuna."

"Ugh," he grumbled, before drinking, the plastic crackling in his hand, crackling again when he set it on the table. "When I got out, I was twenty-two, bare bones broke, and mentally blitzed. What money I had went for booze and smokes, with food coming in a distant third."

"Where did you live?" She didn't remember if he'd told her. "Your house was the one that had burned down, right? The fire you were accused of having set?"

He nodded, ate a bite. "I had a piece of shit trailer. One room with a bed, another with a couch and a kitchen. There was a bathroom, too, though most of the time I stood at the front door and pissed into the wind. Seemed the thing to do after four years of going in a bowl in front of anyone who wanted to take a look."

"I can't even imagine—" she started to say.

King cut her off. "Can't you?"

"Not really," she said, knowing he wasn't talking about pissing into the wind.

"You've been looking over your shoulder for a good chunk of your life. You have no idea who's been watching you, or what they've seen. I doubt anyone's had a camera in your toilet, but one of Tuzzi's spies did have the run of your house. Who knows what the guy may have seen?"

Cady swallowed the soup she had in her mouth and left her spoon in her bowl. She also left her water alone. She wanted a drink, but her hands were shaking, and she didn't trust that she could get it to her mouth and not spill.

"You hadn't thought about him watching you, had you?"

"I only made the connection between Tyler and Tuzzi a couple of days ago, remember?" She closed her eyes, shuddered, clenched her hands in her lap. "I don't care if he saw me undressed, but watching me flossing or poking at zits or showering?"

How many personal rituals did she go through that she wouldn't want anyone, including King, to see? Much less someone looking for a way to ruin her life? Each thing she thought about—shaving, menstruation, even clipping her toenails—humiliated her even more.

King backed his chair toward hers, the legs scooting across the scarred linoleum floor. He draped his arm around her shoulders and urged her close. "I could be talking out of my ass, Cady. He might've done nothing but keep an eye on you while waiting for Malling to get out."

"I wouldn't call that nothing."

"You're right. It's not nothing. But I didn't want you thinking too much about that toilet cam."

"Too late. That's all I *can* think about."

"How 'bout you don't think of anything? How 'bout you finish your soup and climb into bed and get more than a couple of hours of sleep?"

"And what are you going to do?"

"I was thinking of doing the same thing."

"Just sleeping?"

"Just sleeping."

"No bumping naked parts?"

He pulled back, frowned at her as if thinking she needed her mouth washed out with soap.

"Hey, that's what it is. And I've heard your potty mouth say a whole lot worse."

"The look wasn't about your potty mouth."

"Then what?"

"That you've got the energy to go at it again."

She didn't, until she started thinking about it, then realized if he was the one she was going at it with, her energy would never flag.

She reached over and tweaked his nose. "You're the old one, remember? And the one who has dishes to do."

Thirty-five

When King opened his eyes the next morning, it was bright enough outside to be noon. Last night, he and Cady had done the dishes together, made the bed together, then crawled between the sheets and passed out with little more than a hushed good night and a kiss that had gone on forever.

She'd curled up facing away from the window. He'd spooned in behind her and held her for most of the night, waking up once to ease his numb arm from beneath her head and going lights out as soon as he rolled onto his back. He was on his back now, and she hadn't moved except to switch sides. But now that she was facing him he could hear her breathe.

Propping his arms behind his head as Cady exhaled like the brush of a feather against his side, he stared at the ceiling, trying to decide if he was ready to wake up, or if a few more hours of shut eye would do him even more good.

But since his mind had stirred enough to start working, and had turned to thinking about where they were and why they were here, he gave up trying to doze off and instead drifted to the conversation they'd had with their soup last night.

What had Tyler whoever-he-was been doing in Cady's apartment when she wasn't around to see? Boning his supposed girlfriend Alice, obviously, but other than that, what no good had he been up to?

Living as she had for so long, on edge, looking over her shoulder, she wouldn't have been careless enough to leave anything she didn't want seen lying around when she was gone. She took her backpack everywhere, and except when she had it out surfing the Web, her laptop—the only thing she owned of any value—was always in it.

That put Tyler there as a spy. Watching Cady and reporting back to whoever sent word of her comings and goings to Tuzzi. Had Cady said how long he and Alice had been dating? She'd concluded that his crawling into her bed had coincided with Malling's parole, but how long had he been in place?

How long ago had she sold her ride? Was he responsible for her slashed tires? For her botched job interviews and dates soured by graffiti-sprayed cars?

Had he listened in on any phone calls she'd made and spread rumors? Made her private life the stuff of public gossip? Had he come there with a specific assignment or just to keep his eyes peeled? And peeled for what?

That's what King couldn't wrap his mind around. With the Renee massage oil connection, there was no way Tyler was anything but a plant. Alice had been cute enough, so screwing her for the cause couldn't have been a hardship. But it all seemed so ridiculously out there.

As if this entire situation wasn't ridiculously out there? He frowned. Had they talked about the boyfriend to McKie? What if Tyler *wasn't* there to launch a first strike against Cady as she'd suspected? What if—free pussy aside—he was still there because he hadn't found what he was after?

And what if he couldn't find what he was after because it wasn't there? Because it was with Cady all the time? Before climbing into her bed, he'd made sure she was passed out. Had he doped her drink? Or left it up to the alcohol to wipe her out, clearing him to search her backpack, her laptop . . .

King rolled onto his side, propped up on one elbow, nudged his partner in crime. "Cady?"

"Hmm?"

"Wake up?"

" 'M awake."

"What's in your backpack?"

"What?" she grumbled.

"Your backpack. What's in it?"

She straightened her legs, rolled over, and pushed her bangs out of her eyes to look up at him. "I don't know. The usual stuff. Wallet, lip balm, undies, meds, girly hygiene things, and lately a full change of clothes and something to sleep in. Your guns."

So she had noticed. "I'm working on that."

"Good." She stretched, arched her back. The sheet slipped down to bare one breast. "I've got a backache from carrying them around."

"If you've got a backache, it's from boinking like a bunny, and from hauling your laptop everywhere," he said, pulling up the sheet or else they'd never finish this conversation.

"I'm used to my laptop."

"Yeah. About that."

"Yes, I know. I'm online way too much, but since I don't exactly have a lot of things going for me in real life . . ."

"This isn't about you being online."

She grumbled as she propped up on both elbows. "I might be able to keep up if I had coffee."

"And if you hadn't dragged me off to the backyard last night, you'd be drinking a cup even now."

"I knew that would come back to bite me in the ass," she said, rolling her eyes and yawning.

He leaned toward her and growled. "I'm going to bite you in the ass if you don't listen to me."

She sat up and cupped her ears, the sheet falling to her waist. "Better?"

He forced his gaze back to the ceiling. "Your laptop. On the Ferrer shoot. You had it with you. You had it when you climbed into my truck in the garage. We didn't have to grab it when we went back for your things because—"

"Because I had it with me . . . and?"

"Did your roommates ever use it?"

"I don't think so. They both had their own."

"And Tyler? That night he was in your room. Could he have used it?"

She shrugged. "I suppose. Like I said, I didn't know he was even there until I woke up to pee."

"What's on your laptop, Cady?"

"What do you mean?" she asked, and frowned. "The usual. Music, photos. All my saved e-mails."

"What else?"

That question she didn't answer right away, squirming in the bed as if thinking of getting out. He grabbed her nearest wrist to keep her from going anywhere. "Cady? What's on your laptop?"

She rubbed both hands over what she could of her face, threaded her fingers into her hair. "I have a folder of stuff from Kevin."

This time he didn't care that she was half naked beside him. King sat up, plumped his pillows behind him, and leaned back. "What kind of stuff?"

She shrugged. "I don't know. Term papers. Research, maybe. He worked for the campus paper, so articles? I never thought about it when he was alive, and after he died, I couldn't bring myself to go through it."

Interesting. More stuff he hadn't known. "So he was in school at the same time?"

"Same time, same place, two years ahead."

"And it's never occurred to you that he might have had something that Tuzzi wanted?"

"Not really, no. The folder was on a flash drive he gave me before the thing with the heroin and the mascot ever happened. He told me to hold onto it. That he'd backed up some of his papers because his hard drive was flaking out. I kept it all, then after he was gone, transferred the files to whatever laptop I had at the time." She pulled her knees to her chest, propping her chin there in the cradle. "It's like the only connection to him I still have."

"Is the folder password protected?"

She nodded.

"Do you still have the flash drive?"

She nodded. "It's in my wallet."

"Your wallet that's always in the backpack you carry everywhere."

She turned, looked at him and frowned. "You think that's what Tyler found? That he wasn't watching me pee or shower or change tampons. He was snooping in my backpack."

"I don't think so." King shook his head. "If he'd found the flash drive, he would've taken it. It's more likely he found the folder on your laptop when you were out of the room showering or . . . doing those other things."

"That makes more sense. I know the flash drive is still there. At least it was the morning you skipped out on the bill at McCluskey's and I had to pay for my cinnamon roll and everyone's coffee."

Speaking of coffee . . . He tossed back the covers. "Get dressed. We're going to find coffee and breakfast, and buy food. Then we're coming back and you're going to show me what's in that folder."

"You want to wait? Shouldn't we look at it now?"

He shook his head, digging for and finding new boxers, T-shirts, and socks in the duffel of things McKie had provided, but he stuck to his broke-in jeans.

"McKie's the only one who'll know what to do with the information. Whether he gets here in two hours or three isn't going to make a difference. And that's assuming we do find more than your brother's homework."

"I guess you're right."

"Hell, yeah, I'm right," he said, whipping the sheet clean off the bed. "I'm a lot more than a pretty face."

Thirty-six

There was one thing King had yet to hear from Cady, and that was the story about the original prank that had started this whole mess eight years ago.

Demanding that she share the details would hardly put her in the mood to share. She didn't like going back into her past. He couldn't blame her for wanting to stay away.

That meant he had to convince her that telling him what he wanted to know wasn't going to hurt. Unfortunately, that was one thing even he didn't believe.

He'd listened to McKie's version of events in the hospital cafeteria, but his head had been aching and he'd been too focused on Cady and that had been a long time ago.

He knew more about her now, and now he needed more about what had happened. He needed facts so he wouldn't make a wrong move, and he needed them from Cady.

She sat across from him in the small restaurant whose ambience was not that far removed from McCluskey's. It was like eating in the family room of somebody's home. One that also served up country fare in country portions.

None of the skinny small food city portions he'd bitched about to Simon and Micky every time they'd gone out to eat at one of the trendy posh locations his cousin's wife had swore he had to experience.

He'd sworn *at* the experience, but he didn't think that's what she'd had in mind. She'd called him names, insulted his taste, and then ordered him a second meal of real food delivered once they were home. She'd also sneaked more than a few bites off his and Simon's plates.

Watching Cady eat now, he couldn't imagine her sitting still for a plate that arrived with two asparagus spears tied together with a string of red onion, a half dollar slice of grilled potato, and a lamb chop the size of his toe topped with cheese that smelled.

She tucked into what he thought was her third waffle and caught him looking at her. "I'll get a job one day, I swear. I'll get a job and I'll set up an automatic deduction from my check to pay you back for the food."

"It's good to see you eat."

She stopped eating long enough to give him a look. "I've always been able to eat. I may not know when I turned into an oinker, but there's nothing that gets in the way of my appetite."

This was where King kept silent.

"Looking over my shoulder, grieving for Kevin, getting the crap beat out of my face . . . none of that has stopped me from eating, has it?" she asked, obviously a rhetorical question since she didn't wait for him to respond. "Neither did the trial or getting booted from my house. You're looking at a one woman eating machine."

"Tell me about the prank," he said, propping one arm along the back of his side of the booth and thinking it best not to pussyfoot but to get it out there and over with, especially since she'd given him the opening.

"What's left to tell?" she said, dropping her fork against her plate, reaching for her cloth napkin. "What don't you know? I thought Fitz had covered everything already."

"He gave me his version. I want to hear yours."

She'd wiped her mouth, and now tossed the napkin to the table. "I don't know why. I'm sure they're the same."

"Let me be the judge of that." Fitz hadn't been there. He had no way of knowing what Cady did, hadn't experienced what she had, didn't share her memories. Those were the things nagging at King, things he could only get from the source.

"It's not going to work, you know," she said, slumping lower in her padded seat. "Talking about it is not going to make me feel any better about being so stupid."

"I know you want to take it all back, chère. And I know you know that you can't. Talking about it may not make you feel any better, but that doesn't mean it's going to make you feel worse." Was she buying any of this? Hell, was *he* buying any of this? "Besides, if you haven't talked about it since the trial, it's probably time."

She studied him for a minute at least, her eyes alert, her bruises fading from purple to green. "Get rid of it once and for all? Is that what you think will happen?"

Enough with the psychobabble bullshit. "I don't think anything. I just want to hear it."

"Fine." She sat up straight, grabbed her fork, stabbed a square of waffle, and swirled it through a puddle of warm syrup opaque with melted butter. "It was my junior year. I was not exactly a joiner. I wasn't some emo chick holed up in my room, but I did keep to myself. I wanted to get my degree and get on with my life. And here I am still trying to do that."

"You're getting there."

He ignored her when she rolled her eyes. "My roommate, Edie Doyle, got into a big spat with this other chick, Stacia Ashton. She was president of a sorority that was very high profile, and kept giving Edie hell about parking her car in front of the sorority house when she went to the library. Edie was lazy. It was walk half a mile across campus, or park there, cut across their lawn, and hop the brick wall."

"Stacia was Nathan Tuzzi's girlfriend."

Cady ate the bite of waffle she'd been toying with and

nodded. "Edie was quiet on the surface. Underneath, she was something else. She hated Stacia and her friends, thought they were nothing but spoiled rich bitches. She was right, but that's beside the point.

"Anyhow, she came out one night after studying to find her car had been papered with pantiliners." She fought a smile, tried not to laugh, failed. "I'm sorry, I shouldn't laugh. It's not funny, but it is. Or it was. You'd have to know Edie to understand."

"Tell me about her."

"There's not a whole lot to tell. Not only was she quiet and, well, homely, she was mortified that girls talked publicly about things like their periods, or waxing, or using vibrators, or which boys gave the best oral sex."

"She took the mascot for revenge." It was the only thing he could think of to say, not really interested in hearing about the other things himself.

A nod, and she cut into her waffle again. "She pulled all those pads off her car, intending to hand them to whoever answered the door. No one did. She tried it. It was open. She tossed the garbage to the floor, grabbed the Persian cat from the pedestal inside, and took off with it."

Took off and left evidence of her guilt behind. King imagined the rich bitches weren't happy to have to clean up their mess. But Tuzzi . . . he would've been the most unhappy of all to find his product gone.

"She asked you to hide it?"

"Yeah, I have no idea why I took it home except having it around the dorm room would make it easy to find. And I guess I felt sorry for Edie."

Cady grew pensive, and still, her eyes on her plate as she finished. "It didn't seem such a bad thing to do, helping her out, after the way they'd humiliated her. Shows what I know, right?"

And this time when she laid down her fork, King didn't think she'd be picking it up again.

Thirty-seven

Cady paced the small kitchen while King plugged in and booted up her laptop. She'd put away the few things they'd bought—coffee, cream, and sugar; eggs, bacon, and milk; two big potatoes to bake along with butter and sour cream; and the steaks King had chosen for their dinner.

After breakfast in Rosingsville, the small town where her grandmother had kept a post office box for years, they'd stopped for the groceries. It was clear from the reception they'd received at both the diner and the store that word was out—someone was at the Kowalski house.

Cady figured it was best to have King stop at Denton Hardware before they started the drive to the farm. James Denton, the store's owner, had agreed to look after the place after Josephine's death. Cady ran inside to let him know she and King were using the place for a few days.

It hadn't occurred to her until talking to him that her parents could very well have told him she was no longer allowed access to the property. Fortunately, they hadn't. He'd been nothing but pleased to see her, and equally pleased to hear she'd found the place in good shape.

Once she and King finished their errands and were back on the road, she realized the trip to Rosingsville was the first time in ages she hadn't been treated like a pariah by people who had known her in the past.

It gave her hope that she could make a new life for herself away from the place where her old one had fallen apart—or she could do so as long as she closed this final chapter with a big fat "the end" to Nathan Tuzzi.

Whether or not that happened might actually hinge on information she'd had with her all this time—information she'd never dreamed was anything more than Kevin's unfinished term papers or article drafts.

She wanted to kick her own ass for not having the guts to dig into what he'd given her. But reaching back into that time of her life wasn't something that came easily. Those good years spent as a family only reminded her how bad things had been since, how much she missed Kevin, how if she hadn't been so stupid . . .

"I believe we have struck the mother lode," King said, blowing a long low whistle that cut into her thoughts. "If only Fitzwilliam McKie were here to celebrate the moment."

"What is it?" she asked from across the room. She did not want to know. She did not want to see. Asking from a distance was a compromise.

King was still looking at the computer screen, paging through Word documents, toggling windows to scroll down Excel spreadsheets. "It's sure not term papers or news articles. At least not any articles he'd finished. I'm thinking he was compiling research to write the big one that would get him noticed by editors other than those on campus."

"Research on what?" She did not want to know. She did not want to see. She did not want to be reminded of what she'd lost or that she'd done nothing with Kevin's gift.

"Come over here and look," King said, holding up a hand and gesturing her close.

"No."

He turned then. "No?"

"Just tell me." She shook her head briskly. "I don't want to see."

"Cady, this is what you've wanted to happen for eight years. This is what you need to rip Tuzzi a new one. Kevin had the information all along. Buyers, suppliers, transactions. Phone numbers. Bank accounts. Names and addresses. This is Tuzzi's network right here. Top to bottom."

She heard what he was saying, but she still didn't want to see. She still didn't want to know. And now she couldn't move. So why if she couldn't move was she crumpling to the floor?

Thirty-eight

The sun was just setting when King headed out to the garage. He pulled the chain hanging from the overhead socket and the single bulb above popped on.

He stood there for a moment between the old riding mower and the brand new Hummer H3, as if caught between his world and Cady's, when up until now he'd been thinking their worlds were one and the same.

Realizing this little side trip of an adventure was coming to an end had changed that. At least he assumed it was coming to an end. All they had to do was let McKie know what they'd found in Kevin's files.

So far, neither one of them had made the move to do anything of the sort.

He'd come out here to make sure the supplies in the back end of the SUV were secure and make room for the rest of their things since it looked like they'd be packing up soon.

And Cady, well, she'd retreated to the safety of the bathroom's big claw foot tub, supposedly for quiet time to let what they'd discovered about Kevin sink in.

It was pretty obvious neither one of them was ready to face the fact that once they made contact with McKie, things between them wouldn't continue on as they'd been.

They wouldn't have any simple reason to stay together.

From here on, things got hard.

As he opened the back of the Hummer, King found himself shaking his head. Cady'd had it in her possession for years. The smoking gun needed to squash Tuzzi's network like a bug. He still couldn't believe it.

He imagined she was having a hard time believing it, too. Realizing that if she'd looked at what Kevin had given her, instead of shying away because of the hurt, she would never have become one of Tuzzi's victims.

He'd tried to tell her not to beat herself up, but she hadn't wanted to listen to anything he said. He didn't blame her. Not really. All the stuff going on in her head? She had to work it out for herself.

He just hoped she'd remember he was here. That she would come to him when she was ready. She didn't have to talk. She didn't have to take off her clothes. He just wanted to hold her, to let her know he was here, that he'd be here for her as long as she needed him to be.

He just wasn't sure he was ready to tell her that he loved her.

Love wasn't an emotion he had real experience with. He loved his crawfish and sunshine. He loved his bayou country home. He loved his cousin, his cousin's wife. He loved being able to do anything he wanted with his life. He loved that he had a life to do something with.

But none of those loves had crawled into his chest, used a pick ax to carve a permanent spot, then sent out roots to choke and cling and suck his will from his bones.

Not the most romantic way to describe what Cady had done, or at least what it felt like she'd done, but then he wasn't much of a romance kinda guy. He just happened to be the one who had let her.

The fact that he had was a big part of why things post-McKie weren't going to be easy. The girl he'd thought about putting on a bus or into an airplane he now wanted to put in his truck. He wanted to buckle her in and lock the doors and tie her hands to keep her there.

He just didn't know if that's where she wanted to be.

He pushed that train of thought aside and retrieved the gun he'd stuffed in the coffee can of nails. He placed that one and his own on top of his sleeping bag, then dropped to his back with a flashlight, looking beneath the rear of his truck at the tires and suspension.

Not that he'd driven this newest model far enough to wear the newness away, but he wasn't one to hit the road unprepared. Tires, fluids, belts, and hoses. All had to be checked. And since they did, maybe while he was doing it he could figure out what to do about Cady.

He was getting to his feet when he heard her walking around outside the rear of the garage. He tensed, then realized tensing wasn't the way to make the conversation flow.

And so he took a deep breath . . . and came to his second realization.

The footsteps he heard did not belong to Cady. They were too heavy. Too hesitant.

He knew from Cady that James Denton, the caretaker, had to shoo away the occasional trespasser—whether vagrants looking for shelter from the elements or kids looking for a little lovers' lane action.

He was in no mood to deal with either one.

It was the cell phone buzzing like a mosquito that put him in a different mood altogether. This time when he tensed, he did so with good cause, straining to hear the conversation. He picked up a few words, two of them—Cady and alone—being the only ones that mattered.

His trespasser was not a vagrant or a kid. It was someone who'd come after Cady. Someone who knew only the two of them were here, or else thought he was out of the picture and she was on her own.

King froze, wanting to warn Cady but having no idea if he'd walk out of here and find one man armed with a cell phone, or several armed with more firepower than his two guns.

Quietly, he reached for both weapons, tucked them into his waistband at his sides, leaving the tails of his work shirt hanging loose over them.

Then he grabbed the Maglite he'd been using while under the SUV, and made his way along the far side of the Hummer to the shed's wide open door.

The voice had come from the back of the small building. King ducked into the darkness away from the lights spilling from the windows of the house.

He gave his eyes a few seconds to adjust before he began creeping toward the spot where he hoped to find their unwanted visitor. And where he hoped to find him alone.

Pressed to the back corner of the building, King held his breath, listening, the weight of the Maglite in his hand a different sort of comfort than the handguns at his sides, a weight that could also serve as a weapon.

He moved just enough to peer down the back wall, and saw just the one guy he'd hoped for. The intruder hadn't heard him, and King understood why. The wind had picked up in his favor, whooshing through the trees surrounding the homestead, limbs scraping noisily against limbs.

From his one-eyed vantage point, King could also see Cady through the kitchen window and the door he'd left open. Meaning the trespasser, busily texting on his phone, his gaze switching between the house and his cell, could see her, too.

It was then King noticed the gym bag at the guy's feet. He thought back to the first night he and Cady had shacked up in Jersey, and the explosion that had demolished his Hummer.

Then he thought about suicide bombers strapping explosive vests to their chests. Or drivers with no intention of committing suicide slamming their Mustangs into tow trucks four times their size for the cause.

The cause that was standing at the back door even now.

He had to move.

He stepped around the corner at the same time he brought up the Maglite and turned it on, aiming it into the trespasser's eyes and blinding him. "Dude. Private property. No trespassing. You gonna try to convince me you didn't see the signs?"

The kid was too old to be, well, a kid. Late twenties, at least. The age he figured fit most of Tuzzi's thugs.

Cady's age.

Though pale, he was clean cut, looking like he spent his days at a desk on Wall Street, his lunch hour at the gym, his nights on the town. But he had another look. An anxious way of holding himself as if he hadn't been able to shake the tension of being a bitch behind bars.

King didn't want to rouse the younger man's suspicions by coming right out with his. Best to treat the guy as a local scouting a spot for a party and cut away his false confidence when on better footing himself.

If this was who King thought, the one *not* the brains of any operation, that shouldn't take long.

"I saw them, yeah." The kid looked at his texting screen. "But no one's usually here . . ."

"And somehow that makes ignoring them okay?" King flicked the light from the guy's face to the bag near his feet. "You bring enough booze to share?"

The kid's laughter was forced. "I just came to see if the coast was clear. Friends of mine. They're bringing the booze." He gestured with the phone he still held like a lifeline. "I can give them a call and make sure they bring plenty."

"So what's in the bag?" King aimed the light back in the guy's eyes, and nudged the toe of one boot at the duffel.

"Stop! Don't!"

"Or what? It might break?" He paused, added, "Or maybe blow up?"

"It's just that . . . it's not my bag, ya know?" he said with a lazy shrug that wasn't lazy in the least, but stiff, and worried, and . . . scared.

King would worry about being scared stiff later. "And you don't want me getting it dirty."

"Yeah. The guy I borrowed it from can be a real ass."

"Maybe you need better friends. Jason."

Jason Malling's head whipped up, his hand shot to the small of his back. King had his gun pressed to the center of the man who'd-made-the-last-few-days-a-living-hell's chest before he could draw his weapon.

"Hands where I can see them, Jason. Up against the wall, both of them."

"How did you know—"

"How did I know who you were? Because you're stupid enough to think I'm as stupid as you are."

"What?"

"Exactly."

King slid the barrel of his weapon up to rest beneath Malling's chin, reached back, and pulled the gun he'd been going after from his belt. "Carry on the side, boo. Faster draw."

"Who are you?"

"Just someone who happened to be in the right place at the right time. Cady?" He'd heard her come out the back door, and he wanted her close and safe. But he kept his eyes on their trespasser.

"What's going on?" she said, walking up behind him but smartly keeping her distance.

"Cady Kowalski? Meet Jason Malling. Better yet. Meet Jason Malling's gun." He waved her near, gave her the handgun, showed her how to hold it, and where to aim. "Safety's off. If he moves, shoot him."

Thirty-nine

After patting down their intruder, confiscating Malling's gun, phone, and the gym bag he'd borrowed to haul around his crap, King escorted the convicted felon to the kitchen and tied him to one of the chairs.

The fact that King was also a convicted felon didn't influence him to cut the younger guy any slack. He'd served time for a crime he didn't commit, while Malling was still committing, and obviously hadn't wised up at all since the first time he'd been caught.

He'd been out, what? Less than a week, and here he was headed back to do hard time. All King had to decide was whether to turn him over to the Staties or to McKie. The explosive device he had with him might even be enough to perk up Homeland Security's ears.

"Is this the same stuff you used to blow up my Hummer?" While Malling looked on, King emptied the contents of the gym bag onto the table. Wiring. A timer. Detonators. Blocks of C4. Multiple blocks of C4. Enough to make sure Cady and half the farm went up along with the house.

That was the rest of the reason King wasn't influenced to be kind to this piece of shit. Malling was outfitted to take out every living thing in a city block.

Talk about overkill. "Are you paying your bomb maker

by the hour? Or by how much of the Northeast he wipes off the map?"

Malling sat with his hands tied behind him, his torso roped to the chair, his ankles tied to the chair legs. It was hard for him to look anywhere but down. "I don't know what you're talking about."

"How far away were you planning to be before you set this off?" King asked, picking up one of the bricks of explosive material. "Because I gotta tell ya, boo. I'm not so sure anyone in Rosingsville would've made it out alive."

Cady had been standing near the back door, but now she came close and laid her hand on his arm. "Can you not treat that like a football please?"

"No worries, chère," he said, though he set about packing everything back into the bag. "Jason here had some prep work to do before this stuff would do any damage."

"I'd just as soon not see it being bounced around. It's bad enough knowing it's here," she said, crossing her arms and pacing the kitchen behind him. "And thinking about what could've happened."

Straining forward against his bonds, Malling lifted his head just enough to snarl. "You would've been in little pieces if it had, bitch."

King knocked him across the face. "How about some respect, asshole?"

"Fuck you. And fuck her." Malling spat blood. "She got all up in something that wasn't her business, and we're going to make goddamn sure she never forgets."

"We? You got an army out there backing you up?"

"Fuck you," Malling said, and this time he spit at King instead of the floor.

King heard Cady move, so he didn't. He waited, staring down this asshole until the kid lost his cockiness and looked away first. Then King took the wet paper towel Cady handed him and wiped the saliva from his neck.

"Tell me something, boo." He gestured with the now

dirty towels. "Does the man giving you orders expect you to get the job done, or did he choose you because you're a stupid expendable prick?"

"You don't know what the fuck you're talking about," Malling grumbled, his head still down.

"I'm talking about all the times you've screwed up."

"I haven't screwed up once."

"And that's why you're sitting here tied up in Cady's kitchen? Because it was part of your master plan?" King looked over to where she stood with her hands at her sides curled over the lip of the stove.

She hadn't said much at all since he'd handed her the gun and told her to shoot if Malling moved. She'd seemed calm enough then, her grip on the weapon controlled, and calm enough now—her only show of nerves during his manhandling of the bomb.

He had a lot of answers he wanted to beat out of this boy, and he didn't think Cady would object, but having her here to see and to listen, a witness to his interrogation, would hamper him. He'd hold back, take it easy for fear she'd somehow be hurt by what Malling revealed.

Gesturing for her to follow, he picked up the loaded duffel and carried it to the bedroom. Once there, he handed her his cell phone and the card he'd carried in his back pocket since that night in the hospital cafeteria.

He tapped a finger on the phone number, and went with his gut. "Do me a favor. Call McKie. Tell him that in a couple of hours, he can find Malling being held on trespassing charges in the Rosingsville substation."

"Trespassing charges?" She looked from the card to his face, her eyes wide. "What about the gun and the bomb and trying to kill me? Kill us?"

"I'm going to let McKie handle it. If I try to explain all of that to the Staties, we're going to be stuck here for the investigation, and what happened in Cushing Township will come up, and I'll never get back to Louisiana. I figure

Malling can pay a fine for ignoring the signs, and McKie can take it from there."

"It'll take the Staties a while to get here. You want me to call them, too?"

He nodded. "Tell McKie to be here in the morning and we'll give him Malling's stuff along with the flash drive."

At that, she balked. "I can't do that."

"You can. You need to."

She turned away, moved to stand in front of the window. "Kevin told me to hang onto it. To keep it safe."

"You've kept it safe for eight years."

But he knew this wasn't about her doing what her brother had told her. It was that doing what her brother had told her had caused her a lot of unnecessary grief.

If she'd opened the files after Kevin's death, not ignored them, not shied away, Malling wouldn't be sitting in the kitchen, and the evidence Kevin had collected would've put more of Tuzzi's runners behind bars.

He walked up behind her, put his hands on her shoulders and squeezed. "Now you need to put it to work for you. You need to let Kevin finish what he started and take Tuzzi and his bastards the rest of the way down."

Forty

Cady stayed in the bedroom only long enough to make the calls, then crept back to the main room to listen. She didn't trust King to tell her everything Jason Malling said, and she needed to hear it all.

She'd been right in guessing that it would take a couple of hours to get a response to a trespassing call. She'd thought about adding "armed" to the description of the intruder they were holding, but had kept that part to herself.

Possessing a weapon would be a violation of Malling's parole, meaning he'd be stuck behind bars if the troopers discovered the gun. Depending on the terms of his release, he could be stuck behind bars for leaving New Jersey.

She crossed her fingers that didn't happen. They needed him to pay his fine, leave Pennsylvania, and report back to Tuzzi. That was the only way McKie could follow and catch him in the act of making contact.

She climbed into the main room's recliner that sat closest to the hall. It gave her a clear view of the far side of the kitchen—at least the part above the shelves serving as a half wall between the two rooms.

She couldn't see the table or the sink, but the stove, refrigerator, and back door were all visible. And she could hear every noise King and Malling made, as well as every note being sung by the chorus of creatures that seemed to have surrounded the house.

"Here's what I want to know," King was saying. "What exactly are you after? Why blow up the Hummer? Why run us off the road and smoke us out of our room? What is it you want? To scare Cady into next year, because that much you've done, boo. That much you've done."

She frowned. Did King think her weak for being scared? Was Malling going to think her weak? Did she really give a shit if he did?

Malling finally answered. "I don't know why you think I'm going to tell you anything."

"Well, because right now, you're looking at being charged with trespassing. I'm keeping the gun and the explosives off the table. But if you don't talk, I can put them right back on. Make sure they're the first thing the Staties see when they walk through the door."

Cady winced at the string of expletives that came out of Malling's mouth. She had to hand it to King, though, hitting the other man where it hurt without ever lifting a hand.

That's all it took for Jason to capitulate. "What do you want to know?"

"You can start with everything."

"I was born a rich white kid in Westchester County."

"Uh, not that everything, jerk. Start with the break-in at the Kowalski house."

"That shit's all public record. Get a library card. Or take your ass down to the courthouse or wherever you have to go to see it."

Cady heard a loud thud, and assumed King had slammed Jason's gun onto the table.

"How did you know about the flash drive?"

"Kevin told us."

"That Cady had it?"

"No. That it existed. That it was stashed someplace safe."

"And you assumed she had it."

"We didn't assume anything, bro," Malling snarled. "Except that Kowalski was lying. Trying to scare us off or talk us into letting him live. Couldn't do it. He took out Ryland. He had to go down."

"And you made that happen. Being judge and jury and all."

"Us being Ryland's brothers. An eye for an eye."

"Kevin Kowalski was somebody's brother," King said, and Cady's eyes welled. "A real brother, blood and birth, not your fraternity bullshit."

"You calling it bullshit shows what you know."

King paused as if gathering his thoughts, then asked, "Why start looking for the flash drive now?"

"Because I just got out, dickwad."

"I thought Tuzzi had other runners doing his work."

"That work, yeah. Not this."

"Or maybe he realized the flash drive did exist once Tyler found the folder on Cady's laptop."

Malling snickered. "That was so sweet, Renee realizing her new roommate was the bitch who fucked up everything for Stacia Ashton."

"Tuzzi's girlfriend."

Cady assumed Jason nodded, since she didn't hear anything but the legs of King's chair scraping over the floor as he scooted back.

"Stacia's whole future went up in flames when Nathan was convicted."

Cady couldn't sit still anymore. She lunged out of the chair and burst into the kitchen. "And you don't think my family's life went up in flames when your bro," she said sarcastically, "killed mine?"

"Like I said. An eye for an eye."

"And what about Deshon Coral?"

Jason looked away, shook his head. "That wasn't supposed to happen. Stupid fuck should've learned how to drive."

"That's it? No remorse?"

"I needed you to stay put, not go running across the country. He was hired to do that. Not to get himself killed."

"And the smoke bomb?" King asked.

"What smoke bomb?"

"You saying you didn't send a smoke bomb to our room to make sure we were on the street when Deshon came driving by?"

"Maybe Deshon sent it." Jason slumped back, tossing his head to clear his hair from his eyes. "Maybe Kowalski stirred up more shit and has more enemies. But I don't know what you're talking about."

King glanced over at her, looking as worn out as she felt. "The cops on their way?"

She nodded. "You're keeping his phone, too, right?"

"You can't do that."

"Since you were stupid enough not to use a prepaid throwaway, I can do anything I want." He tossed it to Cady. "When our friend shows up tomorrow, let's make sure he gets that. Who knows what his people can do with the information stored in the memory."

Jason groaned. "Fuck. That information falls into the wrong hands, I'm dead meat."

Cady made a big production out of dropping the phone down her shirt. "Maybe one of your brothers will swing by and rescue you."

Forty-one

Cady leaned against the Hummer, waiting for the black sedan they had seen turn off the main road and onto the Kowalski property to reach the house. This was it. The end of the line. She prayed she was doing the right thing. Prayed, too, for King to finish his phone call to his cousin and join her.

She didn't think she had it in her to face Fitzwilliam McKie alone.

The Pennsylvania State Police had shown up close to midnight last night and taken her and King's statements before taking Jason Malling away.

As he'd told her he'd do, King had kept the explosives, the gun, and the cell phone Malling had with him. Those three things were sitting on the hood of the Hummer.

Cady wasn't exactly thrilled by the proximity of the gym bag, but King assured her that if someone as stupid as Jason Malling could haul it around without blowing himself up, she'd be fine until McKie retrieved it.

What she wasn't as fine with was McKie retrieving Kevin's flash drive. She'd been holding onto it, carrying it with her, a talisman she'd kept close for almost a decade.

Giving it up was not as simple as putting it into the government agent's hand. In fact, she wasn't sure King wasn't going to have to pry it out of her cold dead one first.

He seemed to sense her tension as he joined her because he leaned close, dropping a kiss to the top of her head. "I've been meaning to ask you something."

"So ask," she said, irritated by the gesture that seemed so patronizing, even more irritated because she knew he knew that would be her reaction, and was using it to distract her.

"What's with the hair?"

"My hair?" She reached up a hand, checked that it was still there. "What about it?"

"It's just all over the place. Like it doesn't know where to go."

"This style critique coming from a man with a big bald spot?"

He gingerly tested his stitches. "Give me a month, boo. You won't know it was ever there."

"While we're critiquing, what's the 'boo' crap? Are you trying to scare me?"

He laughed, kissed the top of her head again. "You like cupcake or princess or pumpkin better? I can't be calling you chère all the time."

She huffed. "I don't see why not."

By then, McKie was rolling into the driveway toward them. He stopped several yards away, shut down his car's engine, opened the door, and got out.

He shrugged out of the overcoat he'd been wearing, tossed it into the front seat, then shrugged out of his suit coat, too, and did the same.

By the time he got to where they were standing, he'd loosened his exquisite silk tie and the top button of his pristine white dress shirt.

At Cady's side, King chuckled. "You look like a man ready to relax, boo."

McKie held up both wrists. "All that's left is the cuffs. If this information you've promised pans out? I'll roll 'em up right here."

"Get ready to strip to your skivvies then." King reached behind him, handed over the gun, then the phone, then the gym bag. "This is going to blow you away. Literally, if you're not careful."

Fitz gave King a look, then checked the ammo and safety on the first and tucked it into his waistband. He slipped the phone into his pocket after a quick scroll through the contact list that had him both nodding and shaking his head.

The bag came next. He dropped to his haunches, scuffing his fancy shoes in the dirt, and opened it, sorting through the components inside that when assembled and ignited would leave a hole in place of half the Kowalski farm.

"The boy meant business," McKie said, zipping the bag and punctuating his words with a long low whistle as he stood. "But I'm not stripping. Not yet."

King turned to Cady. Fitz followed suit and did the same. Both men waited patiently, expectantly, and her hand began to sweat. She reached for some way to deflect the inevitable.

"Did you find Malling?"

McKie nodded. "Right where you said he would be. He paid his fine this morning, called for a cab, then took off on foot when he found out he'd be waiting till noon."

Even more stupid than she'd thought. "You heard his call?"

Fitz's only response was to cock his head.

"Where is he now?"

"Exactly?"

She gave a quick nod, still avoiding, not yet prepared. She didn't know if she'd ever be prepared.

As she looked on, Fitz pulled what she'd thought was a phone from a holster at his waist. It was a phone, but it was also a PDA-sized PC with an antennae capable of picking up wireless her laptop hadn't even known was out there.

He used a stylus to scroll through several windows, then turned the screen so that she could see the coordinates on the map. Malling had already left Pennsylvania, was in New Jersey, and all too soon would be in Trenton at Tuzzi's front door.

If that was where he was going.

Cady assumed the boss would want a firsthand report of failures as well as his minion's success. "Do you have what you need now? Since you know where he is and can follow him, will that give you what you need? When he makes contact with Tuzzi?"

Fitz shrugged, swiveled the screen back around. "We're at level wait-and-see. Having a lock on him helps, but it's no guarantee."

"Having more would help?"

"Having more that's solid? It would close the deal."

Cady sighed. King nudged her. "C'mon, chère. You know it's the right thing to do. For you. For Kevin. For your folks, even if they'll never know."

She hung her head, stared at her fist. "I'm not as noble as you're trying to make me be."

"Oh yes you are," he said, and before she could change her mind, she opened her palm, offering her whole world to Fitzwilliam McKie.

He didn't say a word, but took the drive and plugged it into a port on his mobile PC.

Cady leaned against King and the SUV because her knees felt like rubber and her stomach wasn't doing well holding down the eggs King had scrambled for them at dawn.

She studied the expression on McKie's face as he pulled up Kevin's documents and read through the lists of names, dates, transaction amounts, and other information her brother had obtained no doubt through questionable means.

But she couldn't read anything of what he was thinking, and he'd hadn't said a word while studying the data. What was he waiting for? Didn't he know what it had taken for her to give up her last connection to her brother?

She couldn't help herself or stand not knowing a moment longer. "Well?"

He closed up the PC and returned it to its leather holster. And then he gave her a bigger grin than she'd known he had in him. "I'm still not stripping."

Cady deflated. After all of that? "It's not enough?"

"Oh, it's enough, Cady. Trust me that it's enough. I'm just not much for going commando in public."

King whooped. "Then that's it, yes? We're done here. It's over."

"It's close enough," Fitz said, leaving an opening King couldn't resist.

"Close enough. But it's not government work, is it, boo?"

At that, McKie winked, and headed for his car.

Forty-two

"Are you ready for this?" King asked, looking out over the same lake where she and Kevin as kids had been sure their fishing hooks would snag the bones of dead bodies, where instead they'd caught bite-sized crappie and thrown them back, where they'd waited for water nymphs to drop their fishing lines into the air and try to catch them.

Was she ready for this?

Oh, what a loaded question. Five words that sounded so simple, but were weighted down with so many years of guilt and pain and anger and loss. Fitz had the flash drive, and when Cady's laptop went into the lake, she would no longer have anything of Kevin to hold onto.

No, that wasn't true. She'd have her memories, the same ones that brought a smile to her face even now, a smile that was no less joyful because of the tears she couldn't hold back thinking of the brother she'd loved.

Oh, Kevin. I'm so so sorry. I shouldn't have been so stupid. I should've had my head in the real world and known no good would come of Edie's silly prank. All of this happened because I was too wrapped up in myself to think straight. I have no one but myself to blame.

But even as she had the thought, she heard Kevin

chastising her. He was the one who'd taunted Tuzzi with what he knew. And Tuzzi was the one who'd pulled the trigger. Yes, she'd been the catalyst that brought the two of them together, but blaming herself for how things had played out between two hot-headed young men was insane.

She cradled her backpack to her chest as King cradled her body against his. "I don't know. I mean, I do know. I am ready. I'm just afraid to think of what happens now. This is all I've known for so long. Letting it go means I have to find something else to hold onto."

He tightened his hold where his arms were wrapped around hers, but he didn't say anything in response. She wasn't sure that she wanted him to. He might tell her to hold onto him. He might say she needed to stand on her own.

He might tell her any number of things she didn't want to hear, or wasn't ready to hear, or would die if she had to hear. He was so much more pulled together than she'd managed to do for herself in twenty-nine years.

The truth was, she had to work out this new chapter of her life on her own. She knew that, which she supposed was one positive mark in her favor. And King, having done the same to get where he was, knew it, too.

"You were right."

"About which of many things, chère?"

"That I should've looked at what Kevin gave me. I don't know why I didn't."

"Sure you do. You were sad. And you were scared."

"Scared about what?"

"Scared that if you looked at it you would quit being sad. That you'd find something that knocked him back to being human instead of this martyr you'd made him. Or maybe the further time got from his death, it became easier not to look because you didn't want to open wounds that were healing."

Everything he said resonated so purely.

"How come you know so much?"

"Because I'm an old fart."

"You're not old."

"I don't know much of anything either."

"It doesn't seem that way. You've known what to do every time we've turned around."

"Ah, well, that's experience, boo. As many times as I've been around the block? I damn sure better know when and where to turn."

"Maybe I'll be as wise when I'm as old as you."

"Hey, now. I'm the only one allowed to say I'm old. But it's experience. You know that. And what you've been through should be more than enough to keep you turning the way you need to for the rest of your life."

"God, I hope so. I can't go through this on a regular basis."

"If McKie follows through on his promises, you won't have to worry about Nathan Tuzzi ever again."

"Making my next life crisis a piece of cake."

"You've got to get beyond this one first, and I don't see you letting go of that backpack."

He'd buy her a new one, he'd told her. He'd promised her a new laptop, top of the line, all the software she could ever want, a webcam for taking pictures should she get a wild hair and sign up at a dating Web site.

She'd hit him then, and meant it.

"If it would help, I'll be happy to do the honors," he said, reaching for her bag.

She shook her head, stepped closer to the edge of the rocky outcropping overlooking the private lake. "I have to do it. I won't be the one letting go if I don't."

The distance between where she stood and the water below was nothing, but it seemed like such a long way down. She knew it wasn't. She'd jumped from here and cannonballed in, sinking almost to the bottom dozens, maybe hundreds, of times.

More than once Kevin had landed on top of her, and she'd sputtered her way to the top for more air, adrenaline bursting into her veins like rocket fuel.

She'd known exactly how far it was to the top, how long it would take, how much of her remaining breath the trip up would steal from her lungs.

But she'd been scared to death every time, thinking she'd never make it. Just like she was scared to death that she'd never make it now.

She hooked her fingers through the carry loop on the top of the backpack and began to spin, turning faster and faster, the weight of the bag pulling at her skin, her bones, her muscles, stretching her arm longer and longer, a rubber band, a bungee cord, extending out over the water.

And then she let go. She straightened her fingers, and the loop slid off, and the backpack went sailing. King caught her before her momentum sent her flying off the rock, too.

She stood in the crook of his arm and watched her Rock of Gibraltar splat on the surface of the water and sink like the stone it was. No fanfare. No heralding trumpet. No dramatic hesitation. It was there, and then it was gone.

She caught back a sob, clenched her hands beneath her chin, and watched the ripples spread in circles that grew and grew as if they would never stop. But they did, silencing, lessening, until the surface of the water was broken by nothing more than insects skating along the surface.

"Well?" he finally asked her after she'd taken a deep breath and exhaled.

"I think I'll be okay. It'll take some getting used to, not having all that weight to cart around." She looked back over her shoulder, caught him looking down. "You'll buy me something that's not so heavy, right?"

"I'll buy you anything, everything you want," he said, and she turned in his arms.

"No. You can't buy me anything but this. This one thing.

Well, two things counting the bag, but that's it. I'll do the rest on my own."

"It's a deal," he told her, hugging her close as they turned and made their way from the highest point of the outcropping hanging over the lake to the lower spot King had decided perfect for parking his Hummer.

Walking beside him, she drifted into a peace she hadn't felt in far too long. She'd thought when looking up at him that he'd wanted to kiss her. She'd wanted him to, but now this was so much better, this companionship, this intimacy that was so much richer and required nothing but having him near.

When they reached his SUV, she opened the driver's side door and gestured for him to climb in.

"Your turn," she said.

He grinned from ear to ear. "This is going to be more fun than I've had in a while."

"Hey. I resent that remark."

"Than I've had in a while with my clothes on. How's that?"

She didn't say a word, made another sweeping gesture as if ushering him into a limousine. He ruffled her hair as he climbed in and started the SUV.

The H3 was packed with all the things Fitz had loaded in for them—things that were to see them through their adventure, things neither one of them ever wanted to see again.

They'd kept out the essentials, a change of clothes and toiletries for the road, but the rest of the supplies—the sleeping bags and cooler of juice bottles and camping gear, even the instant cold packs that had come in so handy—were reminders of the last few days.

So was the Hummer.

Cady had argued at first; what a needless waste, especially after the explosion and the accident and all the collateral damage—to the hotel where they'd stayed that first night, to May Wind's B&B, to Jarrell Bradley's tow truck, not to mention the loss of Deshon Coral's life.

King had argued back. Dumping the Hummer wasn't a waste if it kept him from spending another minute of his life remembering this nightmare of a trip—remembering anything except his time with her, he'd quickly amended when she'd come close with the fork she'd been holding.

And now here they were, about to feed the SUV to the fishes, sending it to the bottom of the lake where it would stir up all the bones she and Kevin had tried to stir themselves so many times. She smiled as she thought of her brother's hook snagging a camp stove or lantern instead.

"Happy fishing, Edgar," she said, and stepped away, watching as King wedged the garden hoe he'd sized and cut to fit between the front of the driver's seat and the accelerator. The tires began spinning, burning, spitting out grass and dirt, the motor whining from being all revved up and restrained.

And then King shifted into gear, bailing out the door and rolling away from the vehicle as it lurched forward, picking up speed before sailing off the ledge of rock and into the air.

It hit the water with a sound nearly as loud as the explosion that had destroyed the first of its predecessors. Cady flinched, then watched the water gulp down the SUV in one big slow swallow.

Once the SUV had vanished beneath the water and the sputtering bubbles had stopped rising, she asked. "Well, boo. How are you going to get to Louisiana now?"

King chuckled. "I've got a plan in the works. It means spending one more night here. Think you can deal with that?"

After all that he'd done for her, she could deal with anything. She just wished she knew what she was going to do with herself, and if he was going to be with her while she figured it out.

She nodded. “I can deal. As long as your plan includes my laptop and something to carry it in.”

“That phone call to Simon this morning? I talked to a man who knows a man who knows his stuff. You’ll be able to web surf your little heart out.”

Forty-three

King settled behind the wheel of the Audi convertible that was delivered the next morning along with Cady's new computer bag and notebook PC.

He belted himself in, and watched Cady do the same. She lifted her face to the midday sun and closed her eyes, the biggest smile he'd seen from her yet spread all over her face.

He turned back to look at the dash, his hands tight on the steering wheel. This was where things were going to get sticky, and could very easily go wrong.

He did *not* want things to go wrong. Not after all they'd been through.

He cleared his throat. "Well, boo? Where do you want me to take you?"

From his peripheral vision, he saw Cady's head pop toward him like a bobble head doll. "What do you mean, where do I want you to take me? I want you to take me with you . . . unless . . . unless you don't want me there."

He wanted her everywhere. He wanted her here and now. But he also wanted her to be sure, because turning around and bringing her back would kill him. "There's no snow in Cajun country. It's hot and sticky and steamy. You're gonna sweat your ass off and more."

She blew a long sputtering raspberry. "What, and you think New Jersey's all ice cubes and lemonade?"

Nothing against the Garden State, but there were plenty of gardens to be found along the bayou. "There're no celebrities needing hair and makeup done for photo shoots."

"I hate doing hair and makeup. Well, I had fun doing yours, but you're a special case," she said, laughing at him way more than laughing with him, especially since he wasn't laughing at all.

At least not much. "We've got Lee Benoit, and Beausoleil, but no Bruce Springsteen. And we have crawfish. A *lot* of crawfish."

She unbuckled her seat belt then and somehow folded and bent her limber body and crawled into his lap. They were face to face when she told him, "You're doing a really lousy job of talking me out of coming with you."

He looked into her eyes, smiled softly, watching her expression grow wary as if she were waiting for a blow. He wondered what it said that they were both bracing for bad news instead of expecting good.

Maybe that they were the perfect match he hoped . . . and why was his throat closing up? He swallowed, rubbed his hand up and down her thigh, and said, "I just want you to know what you're in for."

She pressed her forehead to his, sighed, kissed him gently, then pulled back, brushing his hair behind his ear on one side and avoiding his gaze. "If you want to put me off, King, then tell me you won't be there. Or tell me that you'd rather I stay here. I won't like it, but I would way rather hear you say that now than to hear later that you made a mistake."

"I can't do that, chère. I can never do that." And then he moved his hands to her face, and ignoring the heat burning wet in his eyes, he kissed her.

Her mouth was so sweet, and the tiny sounds she made

as she tried not to cry even sweeter. He slanted his lips over hers, rubbing, tasting, laughing as he did, as he caught her sobs and told her with his touch that she was not a mistake, that they were not a mistake.

And then as the kiss ended, he whispered against her mouth, "I love you."

That started her crying again, her hands coming up to hold his head as her lips moved from his eyes to his cheeks to his brows. Her tears were wet on his skin, her heart beating so hard her chest nearly bounced through his.

"Oh, King. I thought you only loved the sex. I thought you were trying to talk me out of coming because you could have fun with anyone—"

He pressed a finger to her mouth to shut her up. "You thought wrong, chère. You thought so very wrong. I love more than the sex, and I don't want to have fun with anyone but you, and if you thought I was trying to talk you out of coming with me, it's only because I wanted you to be sure."

"Be sure about what?" she asked, talking against his non-silencing finger. "That I love you? That I want to be with you? That I can't imagine not waking up beside you every day, ready for a new adventure?"

He snorted. "If they're all going to be like these last few days? I can do without the adventures." Then he paused, frowning as he went back over what she'd just said. "Did you say you loved me somewhere in all of that?"

"Yes, yes." Her head was back to bobbing, her giggles rising on infectious bubbles that burst all over his skin. "I love you. I love you. And my first adventure? Crawfish. I have never eaten crawfish. I want pounds and pounds of crawfish."

Lord, but this woman tickled him. This woman who loved him, this woman whose appetite and laughter he would never get his fill of. It was hard to tease her, his chest was so tight, but he gave it a go.

"I'll have word put out to Texas and Mississippi that

we're on our way. I've seen you eat, and I don't think Louisiana grows that many mudbugs."

"Mudbugs? What the hell is a mudbug?" she squawked as she scrambled back into her seat.

King hit the button and revved the engine once it turned over, laughing as he put the car into gear. "Oh, chère. You are so going to love Bayou Allain."

Forty-four

They were cruising through Tennessee three days later, taking their time between Pennsylvania and the Pelican State, when Cady turned on the radio.

Authorities have arrested seven members of an organized gang accused of distributing drugs in the tristate region, and allegedly supplying inmates in the New Jersey State Prison. The gang's leader, Nathan Tuzzi of Elizabeth, New Jersey, is currently serving a life sentence for the murder of Freehold Township college student, Kevin Kowalski, eight years ago.

One of those arrested, Jason Malling, was paroled earlier this month after serving seven years for his role in the same crime. This makes Malling's third arrest as he was most recently detained and charged with trespassing on property owned by the Kowalski family in Northampton County, Pennsylvania.

King reached over and turned it off. "I'm not in much of a mood for the news. What about you?"

Eyes closed, Cady leaned back and lifted her face to the warm spring sun. "I'm not in much of a mood for anything that takes me away from being here."

"Sorry, chère," he told her. "Every mile we go is taking you away from being here."

"Literally, yes. But I was speaking metaphorically. I don't have a care in the world and, if it's okay with your majesty, I'd like to keep it that way."

To that, he had only one thing to say. "Damn, but it's good to be King."

Epilogue

Authorities have arrested seven members of an organized gang accused of distributing drugs in the tristate region . . .

The private jet reached its cruising altitude and leveled off for the early transatlantic flight, and the single passenger on board flipped off the television broadcast he'd recorded the day before.

The sun was cresting the horizon with the promise of a bright new day—a new day the man making the trip planned to sleep through. Tomorrow would be soon enough for Fitzwilliam McKie to celebrate all the days to come.

Nearly a year ago to the day, he had buried Oliver, his young brother-in-law who'd been serving time for possession of and intent to distribute heroin, and had been killed on Tuzzi's orders after cooperating with the state.

Weeks later, Fitz had buried Elise, his young bride of less than two years, whose grief had been inconsolable, and who had taken her own life at the news of her brother's violent death.

And now that he had buried everything that mattered to Nathan Tuzzi, taken apart his operation and reduced his organization to ash, Fitz was done.

He'd lost track of Cady Kowalski and Kingdom Trahan

both. He could find them . . . but he had no need. They'd served their purpose in a larger way than he'd ever expected. They deserved to get back to living their own lives—just as he would be getting back to living his.

In fact, as he stripped down to his skivvies as he'd promised to do, tucked a pillow between his head and the window, and finally closed his eyes, he swore he heard Dublin calling his name.

The sound may have been nothing but the echo of his longing, but it sang with a truth that had been clawing at him for a very long time.

It was time for Fitzwilliam McKie to go home.

Try DATING OUTSIDE YOUR DNA,
the latest from Karen Kelley,
out now from Brava!

"Lyraka is different."

Roan crossed his legs. "I've heard that crap before."

"She's not full-blooded Nerakian. Her father is an earthling."

He raised an eyebrow. Okay, Joe had his attention. "I didn't know there were any half-breeds old enough to train, but it makes sense they would mate. The ones I've run across make no bones that they like a good roll in the hay."

"Now you're being crude," Joe admonished.

"Just stating facts. Chocolate and sex are the only things they seem to care about."

"That's not true and you know it."

Yeah, he did, but he'd been in a particularly foul mood since Joe told Roan that he wanted him to stay at the training center a little longer. Now Joe was giving him this new assignment. Roan wanted to get back into field work and out of training. He was starting to feel trapped, and that didn't set well with him.

A leg injury he'd sustained a few months ago had kept him on the sidelines. The doc still wouldn't release him for full duty even though Roan felt fine. He had a feeling Joe was behind some of it.

"Train her, and I'll get you the release you've been wanting," Joe said.

"Are you serious?"

"Yes."

"She must mean a lot to you. Is she that good?"

"You can't imagine." Joe handed Roan a manila envelope. "This is everything I have on her. I know it's not much, but read it tonight."

Roan was still skeptical, but believed Joe when he said he would get him the release. Hell, he'd do just about anything to get back to active duty. He believed there was more to training this chick, though. "What's the catch? There has to be something wrong with her."

Joe shrugged, a little too casually, if you asked Roan.

"Like I said, her abilities are different, stronger than the average Nerakian, but she needs to learn discipline and control."

She was half Nerakian and half earthling, how strong could she be? He assumed she was a warrior so he wouldn't have to actually do that much. A few weeks of his time and he'd be back getting his hands dirty. He could handle that.

"Okay, it's a deal. When do I get to meet her?" He'd known Joe for quite a few years. At one time, Joe had been a kick-ass agent, but when the elite force was formed, Joe had taken over recruiting people who had the potential to be the best of the best. Roan knew it took a lot to impress Joe. So yeah, he was curious.

Joe beamed. "You get to meet her right now." He pushed a button on his intercom. "Go get Lyraka and ask her to come in."

A few minutes passed before the door opened. Roan didn't move from his chair. Nerakian women were beautiful, but it hadn't taken him long to realize they had strange ideas about things.

And they took everything literally. He didn't have that much patience when it came to explaining every little detail. Women from Earth were more to his liking. They knew the score. He slowly turned in his chair, expecting to see a beautiful woman.

There were very few times in his life he'd ever felt as though the wind had been knocked out of him. This just happened to be one of them. She didn't look like most Nerakians. Warriors were darker—dark hair, dark eyes, dark clothes. Healers had long blond hair and usually wore green flowing robes, and man, were they a pain in the ass. He'd only met one, but that one had been more than enough. Each Nerakian had a different look that immediately said what their role on Nerak had been.

But this woman was different. God, was she different. His heart had already begun to pound, and the palms of his hands to sweat just looking at her. She was a walking, talking billboard of every man's sexual fantasy—him included.

How the hell was he going to train her?

Whatever the Seer wanted, the Seer got, be it for his comfort or his whim or his pleasure.

She stood staring at the chair on the raised dais at one end of the chamber, the chair where he sat when the visions came. From the expression that filled her green eyes, she knew it as well.

Had she witnessed his power? Had she watched as the magic within him exploded into a vision of what was or what would yet be? As he influenced the high and the mighty of the surrounding lands and clans with the truth of his gift? Walking over to stand behind her, he placed his hands on her shoulders and drew her back to his body.

"I have not seen you before, sweetling," he whispered into her ear. Leaning down, he smoothed the hair from the side of her face with his own and then touched his tongue to the edge of her ear. "What is your name?"

He felt the shivers travel through her as his mouth tickled her ear. Smiling, he bent down and kissed her neck, tracing the muscle there down to her shoulder with the tip of his tongue. Connor bit the spot gently, teasing it with his teeth and soothing it with his tongue. "Your name?" he asked again.

She arched then, clearly enjoying his touch and ready for

more. Her head fell back against his shoulder and he moved his mouth to the soft skin there, kissing and licking his way down and back to her ear. Still she had not spoken.

"When I call out my pleasure, sweetling, what name will I speak?"

He released her shoulders and slid his hands down her arms and then over her stomach to hold her in complete contact with him. Covering her stomach and pressing her to him, he rubbed against her back, letting her feel the extent of his erection—hard and large and ready to pleasure her. Connor moved his hands up to take her breasts in his grasp. Rubbing his thumbs over their tips and teasing them to tightness, he no longer asked, he demanded.

"Tell me your name."

He felt her breasts swell in his hands and he tugged now on the distended nipples, enjoying the feel and imagining them in his mouth, as he suckled hard on them and as she screamed out her pleasure. But nothing could have pleased him more in that moment then the way she gasped at each stroke he made, over and over until she moaned out her name to him.

"Moira."

"Moira," he repeated slowly, drawing her name out until it was a wish in the air around them. "Moira," he said again as he untied the laces on her bodice and slid it down her shoulders until he could touch her skin. "Moira," he now moaned as the heat and the scent of her enticed him as much as his own scent was pulling her under his control.

Connor paused for a moment, releasing her long enough to drag his tunic over his head and then turning her into his embrace. He inhaled sharply as her skin touched his, the heat of it seared into his soul as the tightened peaks of her breasts pressed against his chest. Her added height brought her hips level almost to his and he rubbed his hardened cock against her stomach, letting her feel the extent of his arousal.

As he pushed her hair back off her shoulders, he realized that in addition to the raging lust in his blood, there was something else there, teasing him with its presence.

Anticipation.

For the first time in years, this felt like more than the mindless rutting that happened between him and the countless, nameless women there for his needs. For the first time in too long, this was not simply scratching an itch, for the hint of something more seemed to stand off in the distance, something tantalizing and unknown and something somehow tied to this woman.

He lifted her chin with his finger, forcing her gaze off the blasted chair and onto his face. Instead of the compliant gaze that usually met him, the clarity of her gold-flecked green eyes startled him. Connor did something he'd not done before, something he never needed to do—he asked her permission.

"I want you, Moira," he whispered, dipping to touch and taste her lips for the first time. Connor slid his hand down to gather up her skirts, baring her legs and the treasure between them to his touch and his sight. "Let me?"

And don't miss Cynthia Eden's
ETERNAL HUNTER,
in stores next month from Brava . . .

She reached into her bag and pulled out a check. Not the usual way things were handled in the DA's office, but . . . "I've been authorized to acquire your services." He didn't glance at the check, just kept those blue eyes trained on hers. Her fingers were steady as she held the check in the air between them "This check is for ten thousand dollars."

No change of expression. From the looks of his cabin, the guy shouldn't have been hesitating to snatch up the money.

"Give the check to Night Watch."

At that, her lips firmed. "I already gave them one." A hefty one, at that. "This one's for you. A bonus from the mayor—he wants this guy caught, fast." Before word about the true nature of the crime leaked too far.

"So old Gus doesn't think his cops can handle this guy?"

Gus LaCroix. Hard-talking, ex-hard-drinking mayor. No nonsense, deceptively smart, and demanding. "He's got the cops on this, but he said he knew you, and that you'd be the best one to handle this job."

Erin strongly suspected that Gus belonged in the *Other* world. She hadn't caught any scent that was off drifting from him, but his agreement to bring in Night Watch and his almost desperate demands to the DA had sure indicated the guy knew more than he was letting on about the situation.

Could be he was a demon. Low-level. Many politicians were.

Jude took the check. Finally. She dropped her fingers, fast, not wanting the flesh on flesh contact with him. Not then.

He folded the check and tucked it into the back pocket of his jeans. "Guess you just got yourself a bounty hunter."

"And I guess you've got yourself one sick shifter to catch."

He closed the distance between them, moving fast and catching her arms in a strong grip.

Aw, hell. It was just like before. The heat of his touch swept though her, waking hungers she'd deliberately denied for so long.

Jude was sexual. From his knowing eyes. His curving, kiss-me lips, to the hard lines and muscles of his body.

Deep inside, in the dark, secret places of her soul that she fought to keep hidden, there was a part of her just like that.

Wild. Hot.

Sexual.

"Why are you afraid of me?"

Not the question she'd expected, but one she could answer. "I know what you are. What sane woman wouldn't be afraid of a man who becomes an animal?"

"Some women like a little bit of the animal in their men."

"Not me." *Liar.*

His eyes said the same thing.

"Do your job, Donovan. Catch the freak who cut up my prisoner—"

"Like Bobby had been slashing his victims?"

Hit. Yeah, there'd been no way to miss that significance.

"When word gets out about what really happened, some folks will say Bobby deserved what he got." His fingers pressed into her arms. Erin wore a light, silk shirt—and even that seemed too hot for the humid Louisiana spring night. His touch burned through the blouse and seemed to singe her flesh.

"Some will say that," she allowed. Okay, a hell of a lot would say that. "But his killer still has to be caught." Stopped, because she had the feeling this could be just the beginning.

Her feelings about death weren't often wrong.

She was a lot like her dad that way.

And, unfortunately, like her mother, too.

"What do you think? Did he deserve to be clawed to death?"

An image of Bobby's ex-wife, Pat, flashed before her eyes. The doctors had put over one hundred and fifty stitches into her face. She'd been his most brutal attack.

Erin swallowed. "His punishment was for the court to decide." She stepped back, but he didn't let her go. "Uh, do you mind?"

"Yeah, I do." His eyes glittered down at her. "If we're gonna be working together, we need honesty between us."

"We need you to find the killer."

"Oh, I will. Don't worry about that. I always catch my prey."

So the rumors claimed. The hunters from Night Watch were known throughout the U.S.

"You're shivering, Erin."

"No, no, I'm not." She was.

"I make you nervous. I scare you." A pause. His gaze dropped to her lips, lingered, then slowly rose back to meet her stare. "Is it because I know what you are?"

She wanted his mouth on hers. A foolish desire. Ridiculous. Not something the controlled woman wanted, but what the wild thing inside craved. "You don't know anything about me."

"Don't I?"

Erin jerked free of his hold and glared at him. "Few things in this world scare me. You should know that." There was one thing, one person, who terrified her—but now wasn't the time for that disclosure. No, she didn't tell anyone about *him*.

If she could just get around Jude and march out of that door—

"Maybe you're not scared of me, then. Maybe you're scared of yourself."

She froze.

"Not human," he murmured, shaking his head. "Not vamp."

Vamp? Thankfully, no.

"Djinn? Nah, you don't have that look." His right hand lifted and he rubbed his chin. "Tell me your secrets, sweetheart, and I'll tell you mine."

"Sorry, not the sharing type." She'd wasted enough time here. Erin pushed past him, ignoring the press of his arm against her side. Her body ached and the whispers of hunger within her grew more demanding every moment she stayed with him.

Weak.

She hated her weakness.

Just like her mother's.

"You're a shifter." His words stopped her near the door. She stared blankly at the faded wood. Heard the dull thud of her heart echoing in her ears.

Then the soft squeak of the old floorboards as he closed the distance between them.

Erin turned to him, tilted her head back—

He kissed her.

She heard a growl. Not from him—no, from her own throat.

The hunger.

Sure, he made the first move, he brought his lips crashing down on hers, but . . . she kissed him right back.